GUIDE ME HOME

GUIDE
ME HOME

ATTICA LOCKE

MULHOLLAND BOOKS

Little, Brown and Company

New York   Boston   London

Mulholland Books / Little, Brown and Company
Hachette Book Group
1290 Avenue of the Americas, New York, NY 10104
mulhollandbooks.com

First North American Edition: September 2024
Published simultaneously in the UK by Viper Books

Mulholland Books is an imprint of Little, Brown and Company, a division of Hachette Book Group, Inc. The Mulholland Books name and logo are trademarks of Hachette Book Group, Inc.

The publisher is not responsible for websites (or their content) that are not owned by the publisher.

The Hachette Speakers Bureau provides a wide range of authors for speaking events. To find out more, go to hachettespeakersbureau.com or email hachettespeakers@hbgusa.com.

Little, Brown and Company books may be purchased in bulk for business, educational, or promotional use. For information, please contact your local bookseller or the Hachette Book Group Special Markets Department at special.markets@hbgusa.com.

ISBN 9780316494618
LCCN 2024936466

Printing 1, 2024

LSC-C

Printed in the United States of America

For every mother whose child knows only half the story

I know *I was done wrong*
I've got to keep on singing my song...

...Lord, I know *I done wrong*
I want you to guide me home.

— Willie Mae "Big Mama" Thornton

Nacogdoches County

THE TRACKS were long gone.

But if you knew where to look, how to set your foot just so, you could feel history beneath your feet. The ghost of an old railroad tie, the slim rise of land where the earth had grown over an abandoned tramline. Evidence of a logging camp that had thrived in these woods over a century ago. Rey toed the rubber nose of his Airwalk sneakers into the damp carpet of sweetgum and tupelo leaves at his feet, overlaid with fallen pine needles, slick and rust red beneath a braided canopy of tree branches. Lingering drops from a light morning shower fell from the leaves, landing, crystalline and cool, in the black curls at the base of Rey's skull, dampening the collar of the company-issued pullover he'd borrowed from his dad when he left home.

Home.

The word had started to bite since he'd made his decision.

He hadn't told his parents. Maybe he wouldn't. Maybe it was better to just leave. Be a memory by the time his mother flipped on the light switch tomorrow morning in the room he shared with his little brother. He hadn't told anyone but Sera that he was thinking of just taking off.

And he wasn't sure she'd believed him. She certainly hadn't bothered to reach out to say goodbye. They hadn't spoken in days, in fact.

It had been warm when he started his walk (*hike* always sounded so white; *¿Qué* hike? his stepfather had said the first time Rey had ventured from their new town, back when he'd thought it fate that the family had landed near a national forest), but he'd brought an extra layer today anyway. There were pockets of the woods that were so tucked away, so walled off by trees as to be crypt-like. Quiet. And oddly cold.

This state could be weird like that. Contrary.

Of all the places they'd lived, he found this one to be the most frustrating to his sense of order in the natural world. It was achingly beautiful — slate-blue sky in the fall, a gem-like sapphire in the spring and summer, set above land so fecund and verdant as to nearly embarrass itself with its showy beauty, every turn scented by pine and the sweet smokiness of red cedar — but the air itself, no matter the season, was often thick and muggy as a wet cotton ball, and you couldn't go ten feet without being met by a pushy mosquito or a gang of gnats or both. Roaches flew here. There were scorpions *and* swamp rats. Going outside required a level of fortitude just barely commensurate with any pastoral pleasure that awaited you. To see its grace, Texas was going to make you put in the work. As Rey got closer to the cave-like atmosphere surrounding the ruins of the old sawmill, he slipped on the pullover. He felt immediately cushioned and comforted by the peace he always felt this deep in pure woodlands. He took in mouthfuls of the air, so clean here it was almost sweet, trying to taste it on his tongue, to swallow and savor this place. If he kept to his plan, today would be his goodbye.

He'd discovered the remains of the ancient mill about a month after his family moved to Thornhill. Though other people had known about it, as evidenced by the graffiti on the two surviving walls, the tops broken and crumbling at an angle. Some of the writing here went back far enough to reference bands from the '70s Rey had never heard of. The first day he discovered the old sawmill, he ran his fingers along the fading words on the crumbling walls. *Trisha Was Here. Lumberjacks, Class of '87.* And *Pink Floyd, The Wall (on a wall, man!).* Then he googled everything the second he was back home with decent Wi-Fi. Free, quality internet service was one of the amenities that came with living and working in Thornhill. Or was it *at* Thornhill? Or *for*? None of it felt right. Did they live where his parents worked? Or did his parents work where they all lived?

He got the Pink Floyd joke after googling it, though it was hardly worth the effort of the search. He did download a few of their songs. "Wish You Were Here" became a favorite of his. For the rest of his life, it would make him think of Sera. He'd looked up anything he could find about what he'd just seen. What were the remains of a stone and brick building doing in the middle of the Angelina National Forest? He soon learned that logging had been huge in this part of the state at the turn of the last century, had made some men very rich and left others dead from the dangerous work of cutting trees taller than most buildings at that time. Moving them from virgin earth to a mill that could turn wood into timber for construction. At one point, there had been hundreds of lumber mills (and their outgrowth, mill towns) in these dense woods. Loblolly and longleaf pine were East Texas gold, harvested for decades until there was nothing left, whole swaths of the state pillaged, left treeless and bald. By the 1910s, the entire industry had shrunk in on itself like a snail slinking back into its shell in shame. Dozens of companies folded, the remaining ones consolidating into a few industry giants.

The ruins of the Hill Mill, as Rey learned it had once been called, got left behind along the way, abandoned because of a new rail line closer to New Orleans or maybe because a bigger mill was built nearby. His research—all done on the company-issued cell phone that he shared with his kid brother—got fuzzy at a certain point. He'd thought it might make a good thesis project for an environmental science major. But that was before his family had been told that, unlike Sera, there would be no paid college for him. When Sera got into Stephen F. Austin the previous year, Rey had brought her to this place in the woods, talking her ear off the whole way from the trailhead to the secret turnoff deep in the thicket about logging routes and timber yields. Though she appreciated the haunting beauty in all that decay, she didn't see in the place a cautionary tale or a shrine to fallen industry as Rey did. A relic of the folly of men. For him, history was a missing tooth his tongue never lost a taste for, especially when it came to the natural world. He was curious about all of it. But because Sera loved the mill site too, saw something fantastical in its existence, it became a special place between them, their pied-à-terre in the woods. Hansel and Gretel's little getaway from the narrow confines of Thornhill.

They brought books there, sometimes music, trading off who got to set a playlist, exchanging stories of where they'd come from, how they found themselves in this little slice of East Texas: Sera by way of Houston and a once perma-existence at the medical center there; Rey by way of South Carolina, which was by way of Iowa and then Florida and Alabama. They brought lunch sometimes—charro beans with pork smoked over maple and mesquite, which Sera would scoop up with homemade white bread drizzled with honey; or a basket of her mother's cornmeal-crusted catfish, of which they could hardly resist pinching off piping hot morsels on their walk to the woods, bottles of homemade hot sauce sticking out of the back pockets of their jeans.

They would make seats of loose bricks and stare up at the pines, the tips of which seemed as impossible to reach as the sky, as Rey's dreams for his future. The more he talked about the "mill project," as he called his research, and the more he prodded Sera with ideas about areas of study, which classes she could take to advance a thesis topic, the more awkward things grew between them, both because Sera asked him to stop—she'd had enough of being told what to do in college, what to study and where to live, from her parents, her father especially—and because Rey became aware of an invisible but real crossroads that had sprung up between them. Sera would go one way, and Rey would, well...well, Rey decided he didn't want to talk about it with her anymore. Instead, he often took on the role of elder statesman of Thornhill—his family had lived there for years before hers had moved in; his had been one of the original families when the town was founded—hoping to make himself indispensable by affecting an expertise about the town's secrets and social mores. Like which laundry machines worked without tokens, the unspoiled food routinely tossed in the trash bins behind the commissary, and the Wednesday-night services at the Baptist church that should be avoided at all costs because prayer requests there too often became fodder for town gossip.

The truth was, besides his kid brother, Sera was his only friend. Which embarrassed him a little...or *a lot,* depending on his mood. On which side of leaving or staying his heart fell on that day. Though Thornhill brass would likely never admit it, the makeup of the town made clear they favored families with younger children. Rey and Sera were two of the only older young people there; most of the "founding" families his had come in with were now long gone. It bonded them by circumstance, the hovering and increasingly pressing question of what came after Thornhill for kids like them. They were both nineteen. She got college. And he got . . . told there was no work for him. His family had recently received the paperwork they'd been dreading, the notice that since Rey was without proper documentation, his time as a Thornhill resident had to come to an end. He was actually supposed to have vacated the town weeks ago.

But he was scared to go out into the world all alone.

As he came upon the old sawmill now, taking in the fern grass and vines of wild honeysuckle that grew along the structure's remaining walls, blood orange blossoms poking through holes where weary bricks had flown the white flag of time, crumbling to the forest floor, he chewed on a soothing thought. *Maybe she's just busy with school.* Why else had she stopped texting and calling? He stepped over the chunk of fallen stone Sera had considered her forest throne, the seat, furry with moss, from which she'd introduced him to J. California Cooper, a story she read from *Some Love, Some Pain, Sometime.* He pictured her bright, round eyes and the dimple of her right cheek, the red tone beneath her brown skin, which reminded this earth-loving boy of rich clay soil that he wanted to run his fingers through. It was possible he didn't realize until this exact moment that he was half in love with her. He felt a sudden exhilaration at the release of what had been at the edge of his waking thoughts for months now, as if a bell had rung in a still room. The clarity was achingly clean and clear: He loved Sera. He felt giddy for half a second. Which was why when he saw — a few feet ahead of him — a snatch of blue the same color as the Thornhill pullover he was wearing, he thought he was seeing *her,* sitting on a low and loose branch, waiting for him. As if his affection had summoned her, as if she had somehow known to meet him here for a clandestine goodbye, had intuited his feelings and had maybe come to say the same. Maybe Sera loved him too. But a second glance revealed he was just looking at a shirt. Thornhill blue, a brilliant azure, with yellow-gold writing. Near the log on which the shirt lay, there were beer bottles and a few cans. Lone Star and Shiner Bock, plus an empty bottle of green-apple schnapps. These were new. As was the shirt. Sera's, he knew at once.

She often turned the company-issued long-sleeved T-shirts into V-necks or modified the fit to follow some fashion idea she'd read online. This one's sleeves had been carefully excised, leaving not even a stray thread. He recognized the altered garment but not its lifelessness. He couldn't understand what it was doing here without its owner. Was she changing somewhere nearby? There was no watering hole in the part of the national forest that sat on this side of Highway 59. It was a trek of several miles to find a pond you could swim in. He called her name, and in the silence that followed, he felt the coolness in the air ice into a creeping sensation of dread. His breath felt sharp; the air stung as he inhaled. He walked even closer and saw how haphazardly the shirt had been left lying on the log.

Discarded came to mind.

Rey stared at it for a while, running time backward in his head, not just back through the thick woods of the national park or all the way back to Highway 59. He tried to go all the way to the last time they were out here together. It was Labor Day weekend. They'd previously discussed camping here for a few days, but she'd told him a party had come up and her plans had suddenly changed. Plans that had included Rey and then didn't.

A red-tailed hawk flew over the treetops, as near as a bird that size had ever gotten to the old mill site. It dusted pine tops, the crowns of oaks, then circled back, hovering long enough for Rey to wonder if it was actually a buzzard. *El zopilote.* He was so far from the culture of his birth country that he didn't even know if this was a good or bad sign, and he was often too ashamed to ask these things of his dad — who was really his stepdad and born here. But still more Mexican than Rey might ever be.

The hawk or vulture spooked him.

He picked up the shirt, gripped it while playing a scene in his mind of returning it to her. He was pleased by the idea of having an excuse to see her again, until he was suddenly seized by a sour feeling in his gut. A terrible thought yanked him up short. Had Sera been out here without him? Had she brought someone else to their special place? *His* special place? Try as he might, he could not make his mind come up with an innocent explanation for finding Sera's shirt in the woods, not one that wouldn't break his heart.

Why were there beer bottles out here?

Cigarette butts in the grass, he now saw.

Was it evidence of a clandestine assignation? Had she taken off her shirt for someone else when she and Rey hadn't so much as held hands, when he hadn't yet worked up the nerve to ask if he could kiss her? He realized he was still holding the shirt, turning it over, wanting to convince himself that it wasn't really hers.

And that's when he saw the rusty streaks of blood on the back of it.

A wide swatch of it along the neckline.

Part of the shirt was lightly damp, but because of the way it had lain on the log, the blood remained stiff and dry. Matte and dulled to a russet brown. Still, Rey had touched it, had stained himself by proximity. He let out a yip of terror, an animal panic.

He stumbled away from the walls of the mill, nearly tripping over a drift of wood. He didn't know what the blood meant, but it told a story that scared him. Seriously, where *was* Sera? How long *had* it been since she'd returned a text? He froze momentarily beneath the weight of not knowing what he should do. It felt wrong, dangerous even, to leave the shirt in the woods. He'd touched it, after all. He knew it would be bad to have any of this on his hands, a boy like him without a real home in a land he'd come to love. Unsure and afraid, he clutched the bloody shirt to his chest as gingerly as he might have held Sera if she'd let him, if he'd been brave enough to ask.

Part One

1.

DARREN WAS just passing through New Caney when he realized he'd forgotten the honey yogurt she liked. He considered Kingwood the last outpost of city life before Highway 59 takes you deep into the piney woods of East Texas. He had just cruised into one of his favorite parts of this drive, where the pine trees crowded the highway into a corridor lined with dark green on both sides, so you could hardly believe there was a world beyond these trees. It called to mind one of the monikers for this part of the state: Darren was behind the Pine Curtain now. It felt late to double back, especially when he should have already been in Camilla. He didn't want to miss her arrival. He wanted to stock the fridge, run a vacuum over the rugs in the living room, and set up the guest room just so. There was laundry still to do, field peas to prep for dinner. He hadn't expected to spend last night in Houston. But the news from his attorneys yesterday had caught him off guard and sunk him deeper into the funk he'd been in for the past three years. He holed up in a hotel and drank past his limit, a line of such incredible elasticity as to deserve a place of study in the physics department at

Rice or UT. He had woken this morning, cotton-mouthed but clear of mind, ready to tell his lieutenant what he could not put off for another day, knowing it was well past time.

That detour was now making him late getting back home.

He was planning to do up the whippoorwill peas with sautéed onions and garlic and stew them with tomatoes, also from his garden, from heirloom seeds that had belonged to his grandmother and her grandmother before her. There would be chicken or maybe grilled salmon, he hadn't decided. Because it didn't matter. She didn't eat much meat, and the real show was always what he could coax out of East Texas dirt, what the land of his birth would provide. There would be collards, or chard if he didn't have enough time, and a dill and mint cucumber salad, followed by baked peaches coated in butter and ground nutmeg and enough brown sugar to blacken a tooth. It was her first trip to the farmhouse in Camilla in a month, and he was determined to roll out the red-dirt carpet for her, was hoping, in fact, to entice her to stay longer this time. Their goodbyes stung, the more years they were together without putting a name on it. He wanted something real with her now, had his heart set on something permanent.

He'd have to stop for the yogurt somewhere on the way.

There was a Walmart in Cleveland, but it was as likely to have the imported foods she favored as the Brookshire Brothers in Coldspring, and if he had to choose between walking into the red-hat circus of a Walmart or the relative calm of a tiny grocery store in a town smaller than half the high schools in Houston, he would take the latter any day. San Jacinto County had a similarly hued belief system, but Darren found that the smaller the town, the fewer the folks to peacock to, the lesser the need for showing out. It made for, at a minimum, a less anxiety-producing trip to the grocery store. And managing his sense of doom was nearly a full-time job for Darren these days.

It was the reason he'd given Wilson when he turned in his badge this morning.

His lieutenant had looked terrible, sallow under fluorescent lights. He was sitting at his desk beneath a framed map of Texas in 1835, the year the Rangers were founded as a law enforcement agency in the state. He was eating a turkey and jalapeño sandwich, his ulcer be damned. "Is this about the Malvo deal?" Wilson asked when Darren made plain his desire to quit. "'Cause they don't have enough to indict you."

"And yet they keep trying."

Frank Vaughn, the district attorney of San Jacinto County, had tried to charge Darren in 2017 and again in 2018 with obstruction of justice and failed to get an indictment for a wholly circumstantial case — one that would require reopening the Ronnie "Redrum" Malvo homicide investigation. But yesterday his lawyers were frank about a harsh new reality: They were up against more than facts now. Vaughn was on the ballot for a congressional seat in 2020 and had hitched his campaign rhetoric to the winds of MAGA terror over antifa and the BLM movement, somehow tying Darren to both, openly painting him as a radical who had infiltrated Texas law enforcement and taken the law into his own hands by interfering in a homicide investigation, tipping the scales in the direction he wanted them to go. Vaughn had been dropping hints about bringing the case back to a grand jury in his campaign speeches, promising to take down an alt-left interloper inside the Texas Rangers. It was all theater, of course. But it was hard these days to know where make-believe ended and the truth held firm. Facts no longer seemed to matter all that much. It had been a maddening, dizzying three years since the election, a kaleidoscope of confusion and chaos — from the first strident insistence that we had not seen what we all most certainly *had* seen at the inauguration to Sharpiegate just a couple of weeks ago, a grown man drawing on his homework to prove he'd actually gotten the answers right. It would be laughable, would seem we were all watching a well-crafted farce, if Darren didn't feel in his bones that we were all going to die before the curtains closed; he couldn't shake this feeling that something truly awful was coming our way. He was deeply rattled, drinking more than ever, and therefore not entirely lying when he'd told Wilson he wasn't well. Jim Beam had been his best companion of the past few years, something to hold on to as he floated through the aimless void his life became when the multiagency Aryan Brotherhood of Texas task force was disbanded without a single indictment in 2017 — the second the new administration was in charge. He held to drink like a blind man to his cane, a way, in this strange new land, to tap a path through each day, sip by sip. He told none of this to Lieutenant Wilson. Instead, he said something vague about his doctor saying he needed a break — throwing out words about his heart, using poetry to mislead his boss into thinking there was something medically fragile about Darren's cardiovascular system when really he was just profoundly, unimaginably sad in this new world. The fever dream that had been the years since Donald Trump was elected.

Years that had laid bare the fragility of democracy.

Turned out the Founding Fathers were just men who liked to talk big all night after tying on a few, scribbling down laws and ideals that contradicted themselves every third paragraph, dreaming up an institution of freedom on a foundation built by slaves. It was all a house of cards. Smoke and mirrors. Just marks on parchment. With holes you could drive a truck through. And a talented huckster got behind the wheel of one and drove it all the way to the White House. It was reported that he had told over ten thousand lies since taking the oath of office, had broken umpteen laws. Darren would have said *allegedly,* but the president had either committed or admitted to many of these on live television. And no one seemed to care. Not really. People went to work, fed their kids, tucked them in at night, stayed up with the bills, then got up and did it all over again the next day. Because to slow down and really consider what was happening, to fully take in the ways reality itself no longer felt *real,* that it seemed everyone was lying, even if just to themselves about what a precarious situation we were all in, was to wake each night with a bone-rattling terror. The ground had gone out beneath us. We were floating through a mad world without guardrails. Darren was baffled and quietly terrified. And now he was again facing an indictment. According to his lawyers, shit was different this time. The run-up to the 2020 election was frying everyone's brain, making rabid animals out of neighbors and fellow citizens, the people you ran into at the post office. Everyone was mad and confused and sure somebody somehow was cheating them. In this environment, folks looking to park their anger and indignation somewhere might actually indict a black Texas Ranger, might even enjoy it.

The lawyers were clear: This time, Darren could go to prison.

Or be killed.

They said Darren's name and likeness were circulating on right-wing threads on Reddit, Discord, and Facebook pages. All it took was one idiot with a gun to recognize Darren and think he should settle it judge-jury-and-executioner-style, within his rights to take the law in his own hands. The very thing DA Vaughn was accusing Darren of doing.

Seated before Wilson's desk this morning, Darren had to press his fist to his right knee to stop it shaking, and when that failed, he covered his knee with his Stetson.

"They don't know where that gun came from," Wilson said.

"Neither do I," Darren lied.

He pictured the day years ago when he'd walked into Wilson's office to see DA Frank Vaughn sitting before a snub-nosed .38 in a plastic evidence bag on top of Wilson's desk, remembered knowing instantly that his mother, who'd been holding on to the gun as a tool of blackmail, was responsible for getting it into the hands of the district attorney. And he remembered the private tears he'd shed over her betrayal.

"Ballistics tell us that *was* the gun that killed Ronnie Malvo, but it was wiped clean of prints when it was mysteriously delivered to Vaughn. There's no clear chain of custody, no way to prove that gun was in your friend Mack's possession or that you did anything to hide it or try to protect him." Wilson wiped grease from the corners of his mouth with a napkin Darren was fairly certain was on its second or third round of use.

"I'm aware, sir."

The whole thing was a mess, an irony as bitter as chicory root.

When Darren believed that Rutherford "Mack" McMillan had killed Ronnie Malvo, an active member of the Aryan Brotherhood of Texas, and hid the murder weapon on the grounds of Darren's house in Camilla, where Mack had done odd jobs for the Mathews family for decades, Darren *had* looked the other way, tacitly hiding evidence. He didn't want an elderly black man going to death row for ridding Texas of a known racist and a murderer, a man missed by exactly no one, maybe not even his own mama. But it turned out Mack hadn't killed Ronnie Malvo; Mack's nineteen-year-old granddaughter, Breanna, had — over a base entanglement between her and Malvo that involved both drugs and sex. A fact that Darren now realized was a precursor to his current feeling that the world as he knew it made no sense anymore, a first clue that America was a snake eating its own tail. Breanna was sleeping with a white supremacist; a white supremacist was sleeping with a black girl. But by the time he discovered this, the murder weapon had gotten into the wrong hands: his mother's.

Darren eventually coerced a murder confession out of Bill "Big Kill" King, another member of the Aryan Brotherhood of Texas, to close the Ronnie Malvo case—keeping suspicion away from Mack. And Darren himself. He had lied and manipulated evidence, had done a wrong thing for a right reason, sure. But, bottom line, he had lied.

He wasn't entirely sure he didn't deserve to be indicted.

Wasn't sure either that he didn't deserve a medal.

He could keep going like this, vigilante cop settling scores in his own way, meting out his own home-brewed justice, but there would always be a faint whiff of rot coming from inside him, seeping out of his pores. *Because you will never beat them at their own game,* his uncle Clayton was fond of saying. The man in the White House was also making up his own rules and look where that had gotten all of us. The debate over purity in battle versus rolling in mud had worn Darren down, had burned out the light in his heart. What he thought: He wasn't sure if he was a good or bad cop, or even what that meant for a black Ranger, but he still believed he had a shot at being a decent man.

What he'd told the lieutenant: *I'm tired.*

Darren watched as Wilson grunted from the effort of sitting up from a reclining position in his office chair to grab the badge that rested between them on his desk. In one fluid motion, he slid the five-point star across the desktop, dropping it into the drawer, Darren hearing the metal lightly clink against something inside. Wilson looked not just disappointed; he looked like a man who was being abandoned, a wounded soldier left on the field. "Your uncle William would have thought this was the exact time the country couldn't afford to lose a man like you," Wilson said. He had served with Darren's uncle, the first black Ranger sworn into the department, in the 1980s.

"All due respect, sir," Darren said, "my uncle couldn't imagine the times we're living in."

"No worse than what he and your family saw during the sixties, I bet."

Wilson must have caught the fleeting look of annoyance on Darren's face: *And you would know this how?* He closed the desk drawer that now held Darren's badge. "This too shall pass, Mathews," Wilson said, although he looked exhausted by the prospect of waiting out whatever *this* was that they were living through. He rubbed at the bags, both puffy and dark, under his eyes. "This country's been through worse."

"I'm not sure it matters, sir. We are where we are."

"Could use you out there, all I'm saying. Now more than ever," Wilson said.

Darren swallowed his guilt, then rooted around for his anger at being put in this position, at Wilson for invoking his uncle William's name and legacy. Sure, it was a sentiment among black cops these days that "Black Lives Matter" meant a gun and the law had their purpose — safeguarding black folks in every corner of American life. But Darren felt resentful of the idea that black cops somehow bore the sole responsibility for this. Surely it was someone else's turn to do the work of righting the country's racial wrongs, case by trauma-inducing case. He'd devoted his entire career to ridding the state of Texas and the country of racists like the Brotherhood, had compromised his honor to do so, and now they were in every branch of government, sitting pretty.

Wilson gently cleared his throat as Darren rose to leave. "You don't think this makes you look guilty, son, tucking tail and running?"

He *was* guilty. Of a lot of things.

He didn't see it as running so much as saving his soul.

"No," he said.

Wilson glanced back at the desk drawer that held Darren's badge. He fingered the handle, flicking the drawer open an inch, then looking up with something like hope. "Give it some time, Mathews. Huh? Just asking you to think about it, son."

Darren slid his Stetson on his head. "I did," he said. "And I'm done."

2.

THE MATHEWS farmhouse sat at the end of a clay dirt road.

Years before Darren was born, his grandfather had lined the private drive with crape myrtles of a coral color that made Darren think of peaches some days, unripe plums on others. They were planted as a gift to Darren's grandmother. The Mathews family had been on this land for over a hundred years. Darren's identical-twin uncles — William, the Texas Ranger, and Clayton, a former defense attorney turned law professor — had been born in this house. Darren's father had also come into the world through these doors. Darren "Duke" Mathews, the first, was something of a closed book to his only son. When Darren was a boy, the uncles who had raised him were his whole world, the moon and sun, each a source of light, if one was cool and the other fiery. By the time he thought enough to ask after an essential missing element in his life — what was his father like; what sort of man had he come from — William had been killed in the line of duty, and Clayton was even *less* inclined to talk about his baby brother, Duke. Grief bit his tongue. To raise the issue with even the simplest questions — what kind of beer did he drink; was he funny — was to see a pall come over

Clayton's face, a scrim through which Darren could just make out how much it pained and confused his uncle to be the last living member of the family he'd been born into. Married late in life to his twin brother's widow, Clayton had no children of his own. Only Darren. The nephew he'd rescued—to hear him tell it—from Darren's mother, Bell, within days of word that his kid brother, Duke, had been killed in one of the last fights in Vietnam. Darren had been only hours old. Clayton had always had an outsize interest in his nephew Darren's life and choices. Pressing him toward a career in law—one in a courtroom as an attorney and not in the saddle of a Chevy as a Texas Ranger, a profession of which he'd never approved, for either his twin brother or his nephew.

Darren knew very little about his father and would have told you that he'd made peace with that. Because without Clayton opening up about Duke, what choice did he have? His grandparents were gone, his uncle William too. The only person he could ask who knew his father—well enough, at least, to get pregnant by him—was a woman he hadn't spoken to in years now. His mother was another family member he considered dead.

Which was why, when he turned in the driveway of the farmhouse he'd recently painted a pale yellow and saw two cars he didn't recognize, Darren didn't immediately think anything of it. No alarm bells rang. One of the cars was surely Randie's rental from the airport in Houston, and the other was maybe a neighbor's, he figured. They were nosy and endlessly curious about the woman who came for a visit every now and then but was rarely ever seen in town. Had one of them come over to have a look, stopping by with a pie or some eggs from their hens? Did one of them drive a beat-up blue Nissan?

It was the music pouring out of the house that ultimately tipped him off, that spoke to a potential storm of trouble brewing inside. Randie knew where he kept his LPs, sure, knew how to work the old turntable he'd jury-rigged to a modern sound system, but the Bettye LaVette song seeping out of the house like black molasses was the opposite of a siren song. He heard the lyrics as he stepped out of his truck: *The hurt slowly takes its toll. It just ain't worth it after a while.*

He couldn't have sung it better where his relationship with his mother was concerned.

He knew it was Bell before he opened the door and found her standing with her back to him, reading the album cover as studiously as if it were a sacred text. The choice of music, its biting and bitter tone, was the only thing he recognized about her. Having last seen her three years ago, drunk and in a cheap fur coat, he couldn't make sense of the woman before him now. She wore an olive cardigan and khaki pants. Her shirt was tucked in, and her belt matched the modest black shoes on her feet. They were work shoes with a low wedge heel, like the ones she wore when she'd been a maid at a run-down motel near Lake Livingston, only these were pristine and well cared for, no holes or peeling pleather. When she heard his boots on the wood floor, she turned. Their eyes met, and he was reminded that he got his height from his mother's side of the family, the leanness of his limbs. He stood nearly eye to eye with the woman who had betrayed him and disappeared for years. Not that he'd been looking for her. When a bobcat slunk back into the woods, you didn't go chasing after the thing.

His mother's eyes were a deep pecan brown.

They were as bright and clear as he had ever seen them.

He found he could not speak. He had a panicked, irrational thought that he might wet himself. Or, worse, cry. The nip or two of Jim Beam he'd allowed himself on the backcountry roads left him shaky and feeling like he had no self-control. He felt chastened, as if the disgrace of being half in the bag, of driving with whiskey in his veins, had conjured up his greatest shame: his mother. The rising bile of hate he felt toward her scared him, as did the impossibility of holding the hate firmly in his hands. It kept slipping through his fingers like the notes in the song that was playing. The blue guitar plucked at his rage, then bent it till he felt the bruised violet beneath.

Bell finally opened her mouth to speak, but it wasn't *her* voice he heard.

It was Randie's.

"She was here when I arrived."

He turned to see the woman he loved standing at the mouth of the hallway that led to the three bedrooms, including the guest room where she might have already started unpacking her things. He couldn't explain why she bothered with the pretense of it; she hadn't slept in that room even once. She looked a little spooked, confused by the situation they all found themselves in. Until today, she'd never met his mother.

"I'll let you two talk," she said, turning and disappearing down the hallway, leaving behind her vanilla-bark scent, earthy and sweet. He hungered for her in a way that blotted out his other senses. He had a wild thought that he could simply follow her down the hall and recount the nightmare he was apparently having. His mother was in his house, *and, weird, you were there too.* They could laugh about it. And, later, after they'd made love, after he'd spent himself in the thick warmth of her body, the adoring tenderness of her gaze, she would gently poke him about where he thought the dream had come from. *And why now?* And she would say the words she had been laying out like a welcome mat for years now, a gentle invitation: *Tell me about her.*

Could he be dreaming?

There was so much about the world he no longer trusted at face value. Maybe this visit from his mother was just another part of the cosmic joke of the past three years, part of the funhouse sensation that life had turned into a rather good facsimile of itself, missing only a few key details, like gravity, like the sense that there were at least some hardwired principles we'd all agreed on that still carried weight. Instead, nothing felt nailed down anymore. The ever-present dread in Darren's chest sank to a bass note.

Now that they were alone, his mother took her time gingerly putting the album back in its place on the shelf among his other records, sliding it into the slim, empty spot between two collections of original recordings from Don Robey's Peacock Records in Houston, Clarence "Gatemouth" Brown and Big Mama Thornton, the swinging blues of her childhood. She turned to face him again. Hands clasped before her, she looked like a patient and kind schoolteacher. It put a lump in his throat, his mind flashing to himself at six years old, when he'd liked to pretend his first-grade teacher, Miss Billings, was his mother instead of the absent woman his uncle Clayton always said wasn't shit, wasn't ever gon' be shit, whenever Bell's name came up in conversation.

"I'm sorry, son," she said.

"For what this time?" He made no effort to keep his voice down, aware that he was being loud for Randie in the other room, that he wanted her to bear witness to Bell's particular brand of ferity, and for that he needed volume to reach his real mother, not this country mouse before him. "Breaking into my house?"

"For one," she said, her chin ducking slightly, her gaze drifting from the furor in his. She was having a hard time meeting his eye. "Lil' Buckey's boy down the way had a spare key. Buckey Robeson went to junior high with your uncle Petey, my oldest brother. You remember Petey, right? Used to come down from Nacogdoches when he had a little time off at the lumber plant where he worked." Then, when it was clear this line of talk was doing nothing to thaw Darren's icy demeanor, she said, "Well, maybe you don't remember him. Clayton didn't let you around my people much. It was just a janitorial job he had, but it was a good job back then, and we were proud of—"

"Mama!"

The word shot out like a bullet, his lips a loose, malfunctioning trigger, and it jolted him as if he'd shot an actual gun in the room. He wasn't sure if the word was a weapon against her or himself. He'd only meant to stop her from running a prattling con, jamming him up with words. But the *Mama* had come out like a strangled cry. It was pain, naked and hot. But he heard the note of longing in it. She heard it too and pounced on it, seizing an opportunity. "I didn't think you'd see me otherwise."

That she spoke as if this were all quite reasonable, walking into his house uninvited, that she seemed to be waiting for him to embrace her with, if not forgiveness, then some measure of understanding, further made him feel his world was slightly off-kilter, the constant fear of never being sure if the person in front of you was operating from the same set of facts. "You blackmailed me!" he said. "Then gave the gun that shot Ronnie Malvo to the district attorney anyway—"

"I didn't even know that gun killed that man. Least, I wasn't sure."

He thought he saw a flash of glee light her eyes, that she was enjoying this.

"Get out," he said.

"I wiped that gun clean, Darren. I would never have passed that on to the district attorney without making sure first. I just threw them a bone without a scent."

That she could not hear the lack of difference in that distinction caused him to physically recoil in her presence, to stagger back a few inches, to marvel at the fact that he could still stand, that he could, in fact, walk and talk at all, that he had ever stood a chance in this world with Bell Callis as his entrée. And yet he also felt oddly let down, disappointed by a confession that had all the righteous suspense of a tent revival, where everyone who walked in was saved. To hear her admit her crime so mundanely as to quibble over the degrees of betrayal wounded him anew. Somehow, she had managed to fail him again.

Or maybe she had truly freed him now that he was no longer burdened by *What if* or *One day*. They had finally met again, and she was the same mercurial, mean-streaked woman she'd always been, the one Clayton had warned him about. There was no mystery to Bell Callis, save for why he'd drawn the short stick for a mother and what his father, not even twenty when he died, ever saw in her; there was no more puzzle to solve here. Perhaps she had given him a gift. Brought a key not to break in so much as break him out of his lingering attachment to her. She had unlocked a final, irrefutable truth—*wasn't shit; wasn't ever gon' be shit*—and he could be free of her now.

She seemed to sense she hadn't gotten a good grip on him yet.

"Vaughn ain't got nothing on you. I made sure of that. That's what I'm trying to tell you. It ain't gon' come to nothing. Even if they tried to get me to say something against you—"

"Oh," Darren said as it hit him, why she was here.

It almost cut his tongue to say the words: "You're testifying." His lawyers had said Vaughn was serious this time. Was there a new grand jury already under way? Is that why she had darkened his doorstep? To name a price for her silence on the stand?

Bell shook her head.

"Darren, no," she said. "I wouldn't."

"You gave the DA the gun in the first place!"

"I was trying to protect you."

"You're lying."

She sighed in a way that flared with indignation. "I just told you I didn't even know that was the same gun that killed that man. I thought if I handed it in, no fingerprints on it, it would stop them thinking you had anything to do with it."

"I want you to leave."

"Wait, Darren," she said. "This ain't why I came to see you. There's something else I need your help with. It's a problem I run into at the college in Nacogdoches, son."

He laughed at the last word, reached for the freedom he felt earlier.

He was done with her.

He thought of the groceries in the cooler in the car, the dinner he had planned. September in San Jacinto County, he and Randie could eat on the back porch, could feast on a view of the wall of pines that bordered the property. He thought of the bottle of wine they would share at dinner, followed by a bourbon or two of his own afterward, three if the music was good, if they put side one of Freddie King *Live & Loud* on the hi-fi. He only had to get back his key, pray she hadn't pressed its outline in a bar of soap before Randie arrived, and he could go back to the business of being a motherless child. When she at last handed over the spare key, and he told her to leave with the finality of words etched in stone, she looked at her only child and spoke with a directness of purpose that didn't hide her obvious nerves or the hitch in her voice, the tender way it caught and bent when she said, "I'm sober, Darren."

3.

HE DIDN'T believe her.

He told Randie as much over a dinner of buttered rolls and a rough-hewn salad of chunks of cucumber and fat quarters of tomatoes from the garden and a butt of smoked Gouda Randie had found in the back of the refrigerator. She'd prepared the meal for them when it was clear that Darren was in no shape to cook, had lost all interest in food.

"She gave me my first beer, for God's sake," he said.

"Maybe she's finally sorry for that . . . for a lot of things."

"I mean, who gives a kid a beer? What kind of *mother* gives her thirteen-year-old child a beer?" He took a sip of his bourbon and ran his finger around the ring of condensation the glass left on the pistachio-green metal table on the back porch, a table so old it was now vintage and quite chic, Randie had told him. Meals on the back porch were her favorite part of her trips to Camilla. After *him,* he hoped. She wore a thin lilac-colored sweater. Cashmere, he'd guess. It belled at the sleeves like the petals of the flower and showed off the many lay-ers of gold bangles on her bronze wrists. He didn't know where she got her money, how much a freelance photographer could really pull in, or if her late husband, Michael, had left her a nest egg of some sort. Somehow in three years, they hadn't gotten that far. Money, who had what and where and, if this ever became something real, would they share and how. Darren blamed it on her career — why they had not made their relationship official in some capacity — and she lay the blame on his. She traveled from job to job around the country and the world, filling out the in-between times with trips to East Texas, having developed a strange affection for it that she couldn't explain. Strange because she had once blamed the state for her husband's murder, a case that Darren had solved. It was how they'd met, and he was the reason her feelings about the state had shifted. She now saw its raw grace and beauty through Darren's eyes, felt the warmth of its people in the arms he wrapped around her during the nights they spent together. If Texas had made this man, whom she loved and trusted completely, who made her feel safe in ways she never had in her life before, then she would make peace with the complicated state.

Darren's job moved him around less frequently than it had before the multiagency Aryan Brotherhood of Texas task force was dissolved; he had been mostly stationed out of the Rangers' office in Houston, driving up to the farmhouse in Camilla every weekend and holiday until he and his wife made their separation official, about six months after the case of the missing boy in Hopetown, up near Caddo Lake. It made no sense for Randie to relocate, she'd said, to make Texas her home base if Darren was rarely ever in one place. But the divorce was final now, and he'd turned in his badge this morning. He was ready to test the idea of the two of them making things more permanent. There was a ring. His grandmother's, actually. One he'd not wanted to give to Lisa, had feared it wasn't to her taste, as it had no stone, nothing that shone too brightly. It was a band of gold with an intricate engraving, so old it was now vintage and maybe quite chic? Would Randie think so? Was a ring, and the permanent life with Darren it represented, even what she wanted? It was on this visit that he had planned to find out. But then his mother had shown up. And he'd drunk more than he'd intended at what could only loosely be called "dinner." He'd eaten only a few bites between long rants about the viciousness of Bell Callis. Randie, who had stopped after a single glass of wine, was shaking her head. "I'm just saying, she.didn't seem . . . *vicious*."

"That's because you don't know her," Darren said. "You don't know all the stories Clayton told me about what she was like, *is* like, why he had to take me away from her. There's no telling how awful my life would have been if she had been allowed to raise me." He reached for his whiskey again, caught something familiar in the way Randie's eyes tracked his hand, its nearness to the glass. Lisa had worn the same monitoring gaze at times, Clayton too. The look from Randie stilled his hand.

"Of course I don't," she said softly. "Because I've never met Clayton." *Right.*

They each knew of the other, his uncle and Randie, but no, they'd never met. Darren hadn't wanted to share her was the simple truth of it. They had so little time together, a week or two here and there; the longest stretch had been a month and a half around the holidays last year. Darren always found a reason why it was inconvenient to drive up to Austin, where his uncle lived. Clayton still taught constitutional law at the university there, but his course load was light, and he could have likewise come to Camilla to meet Randie. But Darren always managed it so that somehow Randie had just left whenever Clayton made a serious inquiry about driving down to Camilla, returning to his ancestral home and his beloved nephew. *It's been a while, son.*

It was a sore spot for Randie, that she hadn't met his surviving uncle, one of the two men who had raised him. He was hiding either her or

Clayton, and both scenarios spoke to a crack in their relationship. But she misunderstood his reluctance to introduce them, and he was wary of correcting her opinion on the matter. He had vowed not to be the kind of man who drug the problems of his marriage into his new relationship. So he tried to keep from Randie all the ways his ex-wife and Clayton's closeness had put a strain on his union with Lisa, even from its early days when they were high-school sweethearts. Clayton had set his sights on Lisa as a right fit for Darren and had practically been a third party in their marriage, so intense was his investment in the two of them. That Lisa often sided with Clayton about Darren's life choices made him feel ganged up on and infantilized, and it frankly embarrassed him to talk to Randie about it.

But she knew.

"I'm not Lisa, Darren."

He reached across the table for her hand, which necessitated gently pushing the whiskey glass to the side. He held her hand, thumb stroking her skin. "I'm sorry," he said. The setting sun bathed the back of the house in light the color of buttered rum. A breeze ruffled the pine tops in the distance so that they perfumed the air around the back porch sweetly. He felt a surge of overwhelming love for Randie, gratitude for the part of her that was ever a straight shooter. No bullshit and no lies, which she likewise demanded of him. It kept him up nights, the fact that he hadn't been all the way honest with her. She didn't know he'd pinned the murder of Ronnie Malvo on Bill King. Would she marry a man who'd done something so vile? He was scared to tell her and so bore this quiet shame alone, sometimes turning his back to her when he couldn't look her in the eye. He knew she sensed he withheld things. "I don't see how we take next steps if you won't let me all the way in." Randie slipped her hand from his, and Darren filled the void by reaching for his whiskey, taking a hearty sip, ice clinking as he drained it. "Would I have ever met your mother if she hadn't shown up here today?"

"No," he said. "Absolutely not, and you know why."

"She seems sorry, Darren."

"She *seems* sorry, just like she doesn't *seem* vicious," he said. "You don't know her like I do. She can't be trusted, Randie—like, at all. She lies. All the time."

"I know it was an unwelcome surprise, seeing her here, but maybe there's an opportunity for healing, for both of you."

"Heal? What does my mother need to heal?"

"Darren..." Randie took a breath, as if her next words were a large set of stairs it was going to take a great effort to climb. "Has it ever occurred to you that your mother suffered a trauma when you were born?"

"What are you talking about?" He felt betrayed by this whole conversation, mad at Bell for putting on a trickster's costume of a remorseful woman, and mad at Randie for falling for it.

"I know it's this defining story in your family, how, grief-stricken, Clayton nobly saved you from a woman incapable of properly caring for you, but she was also grieving, Darren. She'd lost your father too. And she had her child taken away from her within a day of giving birth. Women are extraordinarily vulnerable postpartum."

"Says a woman who has no children." He heard the nastiness in his voice and felt a vague sense of self-disgust, but he couldn't fully access the feeling, not after this many drinks. Anger—that was still at hand. It was familiar and comfortable.

"Seriously, Darren, I've thought about this. About your story. And hers."

"Why are you doing this?" he said. "Why are you taking her side?"

"I'm only acknowledging that she has one. Truth is, I feel sorry for both of you."

She sighed and looked out across the expanse of acreage behind the house.

Then, quietly, she said, "You've both lost so much."

"She could have taken me back, Randie. She could have fought for me."

"She was a teenager up against your uncles, one a lawyer and one a DPS police officer at that time, men who had way more money than she and her family did."

"How do you know what her family did or didn't have?"

"I got curious a while back when it was clear you didn't want to say anything more about her, and, I don't know, I guess I just wanted to know more about you. I felt we'd hit a wall, behind which some part of you was locked away," she said, trying to hold his gaze, afraid she might lose their connection at any moment. "I looked up some things about the Callis family. You'd spoken so much about the Mathews men and all they accomplished, how your grandparents and your uncles made you the man you are, that I guess I just got curious about the other side."

"You looked up my mother's family?"

Darren felt something seize him then. He stood and backed up to the porch's railing, leaned on it for support, as he searched Randie's face to see if the woman he wanted to marry was in there somewhere. "Did *you* do this? Did you tell her to come here?" He felt his stomach flip and then sink with dread. "Randie, if you . . ."

One thing Lisa would never do, he thought and then immediately felt guilty for the comparison. Randie's brows knit together as she gave him an alien look. "Can you hear how paranoid you sound? Before today, I had never met your mother, Darren, and knowing how you feel about her, the problems you guys have, the ways you both —"

"No, don't do that. Don't 'both sides' my mother and me."

He was so heated, he left Randie on the back porch and walked into the house, bore left toward the kitchen and the bottle of bourbon on the counter. He heard her footsteps behind him. He had to stop himself from turning to face her — he was afraid he might tell her to leave and never come back because she was talking about things she didn't understand; she was dismissing the ways his mother had turned his life upside down. Randie rested her hand on his waist, and he felt his lower body flush with warmth and wanting. They hadn't yet had a proper reunion, not even a real kiss, he'd been so angry after his mother left.

"Darren, look at me." She tightened her touch into a squeeze. He poured himself another bourbon and turned, tried to avoid her eyes but found that he couldn't. "I know how much your mother has hurt you. But even I had no idea that she would have the gall to just show up like this, that she would just walk into your house —"

"This is who she is. This is what I'm trying to tell you." He took a big bite out of the bourbon, welcomed the burn of it going down. "You realize if I go to prison, I might not make it out alive. You think a black Texas Ranger who spent his career trying to take down the Aryan Brotherhood of Texas is going to get a warm welcome in a Texas penal system running rampant with ABT?"

It finally hit him.

He was facing prison.

Randie saw the haunted look on his face, the utter soul exhaustion.

"Oh, Darren," she said, resting her head against his chest. He wrapped his arms around her, then kissed the top of her head, as he stood a good four inches taller than her. He breathed in her vanilla scent mixed with the smells in the kitchen, the bounty from his garden and the open bottle of bourbon. He was at home here, with her.

This was all he wanted.

"She's dangerous, Randie. Always has been. And all that other stuff she brought up, the story she told about some missing girl up in Nacogdoches. You can't believe a word of it."

His mother had not stopped at her announcement that she was sober. Darren had been seconds away from forcibly removing her from the house when Randie came out of the back bedroom to check on him. Bell had quickly started in on a story about a girl, a student at the college up in Nacogdoches where, first Darren was hearing of it, his mother had relocated. Her brother Pete had had a stroke — *Can't tie his shoes, can't half hold a spoon in his right hand* — and she felt she owed it to her big brother to help. *He was the one got me out of this county way back when, tried to get me a chance at something. This was 'fore I had you, of course, which yanked me right back down to Camilla.* She spoke rapidly, as crisp as he'd ever heard the edges of her words. Was it possible his mother hadn't had a drink that day? Impossible to know for sure; he didn't think, in his nearly fifty years of living, he'd ever been around his mother with a dry tongue. She was laying out the story she had come to tell — *To get your help on it, son* — with the speed of rocks rolling down a hill because she seemed to sense that she was on borrowed time with Darren, who had clearly not been wooed by her initial report that she'd finally quit drinking, that she hadn't had a taste in nearly two years.

Randie had then introduced herself as Darren's "friend."

Glad to meet you, Bell had said, taking just Randie's fingertips for a demure handshake.

"My mother is not to be trusted," Darren said now.

"I see that," Randie said. "I'm sorry if I didn't let you know that I see that, that I see what you're up against . . . going all the way back to the beginning." She squeezed his waist and whispered softly into the cool, softly damp fabric of his shirt, "You suffered a trauma too, you know, being taken from your mother at such an early age."

"My uncles did the right thing," he said.

He took another sip of his Jim Beam and caught her watching him, a curious expression on her face, her sloe eyes crinkling in a kind of knowing sadness. "She gave you your first drink in more ways than one," she said, followed by a warm sigh.

4.

THE SEX that night was awkward, rhythmically off.

Darren's mind would not stay with his body, and Randie was also distant, so they seemed like two agitated souls floating above bodies making a valiant, even balletic, attempt at lovemaking. They had the dance moves right, familiar as they were, but one or both had a stone in their shoe, some lingering disturbance that interfered with the release each sought from the other, the exhilaration of being together again.

He was left unsatisfied and lay on his back after, turning over the nagging thought that there was more to his mother's surprise visit than step nine of her professed process of sobriety. He was lying there, thinking about her purported *real* reason for showing up at his home—a girl she thought might be in danger—and how it might factor into some coming con of hers, the shape and time of its arrival he tried to divine by the way it set his teeth on edge. "Are you going to look into it, at least?" Randie asked. She had her left leg entangled with his right, but the rest of her body was turned toward the window, to the view of the picture-book moon, its silvery light dancing through the branches of the white oak along the side of the house. It lit up the damp on her skin, painted her beauty so that he felt stirred to try again, but the earlier agitation resurfaced, cooling the heat between them. "Look into what, exactly?"

His mother hadn't had a name, not one she was sure of, at any rate.

Just said that she couldn't think of who else to talk to about the girl, the college student. "Seems she just up and disappeared. Was just gone one day."

Darren's mother was still in the custodial business, these days working for a maid-service agency in Nacogdoches County — though she had her eye on moving to a live-work gated community just outside of town, if she could convince her brother to leave the home he'd rented for decades. They'd been housemates for the past year.

The missing girl lived in a sorority house off campus that Bell cleaned four days a week. The girl was black, Bell wanted that known straightaway, and with home training, she said. "Any time we seen each other, even just to pass in the hall, me with my bucket and her with her schoolbooks and such, she always give me a little nod, let me know that even if she living in a houseful of white girls, she and me still family in some way. She wasn't stuck-up like the others. She was real nice, what I knew of her."

"Which isn't much," Darren said. "Since you don't know her name."

"Naw, we never did get that far, and I don't snoop around the girls' rooms, don't pick through their papers or nothing. Keep my head down, do my job, go to meetings."

Darren huffed out a tight hot pellet of air. He was having a hard time swallowing this idea of his mother as a bastion of temperance. And anyway, what made Bell think something was wrong? Because a girl she worked for, or who lived in the sorority house that paid the maid service that Bell worked for, was no longer making time to say hi in the hallways? "She's a college kid. Of age, I'm going to guess," Darren said. "I don't see what any of this has to do with you . . . or *me*."

"She reminds me a little of myself at that age, to tell the truth of it," Bell said.

"Weren't you pregnant with me at sixteen? You never graduated high school."

Bell shook her head, expressing disappointment in him.

"Something's wrong, Darren. That girl moved into the sorority house not even a month ago, and I saw her every couple of days or so. She had a single room they put her off in by herself, no roommate like the other girls at the house, and then just this week, the door to her room was closed and locked up from the outside, and no one seems to know anything about it or where she went. I asked some of the other girls there what happened to the one that stayed in the small room on the third floor."

Bell glanced across the room at Randie, sniffing out an ally.

"They act like I don't know what I'm talking about, like maybe I had it wrong and there never was any black girl living in the sorority house. I thought for half a minute I had imagined the whole thing. That all the years of drinking scrambled my mind up some, made it so my own dreams were walking around outside my body."

"Mama," he said with a show of patience so exaggerated it was actually rude. "This is not anything that's your concern. You don't even know something's wrong."

"It's a feeling I got," she said, again glancing in Randie's direction. "And you know how they do with missing black girls, how you can't get no one to pay attention."

"No one is missing."

Randie, who'd been leaning against the cherrywood secretary that had been his grandmother's pride and joy, said to him, "It couldn't hurt to make a few inquiries."

"Petey know a man in the Nacogdoches Police Department, but they say talk to campus security, and campus security say it's off university grounds, and not a one of 'em interested in asking me any questions, wouldn't even take a report from me."

"Not without a name, I'm sure," Darren said.

"Rho Beta Zeta. The sorority. That's a name. They should start there, start with the fact that when I hauled trash out to their dumpster this week, I found a bunch of stuff from that locked room in the bins. I been in that room. Those were *her* things."

"Hmmm," Randie mumbled.

"Right," Bell said, enjoying the telling, her big monologue in the third act. "Something don't exactly seem quite right. Somebody threw that girl's stuff in the trash. Her clothes and some pictures, makeup and a whole bunch of hair products. She couldn't ever make hers lay down quite right. I don't know why these young'uns don't just keep a pressing comb handy, but then again, I can't imagine the house mother would let a black girl down to the kitchen to heat up a hot comb anyway—"

"Mama," he said. Because what the hell was she talking about?

"Now, I know the Rangers step in sometimes when local folks ain't doing what they ought to, and I just can't help feeling like this little girl is being ignored somehow. Why is no one looking for her?"

"Darren," Randie said. His mother had struck a bull's-eye.

He wondered how much Bell knew about Randie.

Her husband's murder in the state had initially been treated with the least amount of care; she was sold half-truths and lazy obfuscations by the local sheriff.

Darren could tell Randie was urging him to do something.

But he was not about to tell his mother any further details about his life. He did *not* want her in possession of the knowledge that he'd just turned in his badge. It was only because he had designs on a proposal to Randie that he said something vague about asking around to see if someone else had filed a missing person report, her parents maybe. He could try to find out a little more, he said. But he was sure there was nothing to worry about, the whole thing likely a misunderstanding.

"You find her parents, you make sure to tell them I got her things out the trash," Bell said, jutting out her chin righteously. "I wasn't about to let them just throw out that child's stuff like she never even existed."

"You moved evidence?" Darren said.

The question was pure instinct, going all the way back to his years in law school.

At the word *evidence,* Darren thought he saw his mother crack a smile.

"So you *do* think something funny is going on," she said.

She had been enjoying herself too much for him to take any of it seriously. She had been having too much fun: announcing that she, a champion drunk, had quit booze; playing a mild-mannered amateur sleuth concerned about a black girl who'd gone missing — giving her a bona fide reason to command her son's attention — a black girl who she'd claimed reminded her of herself, when Bell Callis had, at that girl's age (younger, in fact), been a knocked-up teenager and nowhere near a college campus.

"And who knocked her up?" Randie asked now, finally sitting up in bed, the covers falling to her waist. The windows were original to the house and thin as a sheet of ice over a shallow pond, the glass as cloudy too, especially now, as the heat of their lovemaking still hung in the air, dampening to the touch everything in the room. He should get up and adjust the thermostat, but he felt leaden. The shock of seeing his mother had worn off, and in its place was a creeping sadness. It lived, as it always had, behind the anger. He kept a pint in the top drawer of his nightstand, alongside his Colt .45, a jar of antacids, and matches for the scented candles Randie liked. He sat up too, pulling out the bottle for a drink. Randie turned, watching him. She never said anything about his drinking. He caught looks sometimes, but as with everything else about Darren, she seemed to accept him completely, even as she gently pushed at his complacency, the aspects of his life he thought had been decided years ago. "It's just interesting to me how much you frame your problems with your mother in such a way as to leave out the men who played a part in why your life turned out the way it did."

"My dad died, Randie." He played with the cap on the bottle, twisting it open and then closed. "Can't blame him for not being around for Bell when I was born."

"Not talking about blame," she said. "At all."

Then, kissing his shoulder, she added, "Just what happened."

"Well, he was drafted, so there wasn't much that could have been done."

"I thought you said he was in school at the time."

Had he said that? He knew bits and pieces of his father's life, but they existed in a haze of the world before Darren was in it. His father wasn't real to him. But Bell *was,* painfully so. "Well, how else would he have ended up in Vietnam?" he said, even as something felt off in his body. Randie said that surely his father would have gotten a deferment. Hadn't all the Mathews men been educated? This talk made Darren's head feel heavy, his thoughts fuzzy in the warmth of the room, confused by the tangle of questions. "He died in Vietnam," he said, firmly repeating what he'd been told.

Randie turned her body away from him.

The room was small enough that she reached out a big toe and wiped condensation from the window on her side of the bed. It let in the moonlight once more, threw a gorgeous haze over everything. He was ready to nod off when Randie asked him again if he was going to check on the missing black girl, the Stephen F. Austin student. He reminded her he was no longer a Ranger, that he had no jurisdiction or cause to get involved. If the girl was missing, it wouldn't go unnoticed. Her parents, professors, friends, someone would eventually file a report. "Your mother tried that."

"My mother is not credible or an interested party."

"A black girl is missing, and two law enforcement agencies and the girls at her sorority don't seem the least bit concerned. I would think this would make *you* an interested party. I am, at least. I mean, Jesus, Darren, I lost my husband to this racist state. I can't help but think someone out there cares about that girl and wants to know what the hell happened to her. You could at least alert the Rangers' office in Houston."

"What girl, Randie? We don't know that any of this is real, that my mother didn't make up this whole horseshit story—"

"To what end, Darren? What exactly would be her endgame here?" She'd raised her voice at him.

"Why are *you* getting so upset?" he said.

"Because you're being glib, cynical about this."

"The woman tried to frame me for a fucking crime," he said. "For all I know, she made this up as a cover for the fact that she was just in town testifying against me in front of a grand jury." He uncapped the bottle again and nearly drained it. "My mother is a liar."

Watching him drink, Randie came as close as she ever had to a sneer of irritation.

"I'm just saying, Darren, the reason I'm here right now . . . this whole thing that happened between us, how we found each other in this world . . . is because you were a man who did something when you saw something fucked up going on in this state. You took action in Lark, that shit-ass town. It's part of what I love about you. Part of the reason I'm here, in your bed, is because —"

"So you want me to take on another murder case so you can get off?"

The sharp intake of breath coming from Randie's side of the bed sucked all the warmth out of the room. If he'd thought he saw irritation in her eyes before, it had been replaced with contempt. He knew it was bad, that he'd been crude and cruel. Gross. He reached for her hand, but she swatted it away. She stood from the bed and dragged the entire quilt and comforter in a huge tangle as she walked toward the bedroom door. She turned back and looked at him for a long time. He watched her breath rise and fall in deep waves. He thought to say something, but he was a coward. And drunk. So, so drunk. Randie fixed her mouth to maybe say the same, but then she simply walked out, leaving him alone with the smell of the blood he'd drawn. For the first time since they'd been together, Randie slept in the guest room.

5.

SHE WAS gone by morning. And he was somehow more upset than he'd been the night before. He'd been an ass, yes. But she had been wrong for downplaying facts of his life that she didn't understand, talking down to him about his relationship with a woman she hardly knew. He decided he was furious. That lasted until he drank his way through every bottle in the house. Then, after two days in a stumbling fog, with only his righteousness keeping him half upright, he awoke on the floor, laid low by a hammer-like pulse in his head that nearly blacked his vision, by a hollowed-out feeling in the center of his chest. He beat at it a few times to see if he was still in there, still alive.

Then he rolled over and threw up.

He lay there on his side for a while, trying to divine the events of the past few days in the pool of sick on his grandmother's rug, to tell him what had happened. Bilious and thin, the greenish-yellow liquid was sinking quickly into the fibers. He saw in it evidence that he'd at least eaten in the past forty-eight hours, traces of heirloom tomatoes from his garden and the whippoorwill peas—when in the world had he cooked those?—he'd intended to prepare to welcome Randie to what he'd hoped would be her *home*. He remembered the ring suddenly, his plans to propose.

He felt the hole in his chest open so wide it swallowed him completely. He felt himself disappear into a darkness that was so thick and damp that he thought he'd actually gone through the floor, sinking into the earth below, that Randie walking out on him had buried him alive, and that it was a death he deserved for how ugly he'd behaved, for how callous he had been with her feelings about another person of color potentially in trouble in the state of Texas, another family out there somewhere without answers.

The buzzing of his cell phone told him he wasn't dead. He must have passed out again. The climb to sitting upright enough to get the phone on the coffee table was as messy and arduous as clawing his way back to life. His shirt was creased with sweat and stains he didn't recognize, and he had to wipe his mouth with the back of his hand to clear the filament of vomit on his chin. His long legs cracked at the joints as he unfolded them to reach for his cell phone. He noticed for the first time that the curtains on all the windows were pulled back, and the door to the back patio was open, revealing a view of rolling acres of green behind the house. The scent of pine tickled his nose hairs. Had he slept with the doors open? He thought he heard running water outside — or was it coming from the single bathroom that sat between the guest room and Darren's bedroom? His heart lifted for a fanciful moment, thinking maybe Randie had returned, that he might throw himself at her feet and apologize profusely.

But it couldn't be Randie in the house.

Not when it was her calling his phone now.

He snatched it up, answering quickly. "Randie."

He heard her sigh, a rush of relief in her voice. "You're alive, then," she said.

"Listen —"

"Good."

"This thing with me and my mom, our history, it makes me crazy sometimes. She just knows how to get under my skin —"

"Lisa's on her way, if she isn't already there —"

"Lisa?"

Darren glanced back at the open curtains, heard again the water running in the other room. "You called . . . Lisa?"

"You called me a couple of times, making no sense, unable to answer basic questions. You were . . . very drunk, Darren. I felt you weren't safe. I didn't know if you'd try to drive somewhere or if you might actually hurt yourself in some way. And I had already left by then, flown . . . well, it doesn't matter."

So she was truly gone, he thought.

She sounded so, so tired.

"She was the only person I could think to call. I was too scared to call the sheriff's department out there for a welfare check. Didn't want them coming on a drunk black man, even one on his own property . . . I didn't want you to get shot."

"Lisa," he repeated, trying it on.

"You'll forgive me one day," Randie said. "Or maybe you won't."

He caught a further meaning beneath her words: *Maybe it won't even matter.*

"But you scared me, Darren. I had never heard you talk like that."

"What did I say?"

There was a stretch of silence on the other end of the line. At least a stretch of Randie opting not to talk. Darren heard other voices, phones ringing, wondered if she was in an office somewhere. It unnerved him that he couldn't guess where she would have gone after fleeing his home. He said her name as a question, a hope.

He heard her sigh, followed by "Darren, let's not ... not now, not just yet."

"Randie —"

"I don't know, Darren, I just, I just don't understand what happened, why you sounded so hard, so cold all of a sudden, and the way you spoke to me —"

"My mother, Randie."

This time, her sigh had a bark of impatience in it.

Also disappointment.

"Darren, I've had so many doubts about why we fell into each other, if it was right, or even real, if I was only seeing you through the lens of my grief over losing Michael. You as the hero figure who could somehow fix things, put my life back together. And maybe I didn't consider that I was putting a kind of pressure on you."

"No, Randie, I was drunk, that's all this was —"

"And maybe that's something I need to look at too. My part in that. The drinking."

No, it's my problem, he wanted to say. Bourbon was the culprit here. It had barbed his tongue. The liquor quelled his anxiety, his henny-penny sense that the world was falling apart, but it had made him mean to the one woman he did not want to hurt.

"Look, I picked up a couple of new gigs," she said, speaking fast, not leaving any space between her words so as not to allow Darren to derail the direction she wanted this to go in. "I can't really get into all of this right now or where this goes exactly."

"Randie, don't —"

"Bye, Darren."

It was said so softly that he wasn't sure he'd actually heard her say it until it was clear that she was no longer there. There was just the sound of a late-September wind through the trees and the sprightly whistle of sparrows, whose cheeriness ate at his nerves. He hung up the phone and waited for his ex-wife to come out of the bathroom.

The running water had been for him.

Lisa put him in a cool bath, leaving the bathroom door unlocked so she could pop in every few minutes or so to see that he hadn't accidentally or on purpose slipped beneath the surface of the water. If either of them felt shy or awkward about Darren's nakedness, they didn't speak of it. They were mostly silent together. The water was a blessing on his skin. It didn't sober him up so much as cool his fevered blood. The thumping pulse in his ears slowed, and his muscles felt solid again. His head still hurt, but he could at least foresee a future hour when it wouldn't, could foresee that this hangover would not fell him completely. Lisa told him she was baking the salmon he'd bought for his week with Randie, that Darren needed a good meal, lots of protein and omega-3 fatty acids. "Did I say something? Was I talking when you came in the house?" he asked. It bothered him that he couldn't remember the past two days, that he'd apparently been saying things that frightened Randie enough to call Lisa, who looked at him curiously now. She had expressed so little anger during their divorce as to raise indifference to an art form, a virtue. She had repeatedly told him she was not angry about what had happened, only the how. She was either sitting on a cliff's edge of rage or she had never truly loved him at all. He'd spent their entire marriage in secret fear of the latter. But the look on her face now came closer to regret. She cocked her head and said, "You called me her name, and you asked me — *her* — if she liked the ring."

He pulled his knees up to his chest, feeling wholly exposed now. He slipped the washcloth between his knees, felt around the cloudy, cool water for the sliver of soap.

"I saw it sitting out on your dresser, by the way," she said.

She knelt down and reached for the washcloth to wash his back. "It's pretty."

He told her it had been his grandmother's.

"Figured," she said.

They both fell quiet again, the tinkle of bathwater hitting the side of the tub the only sound in the room. If she was at all gratified by the fact that the woman he'd left her for had now seemingly left *him*, the feeling couldn't stand beneath the weight of her pity. Darren felt it as a presence in the room, a suffocating sadness in the air. He stood suddenly, splashing water over the lip of the tub. Unable to tolerate his nakedness for another second, he grabbed the folded towel she'd left on the toilet-seat lid and covered himself with it. The material scratched at his skin, which felt newly raw. Dripping as he walked, he stepped into the hallway. Lisa followed him toward his bedroom. "Darren."

He didn't want her in there.

He didn't want her in this house.

She had never loved it the way he thought she should, had never shown an interest in the garden or asked to see the spot where his grandmother had washed their clothes in the old pond, would give him a stick and let him pretend to fish while she went about her work. Lisa had never sat on the back porch and shelled peas with him. But that had been one of his and Randie's first dates on the land. She'd put on a Sugar Pie DeSanto record and let the soul sound drift out of the house, curl up and keep them company. This farmhouse, his past and his present, the years ahead of him he wanted to spend here, this dream belonged to him and Randie, if she would still have him.

Lisa sensed this and more.

"I like her," she said, stopping when Darren blocked the way to his bedroom.

She gave him a small shrug and a wan smile, understanding that she had no real right to say anything in the matter. Darren took the gesture as an expression of her discomfort over having gotten a call from the woman he wanted to make his new wife.

"She shouldn't have bothered you."

"I'm glad she did," Lisa said. "Because now I know."

"Know what?"

"She really loves you . . . unconditionally." She looked around the dim hallway, the peeling-in-places wallpaper that had been there since he was a kid. Red roses on a cream background that was now the color of butcher paper. He'd counted the roses as a boy. There were one hundred and sixty-seven between the bedrooms. "I wasn't always good at that part," Lisa said. "I was hard on you, Darren, demanding you fit the image I had of you when we first got together, the life I thought we'd have."

"We were just kids."

Lisa smiled at the memory of them as high-school kids.

"I loved you, though, I did," she said. "Just not as good as she can."

This hit Darren at the knees, proving gravity was no match for matters of the heart. Her words washed clean the air between them, and Darren had an impulse to embrace his ex-wife, to thank her for the truth. But lifting his arm would drop the towel, and he liked the idea that he'd been naked in front of Lisa for the last time. She must have also felt the moment was growing more awkward the longer they stood there.

"Don't fuck this up, Darren."

She took a few steps back and glanced again at the rose wallpaper. He noticed she'd stopped coloring her hair. There were strands of gray at her temples, a growing streak of it on the left side. The look suited her. It made her seem regal and wise.

"You're not as easy as you think you are," she said. "Give her the key to the lockbox, the parts of you I never even got close to. It won't work any other way." She lifted her chin to him as a question: *You understand me, Darren?*

He nodded.

She gave him a tight smile and said, "You gonna be okay? I'll leave the salmon in the fridge. You seem pretty stocked up otherwise."

"I'll be fine."

"Okay." She backed toward the living room. "Hydrate and get some rest."

Lisa turned for the door, then stopped herself. "And call your people, Darren. Call Clayton . . ." she said. "And call Greg. You know he thinks this is his fault."

She gestured between the two of them, meaning the divorce. Darren had been avoiding calls from Greg, his oldest friend and one of the few people besides Lisa he'd known his entire adult life. The three of them had been close once, Darren and Greg like brothers. Which had made the affair sting more. If you could even call it that.

It had happened after he'd left Texas for Chicago, when he'd transferred out of UT to the University of Chicago law school to prove, maybe, that he could excel outside the shadow of his uncle, a professor at the law school in Austin. He'd been sharing a two-room apartment with Greg, Lisa spending every night there with them. The three grew even closer than they'd been in high school, a family of sorts — Lisa and Darren glued together, mom and dad to Greg's unruly teenager. Other times, Darren and Greg were like brothers with an impatient, unamused mom in Lisa, who studied constantly and didn't like, back then, the taste of alcohol unless it was wine coolers.

When Darren transferred, Greg kept the lease because, even then, housing in Austin was a hassle, and Lisa moved in. Darren approved of it at the time, felt good about Greg, who was by any measure one of the most decent men he knew, being around if Lisa ever needed anything. The affair — *sex* was all it was, Lisa insisted — happened the fall semester of their second year of law school, and they were both mortified. Not just because of what they'd done but because of how certain it was that they would do it again. They were studying or in class sixty hours a week, deciphering a lens on the world that was both cynical and hardwired in hope. Law students could be dizzy with it some days, the promise and protection of the Constitution, if you aired that thing out, let it breathe a little and grow. They were high from the exhaustion of marrying ideals to the nuts-and-bolts work of practicing law with other fallible human beings, and they had impulsively reached in the dark for each other as a way both to cope and to bear witness. Yes, they were alive. Yes, it was heady to arm themselves with words that had the power to shape people's lives, to shape their country. Yes, they wanted to quit. And, yes, they both knew they couldn't. If Darren hadn't been going through his own version of that, alone in Chicago, he might have raged at Lisa when she finally confessed that she and Greg had had sex years ago.

Instead, he just felt sad. For his marriage, and for the young, bullishly optimistic people they'd once been. Lisa was now a contracts lawyer at a big firm. Greg had left the FBI, disillusioned. And Darren was a badge-less lawman whose spirit had been broken by the mess of his own morality. Yes, it hurt to think of Greg touching his then girlfriend, and it kept him up some nights wondering if she moaned the same way or bit his neck when she came, the tiny intimacies he always believed were his alone. He had been her first and she his.

* * *

He remembered feeling grateful for the confession, for the way it softened his telling Lisa that Randie was back in his life. She had always suspected something between them, ever since Randie's husband's murder case in Lark all those years ago. And it mildly pleased her to have a bit of righteous anger to hold on to. She never explicitly said, *I knew it*. Just rolled her eyes and began making recommendations for divorce attorneys for Darren. He and Lisa were not meant to go the distance. It had taken a very long time for both of them to admit that. The story of high-school sweethearts who stay together and marry after law school was just too good. It had romanced even them.

Lisa was dating now. And he wanted Randie to be his future.

Lisa stood by the door and watched him for a while, as if she might say something more. About his drinking. About their marriage ending. About when or whether they would ever see each other again. But then she changed her mind and left without a word.

6.

HE HAD no job, no woman, and nothing to do with the days he had planned to spend with Randie. He'd thought this trip he could convince her to take a drive out to Lake Livingston; it had tickled and excited him to think of her in one of his baseball caps as he showed her how to bait a line. She sometimes liked to get in the garden with him. They'd play the music so loud in the house, Gary Clark Jr.'s "The Story of Sonny Boy Slim" would roll out over the sweet peppers and collards in the yard like a benediction, preaching to them to grow strong. And there was the ring, of course. The fact that he had planned to ask Randie to marry him. It cut him in places he didn't know could still bleed. He was ashamed of how he'd acted and terrified that he might lose her.

It was because of her that he decided to "look into it," as she'd suggested. It felt like step one in possibly getting her back, the woman whose love and favor were the only future that mattered to him. He wanted to be worthy of her respect.

And he had nothing else to do.

Just blank hours to fill.

What would a few Google searches hurt? Early in the afternoon after Lisa left, Darren sat at the Formica table in the kitchen, eating the salmon she'd done up in a balsamic glaze he didn't care for, and started with the most basic: *Missing* and *SFA student* and *black.* Which initially yielded nothing more sinister than a black student winning the title of Miss SFA announced at halftime at a school basketball game in March. There was a picture of her standing arm in arm with the white Mr. SFA winner in front of a statue of the university's namesake, Stephen F. Austin, who, as one of the first white men to colonize what was then still Mexico, was widely considered the "Father of Texas." The image of the interracial couple told a story of racial harmony that Austin, an enthusiastic slaveholder, wouldn't have dreamed of.

Darren tried *SFA* and *missing sorority student,* which led to a rain of stories about missing women across the country and included TV listings for two *Dateline* episodes. All missing young white women. He had found nothing about a missing black girl. This had barely killed fifteen minutes, and he was already feeling thirsty.

He'd told himself he wouldn't even think of drinking until the sun went down and that if he could make that goal, maybe he could even go a whole day. And maybe a day could stretch to two, and then even a week. The idea of his mother sober both goaded him and disrupted something fundamental to him. He knew he was a "drinker," but he put that down to forces beyond his control that were both senseless and exhausting to fight; his mother had ruined him, had consistently shown herself to be a malignant force in his life. But if Bell was truly no longer a drunk — and three days into this knowledge, something about the idea was taking solid shape in his mind — then in whom might he bury any impulse to confront his drinking? It was the one gift he'd imagined she'd given him.

He felt a thirst coming for him, a bottomless want, and he was saved only by the fact that he'd already drunk every drop in the house.

He took a deep breath and looked up the sorority, Rho Beta Zeta.

They called themselves Robees on their website, their home page a photo of rows of smiling girls. Four in the front row, two with hair as white as their teeth flanking a pale strawberry blonde and another, slightly taller girl whose hair was the color of orange blossom honey. They stared out at Darren from his computer screen. Behind them were four more rows of Rho Beta girls. Their hair ranged in color from wheat to sand, with textures from flat-iron straight to the limp, slightly frizzy curls frequently unleashed by Texas humidity. The young women's smiles were as wide as truck grilles, their eyes bright beneath fake lashes and pale pink eyeshadow. Coral blush, Darren learned on the About page, was one of the sorority's official colors. They were all in pearls. And pale blue sweater sets. Cornflower blue was the sorority's other official color, to be worn with either violet or pear green, both allowed as wardrobe accents, "but never at the same time," the website's Fashion Guidelines page advised. He spent enough time visiting each of the pages on the sorority chapter's website that he saw photos of Robee girls at formal dances, at pledge lunches, in casual clothes studying in the living room of what appeared to be a well-cared-for sorority house, and in bikinis at a charity car wash. What he did not see was one black face. The sorority did not appear to have any black members, or any Asians either. There was one girl who *might* have been Latina, but it was a crowded photograph and hard to tell. How could a black sorority member go missing if she'd never existed? This whole thing was starting to feel like a silly, useless exercise.

He rose to pour himself a glass of water and put his dishes in the sink. Then he reopened the doors that led to the back porch and let in a

slow breeze moving through the property out back, rustling pine needles that sounded like a thousand whispers at this distance. Sometimes
he liked to imagine it was his people talking to him, the ones who were
gone, who lived in what the air could hold. His grandparents and William, and his father, he supposed. Darren "Duke" Mathews Sr.

He still had a lot more hours to fill before his reckoning at sundown.

He sent an email to his friend Roland Carroll, a Ranger stationed
out of Company A, which handled Houston and a good swath of East
Texas. He hadn't told him he'd quit, even though, as one of the few
other black or brown Rangers in the entire department, he and Roland
were brothers-in-arms. In the email, Darren went about the usual nice-
ties as if nothing was wrong. He asked after Roland's family, wishing
them well, and made a special point to inquire about a woman with
whom their friend Buddy Watson was getting serious. He suggested
they grab a meal sometime, and then he got down to it. Did Roland
know of any reports of a missing student from Stephen F. Austin State?
Could he find out? Black, he wrote, because it mattered. He told him
she was a member of a sorority. A *white* sorority, he felt he should add.
Rho Beta Zeta.

He clicked over to the official SFA University website and scrolled
through the photos and followed the links to dozens of student organi-
zations, lingering especially on ones about Greek life at the school. He
noted the presence of a few of the Divine Nine, the historically black
fraternities and sororities that included such distinguished members as
MLK Jr., Toni Morrison, Zora Neale Hurston, and Wilma Rudolph.
That a black girl would choose Rho Beta Zeta over this rich African
American tradition made little sense and only furthered his feeling
that maybe he was chasing a story that wasn't even real.

But then he saw her.

He'd stumbled on a photo of an event that a large banner told him was held during Pledge Week last year. The caption informed him it was taken last fall. Instead of pearls and sweater sets, it was khaki pants and button-down shirts, all rolled identically mid-forearm, showcasing silver James Avery–style charm bracelets. The shirts were all either cornflower blue or coral blush, with matching headbands on most. The aggressive sameness, the power, or oppression, in numbers reminded Darren of a platoon photo. The picture was taken in what appeared to be the sorority house living room Darren had seen on Rho Beta Zeta's website, with girls sitting in threes and fours at the many tables, which held papers and some textbooks and also party decorations, so it was hard to tell if this was a study session or an event-planning committee.

At a table in a back corner, at the very edge of the image, he saw a dark-skinned black girl with hair that was neither natural nor straight but some confused halfway point. *She couldn't ever make hers lay down quite right.* Despite the crassness of his mother's words and the dated expectations for black women's hair they suggested, they told Darren that he was looking at the SFA student his mother had talked about. She was pretty, but a slip of a thing. *Frail* was the word that came to mind. She seemed to have looked up just as the shutter clicked. But he could find no trace of her on Rho Beta Zeta's official website or their Instagram page, which had hundreds of pics of the Robees' smiling, all-white membership. It seemed the black girl was in the picture one day, and then she was just gone. Just like his mother had told him.

His phone started ringing across the room.

The walk to the kitchen counter gave him time to hope that it was Randie.

But it was Roland Carroll calling, even though Darren had sent the email not even twenty minutes ago. How could Roland have gotten his hands on any missing person information from the Nacogdoches Police Department or the county sheriff that fast?

"Darren," he bellowed, a huff of good humor in his voice. "Now I *know* you was drunk when you called last night." This caught Darren up short. Confused, he said nothing for a few seconds. He had called Roland last night? The idea of it trilled in the back of his mind, like the ring of a distant church bell. There was a pinch of melancholy in Roland's voice, pained disappointment too. "I can't believe I had to hear from Wilson that you quit the department. I know it's been hard, with the separation from Lisa —"

"Divorce."

There was a sigh from Roland. "Aw, man, I hadn't realized it was final."

"It's fine." Darren tried to sound, if not breezy, then at least calm and accepting.

"Still," his friend said, about divorce, "it's hard, man. It's almost like a death."

"It's not," Darren said quickly and left it at that.

"Worried about you, man, is all I'm saying. Buddy, Ricky, and Hector too. Patricia said you're still welcome when we get together at her place in Austin next month." His tone had taken on the lilt of a careful inquiry. "I happen to know for a fact that your paperwork hasn't been fully processed. I think Wilson is stalling, hoping —"

Darren quickly cut him off, choking off this line of thought. "I'm fine, Roland. Really." Then, trying to move away from talk of his broken life, he asked a question that boomeranged right back to it. "You say I called you?"

"About the missing SFA student," Roland said. "You don't remember?"

He didn't, which gave him an odd feeling of dissociation. His heart had done something his mind could not recall. Even though he'd been blackout drunk and angry — at his mother for trying to manipulate him with her lies and at Randie for pressing him to take Bell Callis seriously—his soul had been awake to what they were both saying. There was a young woman who might be in trouble. Even while intoxicated, he'd started investigating the missing student; he had behaved like a Texas Ranger.

"Remind me, please," he said to Roland as he grabbed a slip of paper and a pencil from a kitchen drawer.

There was a long pause on the other end of the line, a desk phone somewhere in the Rangers' office ringing a shrill alarm in the background. Finally it stopped, and in the silence that opened up between the two men, Roland said, "You know, we've all been struggling. We've all fallen down, leaned on a few things we shouldn't have, trying to cope with the insanity of the past few years. Ricky had to start talking to a head doctor after the shootings in El Paso. Patricia still ain't got over all those people that man shot up in Sutherland Springs. And Charlottesville, man, you know that took the wheels off for me." Darren did know. That summer in 2017, Company A was on high alert, had been since the election, had assisted in the investigation of several hate crimes in the eastern part of the state, had feared exactly what was happening in Charlottesville happening here. "Klan marching in broad daylight down the street," Roland said. "Worse than the Klan." With their Scout-like precision, their pressed pants and buttoned shirt collars, they had none of the id-fueled bacchanal feel of the OG Klan, men whose bonfire-like rage burned with at least a modicum of shame, hence the hoods, the midnight ramblings. These boys and men had their faces open to the sun. And even a rookie law enforcement officer knew that any criminal willing to show his face was not likely to leave any victims alive. Watching footage of the riot in Charlottesville in the pained silence of the conference room at Company A headquarters in Houston—where they'd all been called in to work that Saturday as a national emergency unfolded—they turned to each other, stunned over what this meant for the country's future, the state's. If the Aryan Brotherhood of Texas ever got that organized, if they too chose a rebirth in this new political climate—in which the sun shone on them from on high, warmed their pinkish cheeks with the certainty that they were protected all the way up to the White House—then they were done for, men like Darren who had given their careers and lives to the work of racial justice, to righting the ever-listing ship that was this country. You couldn't take your hands off the wheel even for a second. Roland had had to excuse himself. Darren found him in the men's room, gray with worry.

"It's too much, man," he now said. "For all of us. The lies, the violence, the stone-cold hatred that's actually starting to grow, like a nasty mold. It's too much to hold." He paused for a long while, and when his desk phone rang again, Darren heard him pick it up and immediately slam it back down. "But I'm worried about you, man. I know it feels like the country is trying to annihilate folks like us, but please, man, don't try to race 'em to it. Get some help with the drinking, man, or, hell, call me if you need to sometime. Just to talk. We need you, Darren. We need you."

Darren felt a thickness spread in the back of his throat, felt a salty sadness there.

"About the missing girl, Roland. Let me just get down the information."

Roland sighed, as he felt the emotional opening between them whisper closed.

"Get down what? I told you last night, there are no missing person reports involving any SFA student, not with the university's police, not with Nacogdoches PD, and not with the sheriff's department. No student has been reported missing."

"Right," Darren said, looking down at the blank slip of paper. It was the back of a receipt from a hardware store two towns over. Darren had bought chicken wire as a stopgap to keep out the feral hogs that came onto his land from time to time, until he could figure out a better fencing system. He set the pencil down, feeling a tad foolish for getting worked up over something his first instinct had told him wasn't even a real story.

"But I was going to call you even before I saw your email," Roland said. "Buddy of mine at Nacogdoches PD got back to me with something curious about Rho Beta Zeta."

"What's that?"

"There's been no report of anyone missing, but turns out one of their members, a girl who lived in their house off campus, filed a police report."

"Hmph."

"And get this . . . she's black."

"Name?" Darren asked, falling so easily into a familiar investigative rhythm.

"Seraphine 'Sera' Renee Fuller was the full name on the report."

Darren wrote the name on the receipt. "What was she reporting?"

"*Bullying* was the word she used. Though the report doesn't get more specific than that. But apparently, it got so bad she told the desk officer she didn't feel safe living there. 'Complainant reports she is miserable.'"

"What date was this?"

"September twelfth."

So, over a week ago. Darren wrote this down as well. "And did anyone ever follow up on this?" he said.

"Nacogdoches PD forwarded a copy of the report to campus police, but I don't know that it went much further than that. There was never any other report filed by Sera or any other student living at the Rho Beta Zeta house, not this year, at least."

"And this Sera . . . she's black? You're sure?"

"I'm looking at the report now," Roland said. "Listen, I don't know the whole story, of course, but damn if it ain't a coincidence, you asking about a missing black girl in that sorority, and we got a black girl living out there who filed a police report saying she doesn't feel safe. And you know what Wilson says about coincidence —"

"God tapping you on the shoulder," Darren said, repeating his former lieutenant's words, as if cops and God were partners on any case, men like him an extension of His hand. It suggested a level of power that didn't feel safe in a single man's hands, not even his own. Especially not his own. It's not that he necessarily regretted what he'd done, pinning a homicide on a white supremacist who was already a murderer a few times over. But it unnerved him how easy it was.

He thanked Roland and asked him to give his best to Patricia, Ricky, Buddy, and Hector, signaling he was most likely not coming to any get-together in Austin.

Then he let Roland get back to work. And Darren did the same.

He went back over everything, retracing his digital steps. Sera Fuller did not exist anywhere online in the documented world of the Rho Beta Zeta sorority other than the one photo he'd found on the *university's* website of her smiling during a Pledge Week event a year ago.

In the picture one day, and then she was just gone.

Darren stayed at his kitchen table for a long time, sitting with this thought. What it said about his mother and her capacity for truth-telling and what it meant for him, a former Ranger, to be in possession of this knowledge. What was his responsibility to Sera Fuller, who had reported *not feeling safe?* He looked up the address for Rho Beta Zeta on Steen Drive, a Greek row that housed most of the school's sororities. He wrote it on the back of the hardware-store receipt. It was the last thing he did before he grabbed the keys to his truck and started for the door, doubling back at the last second to detour to his bedroom. It still smelled like Randie, and he took a deep breath, storing some of her in his cells. The part of her that saw the best in him. He'd come back for the Colt .45 in his nightstand, the leather of its tobacco-colored holster cracked and patinaed with time, years the weight at his side carried the authority of the Texas Rangers. He hesitated a moment before grabbing it as a private citizen. But then he remembered his lawyers' warning: *All it takes is one idiot with a gun.* That was the trouble with violence, though — it only responded to further escalation.

Outside, he got in his Chevy and followed his compass north.

Part Two

7.

TO GET to Nacogdoches on Highway 59, you passed through Lufkin first, its country cousin to the south. The towns were like fraternal twins for whom genetics hadn't entirely played fair. Oh, they both had a certain undeniable beauty, surrounded as the municipalities were by the big thicket of East Texas, forest-rich land of pine trees and cedar oaks, hickories and maples. Each town, bereft of its initial timber economy, had diversified over time. There was manufacturing in both towns now, and Lufkin had lucked into a few military contracts. But Nacogdoches had the status of being the "oldest town in Texas," a point of pride that encouraged preservation in a way that frankly just made the town prettier, with its charming brick streets downtown, the old courthouse, and storefronts dating back centuries, little bits and bobs of Texas history on every corner. What's more, it was a university town. Stephen F. Austin might not have been Harvard. Hell, it wasn't even Vanderbilt or Emory. But it was a good school that attracted professors and students from all over the country. It had curricula in engineering, agricultural studies, political science, and the arts. It lent a cosmopolitan air to what might otherwise have been just another Podunk on the way to Marshall or Dallas.

The university sat right off the highway, north of the shopping district in the historic town square and the county courthouses. Darren drove past the wide stone wall that announced the entrance to Stephen F. Austin State University, traveling past the familiar markers of most college towns. Fast-food joints and laundromats, bars and chain restaurants, and a bowling alley. Larger than any in which he'd worked a case in some time, it was a sweet town that seemed sure of itself and its purpose — protecting the history of Texas as its stated oldest town while also envisioning the state's future as it educated the minds of its next big thinkers. Or at least turned out decent accountants and nurses, business majors on the road to middle management, plus the young men and women who sought careers in agriculture and the environment, the latter being an area of academic study in which SFA shone. With the university as much a part of the town's identity as its tourism sector that taught all comers about the history of the state (how it went from Caddo hands to the white men who wrested it from the Mexicans), Nacogdoches knew its gifts the way an admired committee chair of a church bake sale knows her pecan pies keep the building fund flush. It had an aura of self-assured pride that never dipped into smugness.

From what Darren had gathered, the school's fraternities were scattershot across the town and its environs, housed in falling-down rentals with sagging front porches or couches inexplicably dotting their roofs, front yards with burn marks in the grass, young men content to live in ramshackle quarters as long as everyone else was made to do it too, as long as they were plenty in number, safe in the womb of their togetherness, their shared professed love for beer and sports and women. But the school's sorority houses — and to be clear, that meant only the white ones; as far as Darren could tell, no black sorority or fraternity had a house of any kind near campus — were all on a spacious, well-maintained circle drive about a mile north of the university. They sat like a row of cake-top confections on display, Tara-shaped sweets iced a blinding white. The columns and trim and snowy-white shutters were set against bricks the color of caramels (Delta Theta Tau), strawberries (Chi Omega Theta), honeycombs (Pi Gamma Phi), cinnamon (Kappa Iota Mu), and butter-yellow vanilla sheet cake (Rho Beta Zeta), the facade of the last flanked by twin live oaks. A better educated man might call the houses' identical architectural style by its correct name: Greek Revival. But to Darren, they would only ever look like a row of plantation mansions.

The front door of Rho Beta Zeta was unmanned and unlocked, so he simply walked inside. Beyond the heavy oak door, it was downright frigid in the house, the air as cold as a glass of sweet tea. And perfumed by a massive floral arrangement that sat on a circular table in the foyer. Pinkish roses and peachy carnations, pale blue hydrangea and hyacinth, colors that Darren recognized as coral blush and cornflower blue. Surrounding the floral centerpiece were two dozen or more tiny picture frames, each barely bigger than an international postage stamp. Encased in each gilded frame was the smiling face of a member of Rho Beta Zeta. He didn't see a single black face.

He heard footsteps and looked up to see two young women rounding the base of a staircase on the other side of a sitting room that lay beyond the foyer where he stood. He recognized one of them from the home page of the sorority's website. She was tying up her honey-blond hair with a scrunchie as she approached. She was short and compact. "Um, excuse me?" she said, tightening her ponytail. Her voice was somehow husky and shrill at the same time so that she sounded a bit like a wounded seal.

The girl with her smiled politely. She had dark brown, almost black hair, which immediately set her apart from the Rho Beta women he'd seen on their website and Instagram. Thus individualized, she seemed real to him in a way the other girl didn't. Remarkable, at least. Like a ruby resting in a handful of rocks. Whatever unspoken rules about appearance gripped this sorority, they didn't apply to her. She had the patient air of someone with only a cursory interest in the events unfolding before her, the calm of the incurious, of one privileged enough to assume no danger from a stranger walking into her home, for surely he was there to deliver some object for her entertainment or pleasure or to cart away a thing she no longer wanted. She deepened her smile. "Is there something I can help you with?"

The shorter one moved in front of the dark-haired girl, as if displaying a willingness to take a bullet for her. "You want me to see if Ms. Marsh is still here?" Her voice rose with a note of solicitation.

"No," the dark-haired girl said in a tone quietly reproachful. "I'd like to know if there's something I can help this gentleman with." Darren stepped forward, closing the distance between himself and the young women, which meant walking into the lushly carpeted front parlor that smelled of damp wood and lavender, acrid in its artificiality. Darren spotted a plug-in air freshener near the base of the maple staircase. He returned the dark-haired girl's smile and told them he was looking for Sera Fuller.

The blond girl's eyes widened ever so slightly.

And the dark-haired girl's smile faltered for the first time.

Darren felt a rush of intuition. He reached for an old arrow in his quiver, impulsively sitting on one of the cream-colored couches in the parlor as if it were a given that he would be invited to stay awhile. Texans, he knew, could be vicious, but they were rarely rude. It was a truth and a lie at the same time, the state's storied friendliness. It masked all kinds of bad deeds. But it was a tool, he'd found, pressing people to confront their ideas of themselves as nice, good people. He'd left his Colt in the glove compartment of his truck. He was unarmed and polite. Were these two young women going to risk how they would feel about themselves if they kicked out a mild-mannered, well-dressed black man? Half the state and the country were bent over backward these days trying to prove they weren't racist. *So, great. Prove it.* He stretched out his long legs before him, crossing them at the ankles, a show of settling in. "Uh," the shorter one said, her tone more circumspect now, "are you, like, her dad or something?" She looked over at the dark-haired girl, checking to make sure it was okay that she had asked this. The dark-haired girl nodded. Darren opened his mouth to answer, wishing he still had his badge. He debated just saying the words anyway, repeating the lyrics to a song stuck in his head — *I'm Darren Mathews, and I'm a Texas Ranger, ma'am.* But he had no real authority here, could not compel them to answer any of his questions. In the brief silence in the room, he heard the whine of an opening door.

He turned and saw, of all people, his mother.

She stood in the door that led to the kitchen. She was wearing a smock and was carrying a broom and a bucket of cleaning supplies. She looked smaller, seemed to be purposely stooping in front of two of the women she worked for — girls a third her age whose rooms she cleaned, whose hair she pulled out of the bathroom shower drains. They called her Miss Bell, and she answered to it, saying she didn't realize anyone was using the parlor, and she would be on her way upstairs. Darren felt a peculiar sadness witnessing her meek manner, the way she cowered in front of them.

Some charge in the air that passed between Darren and his mother told the two girls to pay closer attention. Their eyes moved in perfect synchronicity, as if choreographed, as they looked back and forth between them. Darren could practically see them making quiet calculations in their minds, coming to a split-second decision about whether it would seem rude or inappropriate to ask if these two random black people somehow knew each other. Bell saw the inquiry coming and got in front of it. "I've seen him here before, on move-in day last month. He come with the black girl's people," she said, nodding as she answered a question the dark-haired girl was smart enough to realize she hadn't asked. The girl's lips pursed ever so slightly.

"I'm her uncle," Darren offered quickly, going with the lie.

"I'm Kelsey Piper, president of the Gamma Phi chapter of Rho Beta Zeta," the dark-haired girl said. "Can I get you some water, a can of Coke or something for your ride back?" It was a Southern woman's way of saying that this would be a quick visit, that despite her cheery tone, he wasn't welcome here. "Brit, would you go see what we have in the kitchen to offer Mr. . . . ." She paused, waiting on him to identify himself.

Darren ignored her attempt to get his name. "Is she here? Sera?"

"Sera moved out last Saturday," Kelsey said.

Last Saturday was the fourteenth, Darren thought, two days after she'd filed a police report stating that she was being bullied and was miserable living with these women.

Brit narrowed her eyes at Darren.

Kelsey read her mind. "Which you would think her uncle would already know."

"Her parents asked me to stop by and grab the rest of her things," he improvised. Bell smiled, pleased, it seemed, with her son for being quick on his feet, pleased with the way this put Sera's sorority sisters on the spot. The moment was dislocating for Darren, who felt himself floating out of his skin, hovering over a scene that was as darkly absurd as a bad dream. If you had told him three days ago that he would be in the same room with his mother, he might have laughed till he cried. Tears that ran hot with wild wonder at her gall. For the past three years, he had blamed her for his living forever on the edge of being indicted for a felony. And now the two of them were working in concert to find information about a missing black girl?

He felt lightheaded and in great need of a drink.

He wanted something that might melt him back into himself.

"If you'll show me the way to her room," he said, trying to move this along.

Kelsey eyed Darren for a beat, deciding something.

"She took everything with her," she said. "And I'm afraid men aren't permitted upstairs for any reason. Miss Bell can tell you that's not allowed even on move-in day, which I'm assuming is the reason I don't remember meeting you."

"Must be," Darren said.

"Right." Kelsey stared at him, unbowed by his persistence. She maintained the same preternatural calm, had not so much as flinched since she'd reacted to hearing Sera Fuller's name. But he caught the slightest curl at the corner of her mouth, a clear indication that she didn't believe a word he was saying. The ruse amused her; she wanted him to know that she at least held a grudging respect for Darren for trying.

"Miss Bell," she said, eyes darting from Darren to his mother in her maid's smock standing in the doorway to the kitchen. "I don't believe the bathroom in the president's suite has been cleaned yet." Then she gave her an even bigger smile and said, "I'll thank you now for getting on that, so it's cleaned before dinnertime."

Bell didn't move right away.

Darren watched a slideshow of micro-expressions — umbrage and humiliation and then fury — flitter across her face with the speed of a zoetrope, tricking one into seeing a single fluid movement that gave the appearance of obeisance. She nodded once and carried the broom and cleaning supplies up the staircase, the bucket tapping against the railing every third step, until she seemed swallowed up into the rest of the house. It was the first he'd noticed how quiet the place was. He heard no music or voices through the walls. No footsteps padded overhead that he could tell. It felt more like a nineteenth-century boardinghouse for unmarried women than a sorority house in the new millennium. The air in the room felt tight and controlled, like a collective breath held.

"And she was happy here?" Darren said, coming sideways at the issue of Sera reporting that she was being bullied, hoping to avoid any knee-jerk defensiveness.

He needn't have bothered.

The blonde, Brit, said, "Who cares?"

Kelsey cut her eyes at her at the harsh tone. "Not every girl is cut out to be a Rho Beta."

"We never wanted her anyway," Brit said. "They made Kelsey take her."

Darren felt like he'd lost the thread of the conversation and its meaning. Who were *they* and was this conversation about the same girl? "Sera, you mean?"

Kelsey's beatific smile took on an edge now.

"Your 'niece,'" she said, giving Darren a knowing look.

It was eerie how unbothered she was by his presence, a stranger asking after one of her sisters. Darren suddenly understood that what he'd read as patience was in fact utter indifference. She didn't care about him lying because she didn't care about Sera Fuller. It was not a leap to picture Kelsey as a bully, a mean-girl tormentor. But not a fool. Since they were dropping all pretense, he said, "Just tell me where I can find her."

8.

SHE MENTIONED a place called Thornhill.

Her parents worked there or something, Kelsey said. Sera was some kind of scholarship kid — which Kelsey announced in a way that suggested this explained a whole hell of a lot. At least, Thornhill was the name on the checks that covered her dues and living expenses at the Rho Beta Zeta house. Maybe she moved back home, she told Darren. All this said as she grabbed the area above his right elbow to escort him to the door, pulling at him like an oversize toy she was done playing with. Darren was careful to lean his weight into the gravity of her pull, because to resist, to create any friction between his body and her white hands, was to potentially flip the moment to its photo negative — with Darren seeming like the aggressor. Here on Tara Row, police would be called; he'd be in handcuffs within a matter of minutes. The idea of it woke him to the idiocy of the situation he'd gotten himself into, working a "case" without a badge, a case that held no real mystery. These Rho Beta girls seemed fucking awful. And Sera Fuller did exactly as he might have in the same situation. She'd moved out.

* * *

Outside on the brick front walk lined with monkey grass and sprouting flowers an approved shade of blue, Darren glanced back at the sorority house. Through the panes of glass that flanked the sorority's front door, he saw Kelsey pacing, talking on a cell phone. Her eyes locked with his and she held up her phone and took a picture of him. *Great,* he thought as he headed toward his truck. He had no idea whom she'd called, but whoever it was would now have an identifying image.

Not that he'd done anything wrong.

Not that it mattered, he knew.

By the time he neared his truck, parked at the curb, his mother was waiting for him. In the minutes since he'd last seen her, she had somehow made her way outside. She *psst*'d at him as he walked to his Chevy. She shuffled in his direction, trying to catch up, trailing a scent of menthol cigarettes and cherry Now and Later candy. She had a ball of the taffy tucked inside her right cheek like snuff.

"Why didn't you just tell them people you're a Ranger?"

She had a hand on her hip, miffed at him for robbing her of the chance to flex on those white girls, to brag on her son. "Because I'm not," he said. "Not anymore."

Bell's hand dropped at her side, her voice plaintive and small. "Because of me?"

That she couldn't see the repercussions of the havoc she had wreaked in his life, that she was blind to her own destruction, only deepened his aggravation, lighting a match to it and burning it to rage. Of course it was because of her. The potential indictment on obstruction charges, the threat of prison. Putting the first taste of liquor on his tongue when he was a boy, even the fact that Randie was gone now. It was all her fault, no matter the hangdog look of guilelessness she was peddling. He was sure if she hadn't shown up at the house in Camilla, he would have proposed to Randie by now; they might not have left the bed for the past three days, celebrating. He might be in her arms right now instead of standing outside of a sorority house in Nacogdoches.

"Yes, it's because of you." He slid into the driver's seat. "You have never, not once, *not* upended my whole life, and I honestly curse the day you walked back into it."

"Darren, wait." She walked around to the driver's side, setting an ashy hand, dry and cracked from cleaning, on the hood of the truck. She steadied herself as she came off the curb and went to his window. "Don't leave it like this."

Darren ignored her, putting the truck in gear.

He glanced back at the house. Kelsey was standing at the windows in the foyer, cell phone pressed to her ear, monitoring this entire scene. "Just go back to work," he said to her from behind his driver's-side window. "And leave me the hell alone."

He drove back onto Highway 59, looking for the nearest store.

Liquor was preferred, but convenience or supermarket would do.

Anything he could find heading south, in the direction of Camilla, home, and his last memories of Randie. He had something now. He could call her and say it was all a misunderstanding, could even throw in an *It was nice of my mother to be concerned,* but there was nothing scary or nefarious going on, he could report with some confidence. This was nothing like Randie losing her husband, Michael, to the worst kind of violence. When he saw her again, he would be gentler with her heart, her grief. Be the kind man he was when they'd first met, when he'd protected her body and soul.

He was on the way to putting his future back on track.

He just needed to make one stop first.

Darren pulled into the lot of a small mart and watched two kids on bikes argue over money, exchanging sweaty bills pulled out of back pockets and the elastic of their socks. They finally landed on a plan, who would pay for what, and went inside, looking focused and determined. They hadn't bothered to lock up their bikes, just rested them against the painted brick wall of the store. Darren paused with his hand on the door handle, deciding to stay in his truck until the two kids came back out. He'd forgotten he wasn't wearing a badge, and he didn't want two boys seeing a Texas Ranger buying a fifth of Jim Beam. He sat in his truck, waiting for the two boys to come back out.

It was muggy out, but the sky had deepened into an oceanic teal, a watercolor of a perfect fall afternoon. He rolled down the Chevy's windows to get some air. It smelled of exhaust from eighteen-wheelers and highway traffic on 59 and fish-fry grease. The small store had a YOU BUY, WE FRY advertisement painted on one of the walls, along with a mural of a smiling catfish, his whiskers done up to look like Wyatt Earp's mustache. Darren's stomach rumbled as the moment in his cab gave him time alone to think.

To remember the report that Sera Fuller had filed with police.

It nipped at his heels a bit, bothering him.

On its face, it sure seemed that she'd simply done the right thing for herself and moved out. Moved *home,* as Kelsey opined. But he wanted to know that for sure, certainly before he called Randie to tell her all was well in Nacogdoches County, that the girl was fine, and Randie could come back to him. He reached for his phone so he could look up this place called Thornhill, to find out from her parents' employer where Sera lived. His phone showed he'd missed a call and two texts from Greg Heglund. Lisa must have called him, Darren thought. She must have told him Darren was ready to talk. He wasn't, though.

He wanted to close out this thing with Sera Fuller first.

★　★　★

The top two Google hits for Thornhill were a planned residential community off Highway 59, just south of here, and an agribusiness corporation, both of which were accepting applications. He was trying to decide which Thornhill he should try first — Village or Industries — when he realized they both had the same physical address.

Darren knit his eyebrows, momentarily perplexed by the coincidence.

He threw the truck into gear and pulled back onto Highway 59.

His truck's navigation system put Thornhill seven miles south of Nacogdoches, right off the highway. He hadn't found a home address for a Fuller family in Thornhill. But the housing development itself would have been impossible for even a blind man to miss. There was the smell, for one. It rolled up through the undercarriage of the truck's cab about two hundred feet from the massive stone markers that welcomed him to the town of Thornhill. It was a stinging chemical smell that smarted his nostrils and watered one of his eyes. Ammonia, Darren thought. But something else beneath it too, a smell of active decay, cloying and almost tacky to the touch, sticking to the hair in his nose. He pinched his nostrils a few times to shake the feeling of having been invaded. But when Darren turned off Highway 59 toward the ornate steel gates at the opening of the town, he was struck dumb by how pretty Thornhill was. How tidy.

Over the fifteen-foot stone walls that surrounded the entire town, he saw the tops of buildings whose pointed gables and shingled roofs suggested revivals of early-twentieth-century-style bungalows. They were painted in shades of mint green, daffodil yellow, pale blue, or white with trim in navy. They were all perfectly maintained, untouched, it seemed, by Texas weather, not a shingle out of place, not a stray leaf in the gutters, as if they were freshly taken out of the box of a brand-new toy set. To his right, he saw snatches of a kids' playground with the tallest red slide he'd ever seen. In the distance, stadium lights rose in salute to the Texas tradition of high-school football. Thornhill had its own schools, then. Churches too. He saw a cluster of chapel tops, crosses glinting in the sunlight. If there were synagogues or mosques in town, they kept their faiths and their building designs closer to the ground; he saw no evidence of any other houses of worship. Everything was so bright and clean, so cheerful in its perfection, that Darren half expected to be welcomed with a fruit basket.

Instead, he was stopped at the security kiosk, itself a little Craftsman hut.

Inside, he saw racks of rifles on display, plus a bank of monitors. It was a lot of firepower for a suburban subdivision, and Darren found it odd. The guard was white and slim, clean-shaven, and genial as he asked Darren what brought him to Thornhill today. Darren, the window of his truck rolled down, said the name Fuller with a mix of nonchalance and purpose he hoped wouldn't draw attention to the fact that he didn't know the first name of either of Sera Fuller's parents, who they were, or what their true connection was to Thornhill. "They expecting you?" the security guard asked.

Darren nodded but didn't elaborate.

"I can give you a twenty-minute pass, sir, since Mr. Fuller's shift starts at six."

Darren glanced at his watch. It was 5:32.

The guard smiled kindly while sliding a pass with VALID UNTIL 5:52 printed in bold ink into Darren's car, letting it rest faceup on the truck's dash. "One-oh-seven Juniper Lane."

Well, that was easy. Too easy, Darren thought.

He got an image of Kelsey on the phone as he left the Rho Beta Zeta house and had an irrational but no less invasive thought that she'd somehow called ahead. *You deal with him.* The steel gates suddenly opened, welcoming him into a kind of wonderland.

Behind the stone walls, Thornhill was even more impressive in its cleanliness and sense of order. The colors were brighter — planted snap-dragons in cherry pink and lemon yellow along sidewalks. And the neighborhood was a lot larger than it had appeared from the outside. He'd of course known Texas subdivisions to have their own schools and houses of worship, but as he drove west down the main road, Hill Street, he passed a medical center, a small hospital, a library, and a business park, everything in the same humble Craftsman style, from the schools to the community center to the city hall, all except for a high-rise building in the architectural language of corporate head-quarters everywhere. The words THORNHILL INDUSTRIES topped the brick-and-glass building. The town and the company were both located on the same property, just as he'd found in his internet searches.

The cross streets all had tree names: Ash, Hazel, Magnolia, Tupelo, Cedar, and more. But there were no through streets; each avenue and lane jutted off the main road like teeth on a wide-set comb, each lead-ing to a mini community of houses all facing a shared small green space, a private park just for the families on that street. On Ash, there was a barbecue grill and lawn chairs in the shared green space, plus two long picnic tables. And a swing set.

Thornhill was a family-friendly idyll.

Darren passed mothers walking their kids home from a community pool, preteens on bikes, and a pickup basketball game. One man, with his little boy, wore a blue baseball cap with the Thornhill logo: a house as if drawn by a child's hand, except where a chimney would go, there were two smokestacks of industry shooting into the sky.

Looking for Juniper Lane, Darren somehow arrived in a part of town where the residential streets ended, and the smell was stronger. The town's main road, Hill Street, ended at a brick wall well over thirty feet high. Curious, Darren slowed to a stop. Behind the wall, he saw curls of smoke coming out of twin smokestacks that looked just like the ones on the Thornhill logo on the ball cap. Darren craned his neck, stared through his bug-crusted windshield, trying to guess what lived on the other side. There was wild, ceaseless screeching behind this second set of walls. The earth seemed to shake with it. He could feel the power of machinery going, the beast of industry. Back here, the smell was an actual presence, could have climbed into Darren's truck and driven him back home to Camilla. Suddenly, lights in his rearview mirror caught his attention. They belonged to a Thornhill Police Department squad car, and they were yellow, no more threatening than candlelight. The officer behind the wheel signaled with a honk for Darren to pull over.

Darren was happy to comply. He was lost anyway.

By the time he put his truck into park, the officer was already out of his car and approaching the cab of Darren's Chevy. "Looks like we got a little lost," he said with a smile. His overly cheery tone had the reproachful edge of an exasperated parent poorly masking frustration: *Looks like we had a little accident.* "Can I help you get on your way?"

"I'm looking for Juniper Lane," Darren said. "The Fuller family."

"Other side of Hill Street, heading back east, Mr. Mathews."

Had he shown his ID at the security gate? Given his name? He didn't remember that.

In his mind, he heard the click of Kelsey's camera phone, remembered the feeling of being reported. It was a low-grade paranoia in his veins, a condition he'd been suffering from for a while now. It lent a surreality to the current moment. It was if he'd wandered onto a film set, gotten lost inside a pretty good simulacrum of American life.

Darren nodded to the cop.

But before he could put his Chevy into gear, the officer reached in and grabbed his visitor's pass on the dashboard. "Looks like you got about sixteen minutes left." He smiled again, his teeth so white they looked vaguely blue, like Chiclets. "Don't worry, I'll be sure to give you an escort out when your time is up. Wouldn't want you getting lost again." His voice had dropped into a firm bass, and he tapped the holstered gun at his side, which Darren hadn't noticed before. Thornhill was so sunny and pleasant, Darren might have thought the guy had a daisy in his holster. But this was a clear warning. All the while, the cop never stopped smiling. It creeped Darren out. The smile, the cheerful tap on his pistol, the way the officer treated Darren like a bug that had wandered too close to a clean house for its own safety.

As soon as Darren stepped out of his truck in front of 107 Juniper Lane, he felt eyes on him. The houses sat barely two feet apart, and from behind a window in the home next door, a Latino kid was staring at him, his face partially covered by a dark curtain. He was possibly older than he seemed at first glance, with a long, thin face and a sternum that nearly pulled in on itself. Darren gave him a nod, and the kid immediately ducked behind the curtain. But as Darren walked up the steps to the Fuller house, he glanced back and saw two dark eyes pinned in his direction again. The young man was studying him as Darren walked up the steps to the door of the Fuller house.

It opened before Darren had a chance to knock.

A black man in his fifties stood in the doorway. He had salt-and-pepper hair, clipped close to his scalp. It spoke of low maintenance and a no-nonsense approach to grooming, maybe to life itself. He wore dark gray coveralls with the Thornhill logo in blue and yellow above his heart. His face wore a blank expression, a mask that told little of the man himself, except his seeming suspicion of the visitor on his doorstep. He stared hard at Darren, trying to divine a meaning behind the stranger's appearance. Inside, Darren heard a TV. The high pitch and zany score of children's cartoons. The house emitted a smell that was a respite from the fog of funk that hung over the rest of the town. Through the door came an aroma of oxtails and rice, simmered in tomatoes, onion, garlic, bay leaves, and a bit of brown sugar. Darren heard a woman's voice inside the house, dulcet and honeyed, call out, "Who is it, Joseph?"

Joseph threw the word "Nobody" over his shoulder.

As a brush-off, he said to Darren, "My shift starts in ten minutes."

"Fourteen," Darren said, tightly attuned to the time left on his visitor's pass.

Joseph narrowed his eyes at Darren. He had a cluster of moles above his left eye, and the gesture squished them into the shape of an acorn. "The bus will be here in ten."

"I won't take much of your time. I came about your daughter, Sera."

Darren heard something drop inside the house. A tray or a platter.

It didn't shatter but bounced several times in the silence that followed Darren saying Sera's name. Next door, the Latino kid had come out of his house by now. At the mention of Sera's name, he hopped off his front porch and started for the Fuller house. This, more than anything, seemed to be the reason Joseph let Darren into his home.

The second Darren was over the threshold, Joseph shut the door.

Inside, the house was as nice as it looked on the outside. Not spacious, but immaculately clean and everything so new that the whole place seemed showroom-worthy. The home was two-story and narrow, the front door opening directly onto a living room, where a boy of about nine, maybe ten, was on the floor doing homework in front of a wide-screen television, which was indeed playing cartoons. *The*

Amazing World of Gumball. The boy put down his pencil and sat up, taking in the stranger, as a woman stepped out of the kitchen, wiping her hands on a dish towel, or wringing it, Darren thought. She gave him a tepid smile, curious. She had an oval face and wide, almost black eyes. "Did he say Sera?" she said, a note of hope in her voice.

Joseph held up a hand. "Iris, I got this."

To Darren, he said, "She's at school."

"Stephen F. Austin?"

"You know our daughter?" Iris asked.

"By way of my mother," Darren said, hoping that picturing him as somebody's son would endear him to them. He was aware that he was a strange man asking about their daughter, barely out of high school. "She does some work around the sorority —"

He stopped himself from saying *where Sera lived.*

Some instinct told him to listen more than talk.

"Well, she's at the school," Joseph said, closing the door on the subject.

"Living there?"

"What I said."

"On campus, then?"

Iris opened her mouth to speak but changed her mind. Her eyes darted to the boy Darren assumed was her son, Sera's brother. Darren took in more of the living room. The wall opposite the front door had waist-high built-in shelving. The Fullers had a large Bible and no other books, not even a drugstore paperback. There were school photos on the shelves — of the boy and of a teenage girl whose face looked fuller than the one he'd seen in the Rho Beta picture online. But it was the same girl. She was in a cap and gown the same blue as the Thornhill logo on Joseph's uniform. There was also a sprinkling of porcelain figurines on the shelves — horses and angels with golden wings, a sleeping baby cushioned in a white cloud — the kind of art you pick out of the backs of magazines left behind at a doctor's office. A middle-of-America-white-bread-and-mayonnaise aesthetic that Darren frankly associated with white folks. He might have thought the Fullers had wandered into the wrong home were it not for the smell of the oxtails cooking in the kitchen and the framed photos of the obviously black family everywhere — photos that he now saw included one of Joseph and his son at what looked terrifyingly like a rally for the forty-fifth president of the United States. Joseph had his arm around his son as they stood in front with a sea of red hats behind them.

For a good ten seconds, Darren thought he was seeing things.

Joseph Fuller was a Trump supporter?

It made about as much sense as a hog driving itself to slaughter.

Even putting in for gas.

Darren felt a buzzing confusion about where he was and with whom he was talking, paranoia lighting little fires at the base of his skull, warning signals in the back of his brain. He felt his politics taking over. Or was it just his common sense that told him this fact about Joseph Fuller and his family made them suddenly suspect, unknowable to Darren, at least? He caught Joseph eyeing him closely, taking in his clothes, the contours of his face, as if he were trying to place him, as if he recognized him. Darren felt himself flush, felt a rush of fear, remembering his lawyers telling him his likeness was out there among Trump followers. *All it takes is one idiot with a gun.*

"Are you a friend of Sera's?" her mother, Iris, asked.

"No way this man is a friend of Sera's," Joseph answered for him.

He'd seen Darren studying the photo from the rally, and Darren's distrust of Joseph Fuller was now being mirrored back to him, the older man sneering at Darren's judgment, which he sussed out with the ease of a man who'd many times been on the receiving end of poorly disguised expressions of revulsion. Joseph lifted his chin in a pose of unsullied pride. There would be no apologies in this house. "I voted for Obama. Let's just get that out of the way now. So I don't want to hear none of that race-traitor mess."

"I didn't say anything," Darren said.

But his expression must have betrayed everything.

"You're one of them, huh?"

Iris frowned. "Joseph, he's a guest."

He ignored her. "World's a different place since Obama was in office."

"That I think we can agree on," Darren said. The only thing, he thought, as he was forever dumbfounded by how differently folks saw the country these days.

"I like a man who wants to earn my vote," Joseph said. "Who doesn't assume he's got it in the bag, who doesn't think he can talk down to me. I like a president who sees me as a man, who respects the fact that I think and weigh things for myself."

Darren let out a weary sigh. What bizarro Mayberry town had he walked into?

He got back to the point. "Where's your daughter, Mr. Fuller?"

"Already told you." Then, eyeing Darren, he said, "You a police officer?"

He might have been fishing for what, if anything, he owed Darren, whether he had to answer any more of his questions. But Darren felt an accusation somewhere in Joseph's tone. Were the grim warnings from his lawyers making him hear things too?

Iris stepped forward, newly attentive to this stranger's sudden appearance in their home. "He's a cop?"

"Ranger, ma'am," Darren said, regretting the affirmation as soon as it slipped out of his mouth. It had been pure reflex, a refusal to truck in shame over what had been his life's work. "I'm Darren Mathews, and I'm a Texas Ranger, ma'am."

It was a lie, and it was also his truth.

"Is Sera okay, Mom?" It was the boy, speaking for the first time.

He looked at Iris, an anxious expression on his young face.

"She's at school, Benny," Joseph said gruffly. "She's fine."

Then, realizing he'd barked his anger at the wrong person, he said, his voice softening, "You got her text just yesterday, son." He looked at Iris then, seeming to prompt her.

"That's right," she said, taking a steadying breath. She tucked the dishrag into the waist of her dark blue jeans and smiled at her son. "Seraphine's got her head in the books. We'll see her when she comes up for air, Benny. Soon, she said, remember?"

"So she's living somewhere on campus, then?" Darren asked.

Iris's voice shook a little as she said, "Why do you ask?"

He saw a mother's love in the deep wells of her eyes, felt her fear.

He sensed she was speaking out of turn, taking a chance before Joseph shut her down, which he did just a second later. "Iris, don't say another word to this man."

Joseph opened the front door.

He didn't need to shove Darren out of it because the Thornhill cop he'd encountered earlier was waiting on the welcome mat, his hand on the butt of his pistol.

"Time's up," the officer said.

9.

THERE WERE two squad cars waiting at the curb outside.

Darren halted for a second at the Fullers' front door, not understanding that the squad cars were for *him*. The officer at his side, the same one from earlier, said, "Let's keep it moving, Mr. Mathews." The man's friendly demeanor was gone now, replaced by a look of a cold threat. He gave Darren's shoulder a nudge, the move shoving Darren down the steps. Darren felt a needle shot of adrenaline, reaching for his Colt .45 on impulse. But the Thornhill cop had his own nine-millimeter unholstered before Darren could fully make sense of what was happening. Why did they need four police officers to make sure he got out of town? He wished he still had his badge. A Texas Ranger outranked these glorified rent-a-cops by a mile. But right now he was subject to the authority bestowed on them by the fact that the second they wanted him gone, Darren was legally trespassing. *But why the show of force?* And what's more, he was now fairly certain he'd never given his name to the cop or the guard in the kiosk.

The two squad cars flanked him on the road out of town and followed him back onto Highway 59. The whole way north to Nacogdoches, they hung in his rearview mirror. He couldn't understand why he was being surveilled. Any more than he could understand the dynamic between Joseph and Iris Fuller, his certainty of his daughter's where-abouts matched by her clear doubt. Darren was on the phone with campus security at Stephen F. Austin University by the time he hit Nacogdoches proper. He was loose with the truth. Having already told several lies today, he might as well stretch this thing a little further, he thought; he introduced himself as a *former* Texas Ranger, admittedly swallowing the first word. It was enough to get him past a desk clerk.

No, Sera Fuller had not been reported missing, a public safety officer told him.

Yes, university police were aware of a claim she made to the City of Nacogdoches Police Department about feeling unsafe living among her sorority sisters. The matter was closed when campus police had gone out to interview Sera and some of her Rho Beta Zeta sisters the follow-ing day. "They all reported that the whole thing was a misunderstand-ing and that everything was fine now. Even the girl."

"Sera said that?"

"According to my officer's report, she said everything was fine."

"And this was the thirteenth?" Darren confirmed.

The sorority girls had said she moved out the next day, on the four-teenth. It was weird that she would tell SFA police that she was fine and then move out the very next day.

The campus officer said, "Look, we get all kind of dramatic accu-sations between roommates when they start getting on each other's nerves a few weeks into the school year, and then they make up and the whole thing's forgotten. Or some of the kids who are local, they go back home for a few days to get a break. Says here Sera was living in Thornhill, just down the highway, so maybe knowing she could go home made whatever was going on at the sorority house easier to deal with. You looking to get a hold of the girl, I'd try her people out that way."

Right.

"You're sure she didn't move somewhere else *on* campus? A dorm, maybe?"

The cop made a curious humming sound, and Darren heard the clicking of computer keys. "Not unless she's bunking with a friend, though I know the housing folks don't like that. It's a liability for the university. My first year on the job there was a girl who had her high-school boyfriend living in her dorm for half the semester. Only got caught 'cause some girl on her floor finally turned him in because he never put the toilet seat down." The campus officer chuckled, waiting for Darren to join in, and when he didn't, the cop followed up with "No, for the 2019/2020 school year, I only see here the address on Steen. The Rho Beta Zeta sorority house."

Darren thanked the campus officer, who said, "Sure thing, Ranger."

He clicked off his phone, a bad feeling in the pit of his stomach.

He was growing concerned for Sera Fuller, a girl who was seemingly nowhere, a fact about which no one seemed to care. Darren thought of Iris, saw her deep, almost black eyes and the pinch of grave concern there. He was wrong to say no one cared where Sera Fuller was. Her mother did, and another mother did too. His own. Bell hadn't bought the *And good riddance* story of Sera moving out of Rho Beta Zeta, not when she'd found some of her personal items dumped in a trash bin behind the sorority house, which Bell had saved on instinct. Items Darren now wanted to see for himself.

The combined White Pages for Lufkin and Nacogdoches had a Pete Callis at an address on Lanana Street. Darren remembered his mother saying she'd moved to Nacogdoches in part to help a brother she called

Petey, who'd had a stroke, she said. Until that moment, Darren hadn't been aware that he had an uncle named Pete. He knew little about his mother's family other than that the Mathews men, his uncles William and Clayton, didn't think much of the whole tribe, were known to speak ill of that entire line of his heritage. Darren had heard tales of the Callis men in and out of jail, shiftlessness as a chronic condition, always to support the idea that Darren had been saved from being raised by a band of thieves and ne'er-do-wells. And not a day spent in his mother's company had persuaded Darren against this thinking. Since he was a boy, she was only ever marginally employed and often full of complaints that either Clayton or William had sent Darren over to her place with nothing more for her than a twenty-dollar bill. She too admitted a streak of lawlessness in her brothers, the number of which Darren never got. He'd never met any of them. Not a grandmother on his mother's side, not a grandfather either. No cousins or great-aunts. Come to think of it, he didn't even know if his mother had a sister or if she'd been raised as the only daughter in a house full of rambunctious boys. He thought he remembered her as the baby of the family. But of even that he wasn't sure. Driving toward Lanana Street now, in the heart of the Zion Hill District in Nacogdoches, one of the oldest black neighborhoods in the state, he felt himself driving toward a different kind of mystery.

He had no idea what his uncle Pete looked like, nor could he imagine how his newly sober mother was living. As he turned on her street, he glanced at his rearview mirror, half expecting to see the Thornhill police still on his tail. But he only saw the grille of a small blue pickup truck behind him as he continued down Lanana Street.

The road was lined with clapboard houses, some shotgun-style, some with enough room that a bullet would have to bounce off a few extra walls to do any real harm. A good number of them had no foundations to speak of, whole structures hovering inches above the earth, held in place by stacked bricks or blocks of concrete. They were sweet homes, with patchy but neatly groomed yards. Front porches with green plants hanging and toys and bikes leaned against paint-faded walls. The homes were set haphazardly on their lots, in no way uniform, which gave the neighborhood the beauty of a patchwork quilt. The homes appeared to have sprung up as mercurially as the money it had cost to build them, with late-edition add-ons to some, back rooms growing like appendages, and converted lean-tos turned into outdoor living rooms. It spoke of the grace of improvisation, of the oldest black art form: making do. There were a few families outdoors, as the night was relatively mild. Darren drove past a dominoes game, a brother playing Junior Wells on the radio of a parked El Camino. He drove past Zion Hill Baptist Church, a hauntingly Southern Gothic structure that was one of the most beautiful buildings Darren had ever seen. Finally, he arrived at a white clapboard house with a porch painted green. There was a gentleman wearing a barber's smock standing on the porch. He was silhouetted by the beam of a mechanic's work light hanging from a hook, so Darren couldn't see his face in the shadows of dusk.

He parked his Chevy, whose navigation system told him he'd reached the home of Pete Callis. The man on the porch looked up when he saw Darren get out of his truck.

"Pete?" Darren called to him. The man was cutting the hair of an older man sitting in a kitchen chair set out on the front porch. The man in the chair had a ratty towel around his neck that he kept closed with one hand, clutching it around his throat. It was this man who said, "Who's asking, and I'll tell you if he's here or not."

Darren heard the man with the clippers chuckle, then go back to cutting hair.

The man in the chair cocked his head so he could see Darren better. His barber grunted and gently pushed the man's head back where he needed it to get the cut right.

"Darren Mathews," he said, feeling foolish. "One of y'all is my uncle?"

The man in the chair let go of his grip on the towel. It fell behind him as he started to stand. He needed help from his barber, who held out a sturdy arm for Darren's uncle Pete to grab hold of. As he stood to his full height, Darren felt a sense of familiarity wash over him. "Well, come on, then, and let me get a good look at you, son."

As Darren crossed the grass to the steps of the front porch, he felt a strange tremble in his knees, felt it radiate up through his torso and out to his fingertips. For a moment, he worried his need for alcohol was finally shaking him from the inside out. A wave of feeling was coming over him, a mix of nerves and a curious excitement. He'd lost a great deal in this lifetime. A father he never knew. His beloved uncle William. He wouldn't have put money on meeting any new family this late in his life.

"That's Bell's boy, all right," Pete said as he held out one arm for a welcoming embrace, the other hanging lifeless at his side. Darren remembered again that Pete had had a stroke as he hugged his mother's brother, felt the firmness of immediate affection for Darren in one side of the man's body and the faint struggle to make his right side do what the left was doing. Darren felt an unexpected tenderness for the man who seemed to love Darren on sight, no questions asked. When they broke apart, the two took each other in for a moment. Pete Callis was near seventy and thicker than either Darren or his mother. His hair was unnaturally black, and Darren wondered fleetingly if the barber colored his uncle's hair as well. Pete smiled widely and looked more like Bell than Darren had been prepared for. He'd never seen her face in any but his own.

"Bell told me you was in town," he said, slapping Darren on the back with his good hand. "But she ain't tell me you was coming out this way. Woulda put on something special for dinner. We was just heating up some of what was left over from last night."

"That's all right, I wasn't planning to eat," he said, even as his stomach rumbled in objection.

He hadn't eaten since he'd left the farmhouse in Camilla over four hours ago.

His plan was to get a hold of Sera Fuller's things and leave.

"Well, go on inside, then," Pete said. "Your mama'll be happy to see you."

Would she?

Last they'd seen each other, he'd been harsh and unforgiving.

And now here he was at her doorstep.

Pete seemed to pick up on the ripple of tension, maybe knew that Darren and his mother didn't have the best relationship, didn't have much of one at all. "Go on, little Duke," he said. Then, catching the look on Darren's face, he said, "Sorry, you just remind me so much of your daddy. Time you got out the car, I was thinking, *If that boy don't walk like Duke, don't got me seeing ghosts, then I don't know what.*"

Hearing his father's nickname, Darren was thrown back on his heels. He tightened his grip on the porch railing.

"You met my father?" Darren said, voice rising on a note of disbelief.

Pete smiled, tickled. He glanced up at his barber with a wry smile that said, *Can you believe this kid?* Then, he chuckled. "Boy asking me if I knew Duke Mathews."

The barber didn't react to the name Duke Mathews, ignoring the suggestion that he even knew who that was and causing Darren to wonder about the extent of Pete's stroke. Had he suffered more brain damage than was obvious in his gait, in his bad arm? From what Darren knew of his parents' dalliance — quick and ill-advised, according to his uncles — there was no way Duke had ever met a brother living in Nacogdoches. "I'm going to go in and see Bell," Darren said, the name resting funny on his tongue. "She's got some papers and some things she wanted me to take a look at."

"That poor girl, I know. I hope you find her," Pete said.

The screen door creaked when Darren opened it and stepped into a tiny sitting room at the front of the house, overstuffed with two couches and a large, low-lying dark wood coffee table he almost tripped over. Music was playing on a boom box set on a dining-room table that was shoved up against a wall. It had bills and newspapers and a laundry basket on one side of it, the other side with two place settings. Fork and knife on plastic place mats with poinsettias on them, and two glasses of orange juice. The music was Irma Thomas, "Ruler of My Heart," a swinger from the sixties. He heard his mother singing over the sound of running water in the kitchen. *Ruler of my heart, robber of my soul . . .* It felt wrong sneaking up on her like this, during what felt like an intimate moment, a woman singing about a broken heart. He cleared his throat loudly.

"One second, Pete."

She was just pulling two plates out of the oven. They were covered loosely in foil, swirls of steam escaping the sides, and Bell had fashioned two dishrags into impromptu pot holders. She was starting for the dining-room table when she looked up and realized it was Darren in the kitchen with her and not her brother Pete. The sight of her son stopped her in her tracks. She stared at him for a long moment, a mix of surprise and something akin to tempered relief, a look on her face that suggested any joy at her son's presence was not yet earned. Then the plates got too hot for standing still and she started walking fast.

Darren ducked out of the entryway to the kitchen to allow her to get to the dining-room table quickly. She set the two plates on the plastic Christmas place mats and then looked up, as if she wasn't sure what to do next.

She asked if she could fix him a plate, that it would do him good to sit down and eat something. Darren ignored this and got down to it: He had more information now and wanted a chance to take a look at the things she had recovered from the trash bin out back of the Rho Beta sorority house. He presented all this with a flat affect that suggested no warmth. Bell gave a little nod of appreciation for her current standing with Darren. This would not be a convivial visit, no sitting down to tea and talk, no baby steps toward reconciliation. By showing up at his house three days ago, his mother had put him back on the clock. He was here to do a job, to gather what information he could to find Sera. "Okay, give me a second," she said. Then she hollered out to her brother on the front porch, "Petey, your plate is on the table."

"Butch is almost done," Pete said. "Be in there in a minute."

"You want me to put it back in the oven?"

"You sweet for that," Pete said. "But I'll be in in a second."

Brother and sister had an easy rapport. She was warm with him, doting.

In fact, being inside this low-ceilinged four-room house, the walls close, the light dim, and the smell an inviting mix of warm laundry and the home-cooked meal on the table, butter beans and chicken smothered in gravy and onions, Darren felt he'd walked into the kind of home he'd expected when he first met his mother — not the trailer, the run-down tin can that smelled of cheap beer and cigarettes, where he'd actually first laid eyes on Bell Callis when he was an eight-year-old boy, holding his uncle William's hand, anxious and a little scared to meet this woman he'd only heard about. His mom.

He followed his mother on the narrow trail of low-pile carpet through the house, noting the many unframed watercolors that were taped to the walls, each a variation on a theme, weepy images of the famed Zion Hill Baptist Church — the clover-like windows and Gothic arches, the intricate woodwork and morning light on the cross. Shortly, they arrived at a bedroom. It was tiny, with bright blue shag carpeting that at first glance gave the impression of a bearskin rug made out of Cookie Monster. The walls were a pale blue, giving the decor a seventies ombré effect. In keeping with the look of the decade, the bed was covered with a knotty macramé-style blanket. And resting on top, in neat rows, were hair combs, school papers, a few items of clothing, photographs, toiletries, spiral notebooks, and a bulging pencil case. Bell had taken the time to cover the bed in sheets of wax paper rolled out from a box of it in the kitchen, protecting the "evidence," as Darren had called it, or her bedspread, or both. For this was clearly Bell's bedroom. The faint scent of cigarettes, a pack of which he saw resting on the edge of the dresser, next to her car keys for the Nissan parked at his house just a few days ago. That she had saved and protected these pieces of Sera Fuller's life moved Darren twice over. She'd done it for Sera, yes. But she'd also done this for him.

"You knew I was coming?" he said.

"I hoped."

She tapped her fingers against the doorjamb, letting the moment hang.

"Well, I'll leave you to it, then," Bell said, turning back toward the living room and the messy dining-room table where her dinner was waiting.

"Actually, I'd like you to stay."

He told her the items would mean more with any context Bell might offer, having been around the girl, having cleaned her room and found all this in the trash. "Let's start with the exact day that you found these items behind the sorority house."

Darren caught a flash of a smile on her face. She had reeled him in after all.

Only this time he didn't believe there was any game behind it, other than the thrill of having captured Darren's attention. And he was willing to give it to her if it meant finding out more about Sera and where she might be. "You were at my house three days ago, on the twentieth," he said, squeezing any hint of reproach out of his tone. There was no time for rehashing the anger he'd felt over her stealth arrival at his home. "How long before that had you discovered these items in the trash?" he said.

"The day before. It's what made me decide I needed to find you."

"And it was all dumped loose like this, or was some of it in bags, like trash bags?"

"It was thrown in there just like this, all over the place. I'm not even sure I got all of it, but I also wasn't trying to get caught digging through them people's trash. Woman before me got fired just for telling one of the girls that a peach in her room was gon' go bad if she didn't eat it soon. The girl complained that she felt pressured to eat the peach on the spot or hand it over to the maid. She said it felt like extortion." Bell rolled her eyes.

"Why do you work there, after the way that girl talked to you?" He thought of Kelsey ordering around his sixty-two-year-old mother, how angry it had made him.

"It's a job, Darren. A good one. The service that hires me out, they pay twelve dollars and twenty-five cents an hour to clean the sorority houses. Ain't much, but it's the best job I've ever had. Don't have health insurance yet, but I'm hoping to use this job as a step up to something better." She sounded focused and clear-eyed, something he was still getting used to. Darren looked at all the materials on the bed.

"You got some latex gloves, kitchen gloves or something?"

"Even better," Bell said, sounding to Darren a little too enthusiastic as she stepped out of the room. A few moments later, she returned with two sets of tissue-thin black gloves clutched in her hand. "Petey started dyeing his hair last year. Don't tell him I told you. He's had a rough enough time of it with the stroke, don't need me adding on about how he looks like he tripped during a roofing job and tarred his own head."

Darren chuckled despite himself.

It felt strange having a secret *with* his mother, one he'd been invited into.

She passed out the gloves and they got to work.

10.

HE COULDN'T understand why Bell wouldn't let up about the girl's hair. She showed him three different products Sera had been using that weren't for her grade of hair, told him coconut oil don't work for everyone, but most folks don't know that. In some ways, it was easier these days for the girls to stay off the chemicals, but it was more confusing too. When she quit pressing her hair when she was a teenager in the early seventies, you could go with either a tin of Royal Crown hair grease or whatever you could get off the stove. "Nobody'd ever heard of olive oil back then, but a girl I went to Nacogdoches High School with put canola oil in her hair, and that shit grew me about four inches my senior year," Bell said, as she studied a brush she'd found. She ran a gloved hand over the multiple rows of teeth, which came apart with a flick of her finger. "This one supposed to enhance curls. I seen that on YouTube. But she must not have been using it right." It wasn't that the girl's hair was ugly, Bell said; it just neither laid down smooth nor stood up with any personality or pride. "Confused is what I would call it." Darren was only half listening as he flipped through Sera's schoolwork, loose papers, and a fat spiral notebook from which a typed term paper and her class schedule slid out onto the bed. Something Bell said finally hit a landing pad in his brain.

"You went to high school here, in Nacogdoches?"

Bell nodded as she ran her gloved hands over a bundle of clothes. "My last year, yes. Nacogdoches was one of the first in East Texas to integrate their high school. This was years and years after that court case out of Kansas, mind you, 1970. Two years later, Petey took a job up here so I could enroll. He knew I was smart, thought it was a limit to what I could learn coming out of Camilla in San Jacinto County. Same reason your uncles sent you to high school in Houston when it was your time. It was Petey's idea for me to live with him. He got a job out here just so I could make the transfer and say he was my guardian. He swept floors at one of the timber mills, worked his way up to janitorial supervisor. He did all that so I could get what the white kids was getting."

Darren frowned and said, "I didn't know."

A cover for *I don't believe you.*

"Wouldn't had no reason to. Time you were born, I was back in Camilla."

He rolled the story around in his mind. "But you had me when you were sixteen. How would you have finished your senior year of high school here in Nacogdoches?"

It sounded like a fantasy, a dream she might have had a long time ago.

Bell started to address his open doubt, but then she stopped suddenly. "Darren, look at this."

She held a white slip of paper, stained in places, likely because it had been in the trash. It was smooth, though, barely a crinkle in it. There was a note on one side, written in pale blue ink. Cornflower blue. *Jesus, even their pens are color-coordinated,* Darren thought. He took the note from his mother, taking in the block-style print, the handwriting of kids who never had to study cursive writing in school. It was gawky, awkward-looking. The note said: JUST CHECKING ON YOU AFTER LAST NIGHT.

It was signed *Michelle.*

"Hmph," Bell said, as if the note alone proved something. *What,* he didn't know.

"We don't know this note was for Sera."

"Except it was mixed up with all the rest of her things."

"There's no way to know when it was written, or what 'last night' means."

Darren handed the note back to his mother, asking if any of it rang any bells.

Bell studied it for a few moments. "It's a girl there named Michelle, I think. Been around since I started." Then she smiled at the note. "It's nice to think of one of them girls checking in on her like this." She gingerly set it on top of a piece of wax paper, then went back to looking through Sera's other things. From inside a bundle of clothes, a pill bottle rolled out. "Look here," she said, holding it out for her son.

Darren set aside Sera's schoolwork. He reached for the pills and turned the bottle over, squinting to make out the small print, before glancing around the room to see if there was another light he could turn on. He caught his mother giving him a wry smile. "Gon' be needing readers before long." She cocked her head a little to take him in, her grown boy. "You can borrow a pair of mine. Got a set of 'em in that top drawer."

Darren made a point of needing no such thing.

"Lenarix," he said, reading the label.

"Never heard of it."

"Me either," he said, already googling the medication on his phone.

Darren gave a low hum about what he saw.

"Sera has sickle cell," he told his mother.

"Aw, no . . ." Bell seemed genuinely saddened to hear this, as if receiving news about a relative she hadn't seen in a while but for whom she still held fond feelings.

"She seem sick to you?" Darren asked.

"I always thought she was kind of thin. She didn't seem strong, is what I'm trying to say. But I never saw her fall out or nothing. She appeared to make it to her classes."

"Maybe she had a medical episode of some sort."

Could the girl have fallen out somewhere and needed help?

"Maybe her parents *do* know where she is," Darren said. "Surely they're keeping tabs on her, checking in to make sure she's doing okay, especially living away from home with a serious medical condition." He told his mother about the trip to Thornhill, the fact that there seemed to be something odd and unsavory about Joseph and that Sera's mom had looked scared. But they insisted they were in contact with Sera.

They'd received texts, he'd been told.

"I don't see how," Bell said.

Darren looked up to see Bell holding a small black cell phone.

It was a flip phone, ancient-looking by any nineteen-year-old's standards, but it had her initials scratched into the side. Darren took it from his mother and opened it, mashed every button.

The thing was dead.

"Did you say this girl was from Thornhill?" Bell asked.

Darren was slow to respond, still noodling over what it meant that they had the girl's dead cell phone, retrieved from the trash four days ago, after he'd just heard the Fullers suggest they were in constant contact with their daughter via text. Their daughter with a life-threatening illness. "What?" he said, looking up at his mother, who was shuffling through a thin stack of photographs. He wanted a look at those too.

"Thornhill."

"You know it?" he said while holding out his hand for the photos. Bell, who was perched with one hip hiked on the edge of her bed, passed the photos to Darren, who was now sitting on the carpet with his back against the wall. He had the cell phone at his feet, Sera's notebooks spread around him. He started flipping through the photos — shots of trees, forestland. They were beautiful. Sun-dappled and a brilliant dark green, the oaks and pines in these pictures were majestic. Simply stunning. Sera was in a few of them, back against the trunk of a tree, her gaze turned to the sky. He wondered who'd taken the pictures, with whom she'd spent time in the woods.

"I put in an application to work there," she said. "I'm still waiting to hear."

Darren looked up. "What exactly is it they do? What business are they running?"

"It's a processing plant, what I heard. Pork or chicken, one of them. Hard work, them kind of jobs, but it comes with free housing out there, all kind of extra perks. She was doing good if her people was living and working out there. It's pretty, real clean."

Darren considered the house they were currently in; it was dated, for sure, and there were scuffs and marks on the wall, loose doorknobs, and a few water stains on ceilings, but there was still something inviting about the place. Cozy. The closeness of its walls gave the feeling of strong arms wrapped tightly around you; it felt protective and capable. But Bell said she wasn't sure of a future here for her and Pete, who, she reminded him, weren't getting any younger. It was a struggle to make rent and pay his medical bills. "Even after Obamacare, he still come out of pocket for all the kinds of therapy he need since his stroke. Physical and occupational, they call it," she said. "He's having a good night. But he forgets things, and sometimes the words he's looking for be swimming around in front of him like slippery catfish, a thing he can't catch in time."

Darren thought of Pete saying that he'd met his father, Duke. He wondered if that had been the older man's mental confusion talking. Bell sighed, still ruminating on their current situation. She said, "It's just my little paycheck now."

"Isn't he on disability or anything?" Darren said.

"Yes, but it's the doctors' visits that's eating at us. A lot of the good ones don't be fooling with Medicaid. And Medicare don't cover it all. It's a rehab facility in Lufkin I drive him to a few times a week. I come out of pocket almost a hundred dollars every time he has a session."

She joked that at this rate, Petey ought to be able to whistle and ride a unicycle before they were finished with him. But she guessed she'd settle for him being able to use his right side to do a few odd jobs again. The listlessness of his days wore him down.

It was exquisitely strange listening to his mother talk of caretaking for another.

Either age had brought her here, to the tenderness of life, an understanding and appreciation for its utter fragility, or there had always been a gentle spot in her soul that had just never found a need for expression, certainly not as his mother. He felt bitter about it, but also tired. Of this day that had begun with a ghastly hangover, of the hours he wasn't spending with Randie, and maybe, just maybe, he was tired of hating his mom. Especially since the one he knew to hate didn't appear to be in this room. There was a Bell Callis in his mind for whom he still felt rage. But the quiet older woman before him now elicited only compassion, raw and unexamined, a pure human impulse to care, to have fellow feeling about the person in front of you. The emotion confused him and made the fatigue spread throughout his body, a weight in his bones.

"We should give these things back to her family," Bell said after they'd been through most of the stuff. Darren nodded. He'd like an excuse to see the Fullers again.

He checked the campus health center anyway, plus every urgent care and hospital he could find in a two-county radius. There was no one named Sera Fuller who had visited or checked into any of those places. He had again donned his old identity, repeatedly introducing himself to hospital staff as "Ranger Darren Mathews" and using an old trick: bypassing nurses' stations and asking the switchboard to patch him to the desk for volunteers, sweet older women who made sure flowers got delivered to patients' rooms. They sometimes took messages for patients too, and they frequently said more than they should.

Meanwhile, Bell had reheated her plate and set it back on the table to share with him. Darren was too hungry to be anything but grateful, so they ate from the same plate. Bell barely picked at her side, making sure Darren got a hearty portion of smothered chicken. He in turn hardly touched the butter beans. "Never been a fan," he said. Bell lowered her head, pushing a few of the pale, waxy-looking beans around on the plate. "I didn't know that," she said, soft and wistful.

She took a sip of her orange juice. It was freshly squeezed, and Darren had already had two glasses of it, the sweet tartness of it lighting up places on his tongue that longed for something else, something he'd told himself he wouldn't have as long as he was in his mother's presence. He would not let her see him drink.

He still hadn't accepted her tacit invitation to spend the night.

He could still get a hotel, a bottle of bourbon.

"Kind of shameful, all the things I don't know about you," his mother said. "What food you like, your favorite song, what went wrong with you and Lisa..."

He felt his guard go up again. How did she know about the divorce?

"At least, I assume something went wrong, what with that other woman in the house in Camilla."

"Oh," Darren said. *Right.*

He put off talking about it by saying he needed to call his old lieutenant.

He'd been throwing the title Ranger in front of his name because the truth was, he felt the need for the weight of the Texas Rangers behind this. He needed their help. Sera needed their help. It was coming on nine at night, and he had no choice but to call Wilson's home line. He was prepared for Wilson's exasperation, even his irritation, at Darren's apparent flip-flopping, quitting and then wanting to be put on a new case.

What he did not anticipate was that Wilson had been waiting for his call.

"Making me regret I didn't fire you years ago," his former lieutenant barked into the phone once Darren identified himself. He'd been to Wilson's home only once, for a dinner Wilson had put together for the twenty-fifth anniversary of the swearing-in of Darren's uncle William with whom he'd served. He remembered the dated kitchen, wood paneling and linoleum, canary-yellow trim on all the cabinets. Darren pictured Wilson in after-work clothes and slippers, talking on the wall phone next to the refrigerator. "Back when I was getting calls from Austin that maybe we ought to put you on leave again, some all out calling for your head, with you wrapped up in two grand jury investigations in less than three years. I mean, my God, Mathews, this is the kind of vigilante shit that's got people questioning what side of things you belong on, whether you're an honest man of the law that we all done swore to follow, or if you're out here making up different rules for yourself." Unsaid but lit vibrantly beneath his acid tone was the implication that Wilson, too, was questioning these things about Darren, after years of insisting that Darren was a clean cop. Before Darren could mention the name Sera Fuller, Wilson said, slowly and firmly, as if going over important safety measures on a firearm, "There is no missing girl, Mathews. You're scaring that girl's family for no good goddamn reason. They are in contact with their daughter. There is no concern or dispute about that."

"Who called you?" Darren said. "That security detail out in Thornhill?"

"Police department. They are the municipal authority in that town."

"It's a glorified subdivision, a neighborhood attached to a job site."

Wilson let out a sound that was both a sigh and a grumble. "They are an incorporated city, and they have their own police department recognized by the Texas Rangers as autonomous and absolutely none of our business unless they call us in —"

"Or we see something wrong," Darren said. Because that was the law, the code.

Wilson was quiet a moment, hearing something in Darren's voice that gave him pause.

Darren slid into the silence.

"I am in possession of the girl's cell phone. Out of battery, by the way."

"I don't want to hear another word about it, don't even want to guess what you're up to that you got a hold of this girl's property."

"What I am saying, sir, is how can the parents be in contact with Sera if I have her cell phone?" Of course, even as he said it, he realized there was no chain of custody here that would stand up to scrutiny. His mother had fished it out of a dumpster. Wilson could even argue the girl had another phone. Darren might have stood down — except the echo of something Wilson had said finally hit him. "Why would they be scared, sir, if they know where their daughter is?" He remembered the look in Iris Fuller's eyes. "And *who* told you they were scared, sir?"

This time the silence stretched so long Darren thought it possible that Wilson had hung up on him. That might have hurt less than what came next. "Mathews," the older man finally said. "Listen to me. You do not have a badge. You are not a Texas Ranger. I don't know if it's the drink talking —"

"Sir —"

"No, son, let me speak," Wilson said. He lowered his voice, but it lost none of its steel. "You are William Mathews's boy, for all intents and purposes, and I have loved you, son, because of it. Because I loved that man. And I have protected you in ways you don't even know. Folks coming for you in 2016 when Mack was first accused, folks coming for you now. And I ain't ever want to believe that you was struggling as much as I've come to see that you are, and maybe that's where I have failed you. But you need to understand there's a hurricane of shit coming your way."

"I just think we need to find this girl, sir."

Wilson ran right over him, still talking, his voice trembling in a way that unnerved Darren. He felt Wilson about to cross a line within his own heart. "I'm not supposed to know this, Darren, and please don't ask me how I do, but the grand jury is out with your case. They're deliberating. Two days now. You go to trial, and I don't want to have to get on the stand and testify that you was up in Nacogdoches County impersonating a police officer while you're facing prison time. So I'm going to hang up now, Mathews, but not before I tell you to quit this shit, son. Go home. Get some rest."

Wilson took a deep breath and then added softly, almost sweetly, "Bye, Darren."

He heard a rough click, and then the line went dead.

Darren's hand dropped and he stared down at his phone. When he looked up, his mother was sitting across from him with two bowls of vanilla ice cream. She slid one across the uncluttered part of the table that was reserved for eating. Darren felt a stab of pique, of exquisite vexation at the absurdity of his mother offering him ice cream right now. She was playacting motherhood. The home-cooked meal, a dish of dessert presented lovingly. When he'd just gotten news that because of her shenanigans, there was a grand jury debating his fate. He had to nearly stop himself from tossing the ice cream back in her face. He was so angry his head hurt. His teeth ached, his jaw was so tightly clenched. He realized it had been maybe eighteen hours since he'd had a drink.

He remembered Wilson's words, the disappointment in Darren.

It made him sink down into his chair, so far that his neck rested on the wooden back. What the fuck was he doing in his mother's house? The woman who was the reason he might be charged with obstruction of justice? He let out a laugh, opened his mouth and howled, laughing until he cried. Bell looked confused at first and disappointed and then sorry. "Let me guess, you don't like vanilla ice cream either."

"No, Mama," he said, painting the word red with irony. "I don't."

"It's for the sugar," Bell said. "I can get you something else if you like. But I find the sugar helps when the cravings come on, which, honey, I hate to tell you, two years on, they still do. Little bite of something sweet seems to calm down the thing inside that hollers for you to drink. Petey got some raisins in there, maybe even a pack of M and M's."

Darren sat up and stared at his mother, feeling a strange new thing come over him. It was pure gratitude. It caught him against his will. In this tiny little house, walls so close he could kiss them, he felt strangely safe all of a sudden, protected by his mother's watchful eye. She had seen him, seen where his mind and body were going, and offered a solution. "Thank you," he said, because he very desperately did not want to drink. Not if Randie was gone because of it, not if he'd lost Wilson's respect.

"Not saying you couldn't do it on your own, but if you wanted my help with it, I'd give it to you, Darren. We could start with right now. Tonight, if that's all it is. Stay here. Don't drive off to how you know this will go if you get to a hotel room. I can walk you through one night at the very least. If you would let me do that for you, son."

His eyes were still wet.

And the ice cream was melting.

He reached for the bowl, the teaspoon with a rose imprinted on the handle cradling the scoop of ice cream. He carved out a bite, let it melt on his tongue. The sugar was its own kind of rush. The cold and creaminess of it reminded him of country summers as a boy. Darren looked at his mother, and he nodded.

Part Three

11.

HE HADN'T so much agreed to stay at his mother's house as he'd been unable to get off the couch, the reality of the conversation with Wilson still vibrating through him over an hour later. His disgust over Darren's meddling, which hurt Darren but didn't stop him from finally calling his friend Greg. He might not have been with the FBI anymore, but maybe Greg still had friends in the Bureau. Maybe he could help Darren break into Sera's phone. But what had truly poured lead in Darren's blood, unable to move from his mother's couch, was Wilson's news that a grand jury had his case, cells in his brain waking one by one to the news of how close he might be to prison.

The timing of it was gnawing at him.

His mother sat on the other end of the velour couch, which was a burnt-umber color with large pink and orange roses sewn into the fabric. It too spoke of a home decor barely touched since the seventies. The cushions on his side of the couch, a favored spot he guessed, were worn down so much that he sank into the furniture and sat at least an inch shorter than his mother, knees scrunched and poking up like two pogo sticks. The edge of the too-big-for-this-room coffee table was pressing against his shins. He felt his mother's eyes on him from across the couch. She had changed at some point into a housedress and slippers. He had never seen her in a pastel color of any sort, had never thought of her as a woman who would ever let lace grace her collar. But here she was, wrapped in a confection of quilted fabric and dewdrop buttons. She had her legs tucked up under her, and she was facing him. Darren heard running water and assumed Pete was washing up for the night. This was an early-to-bed household.

"Sometimes it helps to talk," Bell said. "It's the silence, sitting up alone, that gets you, gets your mind to racing and worrying, that makes you hope the hammer of a beer or six will calm it all down. Talking to somebody can put a shape on all the wild thoughts and feelings, a shape you can hold in your hand. Tames it some. When I decided drinking wasn't doing nothing for me no more, Petey and I used to stay up hours and talk."

Darren felt a flush of heat run up his sides.

He'd let his guard down, gone soft in her presence.

"Why did you give the gun to the DA?"

And were you in San Jacinto County three days ago to testify in front of a grand jury?

Bell swung her legs out from under her and sat up straighter. "I told you, son, I didn't know that gun was used in a crime, had anything to do with the killing of that man that was in the Klan —"

"Aryan Brotherhood. Ronnie Malvo was in the Aryan Brotherhood of Texas."

"See, I didn't know a thing about it." She kicked off a house shoe to scratch the sole of one foot with the toe of the other. "I found it when I was seeing to the house in Camilla that time, like you had asked me to. But, Darren, I ain't know it was wrapped up in this other thing. How could I? I took it for safekeeping, trusting myself rather than anybody else getting they hands on it. I was just trying to keep it . . . keep *you* safe."

"By giving it to the district attorney?"

"Wiped clean, son. You keep missing that bit. That gun is totally useless to them." Her voice had inched up an octave, and she was talking faster, as if she were sweeping up her words almost as soon as she dropped them, leaving no trail for him to find his way out of this. He thought he heard the low growl of a wolf in a pink housecoat. "You forget, me and Petey been around rough characters in our family. I know how to disappear a gun or render it a piece of junk for any case they trying to build. Our brothers, couple of great-uncles on my side, even my mama, all knew more than a few ways to set fire to the best-laid plans of men in authority." Reminding him that he came from a line of hustlers on his mother's side, men and women who were master blacksmiths, bending laws and rules and the truth to a shape that suited their ends.

"It's how we survived," she said, patting his leg. It was so tempting to believe that his mother had done all this to protect him. But he also felt the danger behind the temptation, felt afraid of making the mistake of trusting her again.

"Wasn't it, Petey?" she said as his uncle walked into the room.

He was wearing an ancient HILL LUMBER CO. T-shirt and gray sweatpants that were stained in a few places, all on his left, working side. He smelled of toothpaste and freshly rolled deodorant, and he walked slowly from the hallway, wiping at his mouth with the back of his good hand and shuffling his bad leg behind him. He didn't seem to understand what all he'd walked into, but he took in the pinched expression on Darren's face and gave him a shaky smile. He said, "Aw, Bell, I don't think it was half as bad as all that, and even if it was, we here now, living good, paying our bills."

"One of us, at least," his mother said sharply.

It felt cold to Darren, a little mean.

This, he thought. This was the Bell Callis he recognized.

He stood suddenly, banging his shins into the coffee table. He had to get out of there, had to get away from the feeling that he had somehow fallen prey to his mother once again, but in ways he didn't yet understand. He felt angry and unsafe, at least unsure of his own read on things, whether he could take any of what was in front of him at face value, most especially where his mother was concerned. He stepped around the coffee table, edging past newspapers and shopping bags filled with just the right shoe from half a dozen pairs, and passed a coat-rack, where his mother's CHEERY CLEAN MAIDS smocks hung limply. He let himself out the door and onto the front porch.

He wanted to call Randie, was desperate to hear her voice.

He had his cell phone out, was two rings in, when down the street, a darkened car caught his attention. In the dim light, he couldn't be sure, but hell if it didn't look like a police squad car the same bright blue as the ones driven by Thornhill cops. Darren stepped into the road to get a closer look at the exact moment that the car peeled away from the curb and flicked on its headlights. They blinded Darren and streaked his vision with jagged, white lines as the car came within a foot of his kneecaps, then swerved suddenly and went around him, speeding off down Lanana Street, its taillights blooming red on his chest, which rose and fell with . . . not panic, exactly. Because he seemed to understand at once that if he had truly seen what he thought he had—a Thornhill police officer keeping tabs on him—then panic was too impulsive a reaction, a luxury he didn't have. *If* Thornhill police were watching him, he needed to be careful. They had already reported him to the Rangers; it was only so long before all of this got to DA Frank Vaughn in San Jacinto County, news that Darren was again acting outside the law. *If* that was a Thornhill police vehicle, he reminded himself. Tired as he was, he suddenly wasn't so sure, still felt like the world was playing tricks on him. Because why would Thornhill be tailing him all the way to Nacogdoches? He looked down and saw that he'd let the call to Randie ring through to voicemail. That she hadn't answered his call made anything he wanted to say to her moot.

He hung up and walked back to the house.

From the porch, he could see the storied Zion Hill Baptist Church, the blackness of its scalloped windows strangely inviting. To keep from drinking, maybe he could spend the night in there. Just him and the ghost of Christ. He heard the screen door creak open. The step-shuffle gait told him it was his uncle Pete. *Uncle.* The idea of it still felt new. "Your mama in there making up the bed for you," Pete said. "Moving that gal's things to the side. Bell said she ain't mind sleeping on the couch for the night."

There was a question at the back of his throat.

Darren hadn't said yet whether he was staying or going.

"Just getting a little air," Darren said, committing to nothing.

"She get a little bite in her sometimes, been knowing that since she was a kid, but tell you what, you done lit her up for a lifetime coming here like you done." Pete shot Darren a lopsided smile before shuffling over to the chair where he'd been getting his hair cut earlier. It had a metal frame, and the seat was a dark yellow vinyl with green and turquoise paisleys on it. It felt familiar, but he hadn't seen its match anywhere inside the house. Darren wondered absent-mindedly where it might have come from. The light that hung when Pete's buddy Butch was cutting his hair was gone now, and Darren could see his uncle only by the lone streetlamp on this block of Lanana.

Pete pulled out a pack of cigarettes identical to the ones Darren's mother smoked. "And before you say anything," Pete said, "Bell done tried to get me to quit, even though she steady smoking herself. But I figure what difference it make now?" He rested the cigarettes on his bad leg, which gave off no twitch and lay so still, it acted almost as a narrow tray. "I'm coming on seventy now, and I can't work or cook or fuck no more, ain't got enough money for all the doctors in the world to put me back together again, and I don't want all this on Bell," he said, suggesting he was maybe courting another stroke, a bigger one this time. "I want to do what I want with whatever time I have left." His was a matter-of-fact understanding of the limits of what this world would do for him. With his good hand, he flicked a lighter he'd fished out of his pocket. Something in the hot glow off the flame brought forth a memory for Darren. He suddenly remembered where he'd seen a chair just like this one. At his mother's trailer, one just like it used to sit next to the trailer's steps. He'd sat on it as a boy, his bike leaned up against the side of her home, while he listened to his mother talk, sad story times that often involved long stretches of silence, of staring off into the pine trees that surrounded her rented trailer, of painstakingly cataloging her many regrets. He looked back at Pete, the cherry of his cigarette glowing brighter when he inhaled.

Darren nodded toward the chair he sat on.

"Bell had one just like it at her place back in Camilla," he said.

"They was my mama's. Your grandmother. I took 'em with me when we first moved up here back in '72, when we didn't even have a bed to sleep on. Mama said, 'At least you two gon' have a place to sit. At least I done that much for you.' She was sad to see me and your mama come up here without a pot to piss in, sad to see her only girl go." Pete took another drag, coughing a little at the back of the inhale.

Darren puzzled over the fact that Pete had said *we*.

He remembered something his mother said earlier that had made little sense to him at the time. "Mama said something about finishing high school in Nacogdoches?"

The math of this proposition didn't add up right. His mother had him when she was sixteen. By her "last year" in school, did she mean the year she dropped out?

Not at all, Pete told Darren.

It had been Pete's idea to move Bell to Nacogdoches so she could jump two grades and enroll in the new integrated high school out here as a senior.

"Jump grades?" Darren said.

"Your mother was brilliant," Pete said, nodding. He tapped his cigarette against the metal arm of the chair, sending a rain of gray ash onto the porch floor.

"*My* mother?" Darren said, as if Pete had said she flew clouds for a living.

He'd never heard his mother spoken of this way. He leaned against the porch railing, trying to read the knowing smile on Pete's face as his uncle said, "You too young to appreciate the promise of integration, what it dangled in front of us, the doors we were all sure it would open. And did, for a while. Of course, Texas was slow as molasses with it. Your mother was already taking classes past her grade level, might have made valedictorian at Lincoln, the colored high school where we grew up, but that was with old books falling apart, castoffs from the white schools in Houston or Tyler or Dallas. The Texas Department of Education would ship whatever they had lying around and left over to the colored schools. We was the last stop before the trash bin."

Darren got a sudden image of Sera Fuller's belongings tossed in a dumpster behind a sorority house. It rattled him still, the lingering question of where the girl was.

"Your mother and me," Pete went on, "we was the two always trying to walk a straight line, more so than our brothers, more so than either of our parents. Never got in trouble, never had no run-ins with sheriff's deputies. And Bell, like I said, she was real smart, all As. On every little committee they had. She could have been somebody. A teacher, sure. That was the lane for black folks back then. Office job somewhere, if you were lucky. But maybe she could have even gone past all that. She could write, she liked science, wasn't nothing that girl couldn't do." Darren remembered then his mother saying that Sera Fuller had reminded her of herself at that age, a thing that at the time he couldn't imagine, flat out didn't believe was more than a line. But here was her older brother saying Darren's mother had been a keen student, a girl with a bright future for herself. "I wanted to get her to a better school," Pete said, ashamed to admit he thought that *white* meant "better." "It's what we was all told was gon' be better for all of us. So, yes, when I heard they had finally integrated the high school in Nacogdoches, I got a job here, doing any old thing I could." He took another drag on his smoke. Darren waited through the exhale. Mainly because he didn't know what to say.

Pete had described such an act of uncomplicated generosity that Darren kept trying to turn it on its side, to see it from another angle, a way that Bell had played Pete or the other way around. It was all Darren had ever known about the Callis family.

This story matched none of the tales he'd heard about his mother's family from the uncles who'd raised him, William and Clayton. Clayton, especially—who held the whole lot of them, but Bell in particular, in contempt, ever pressing upon Darren the necessity of spiriting him away as a baby. But Pete was now painting a story of sibling love and devotion, of the sort that Clayton and his twin brother, William, hadn't been able to sustain when both had been alive. They'd had an irreparable rift, first over a woman—Naomi, who had chosen William over Clayton (and then, in a messy East Texas soap opera, returned to Clayton years after William's death). The second and final rift between the brothers was over the fact that William chose to become a Texas Ranger. A career in law enforcement was something that Clayton, a black criminal defense attorney, couldn't abide. The brothers were not even speaking at the time of William's death, in the line of duty; had not in years looked into the truest mirror of themselves. The break between the two father figures in Darren's life had cleaved his world in two, further compounded by William's sudden death years later. The one-two punch of it had broken Darren's heart. It was after William's death that bourbon became a daily companion. His mother might have given him his first beer. But the break between his uncles and the loss of the man he looked up to more than any other had poured Darren his first whiskey. And now he was learning that Bell had quit booze so she could take care of the big brother who'd tried so many years ago to take care of her—to give his sister what, as he said, they all thought was the best that the country had to offer. A white school, clean books. A future where your government was on your side, wanted the best for you and yours. He looked at his uncle Pete, smoking in silence, as Darren ran through the pieces of Pete's story of sacrifice. Sweeping floors, Bell had said.

Worth it, Pete said now.

"Got what job I could out here at a lumber mill. Till they shut down, merged with a company out to Georgia and such."

Darren again read the name on Pete's ancient T-shirt: HILL LUM-BER CO.

The name tickled something in the back of Darren's mind.

Both men grew quiet as another car passed on Lanana, its lights sweeping across their faces. Darren felt something had been swirling in the back of his throat since he'd arrived at Pete's, a heady question that had lodged there, begging to be asked.

"Did you really meet my father?"

"Duke?" Pete smiled.

He tossed the cigarette onto the porch floor and stubbed it out with the toe of one of his slippers. They were gray and brown, worn almost flat at the heels. "Told you you look just like him. Not the height. That you get from me and your mama's side. Every Callis I ever knew was tall. But it's in the face, your eyes. They bear down, intense-like, just like your daddy. And it's a light behind 'em too. Plus it's just a feeling I get off of you. Duke, he was a good kid, lot of promise, and he had a good heart. Some of that I can just feel coming off you, son. Same as I saw in your daddy."

Darren had never thought of himself as having a *daddy*.

Oh, he had a father, for sure. Someone had made him.

But no daddy had ever kissed him good night, no mother either.

"He would have got a kick out of you," Pete said, reading his mind.

Darren felt a bloom in his chest, a rush of warmth spreading through his body.

"The truck, boots, and all that, shit-kicking these fools out here." Pete reached for the pack of smokes on his leg but needed some help fishing out another with only one hand, help Darren wasn't inclined to give. Pete sighed. "I wish he hadn't gone there."

"Vietnam?"

"I'd have gone for him if he'd have, if he'd . . . if he'd just asked me," Pete said, verbally stumbling as he reached for words, emotion clogging pathways in his brain. "I could have gone."

Darren nodded, though he didn't entirely understand. "Did you get called up too?"

Pete grew quiet again.

He caressed the outside of the package of cigarettes, flipping the lid open and then closing it over and over, the sound a soft scratching in the dark, like a cat begging to be let in for the night. Inside, Darren heard the television. He wondered if his mother had settled onto the couch, her proclaimed bed for the night. He wondered if he would end up staying here tonight.

"Called up where?" Pete said, confused now.

Darren pinched his eyebrows together, no longer sure that he and Pete were still on the same road in their conversation, still heading in the same direction.

"Vietnam. Where my father was killed. You just said you knew him —"

"Of course I knew him," Pete said. "Boy lived in this house for six months."

12.

"OR MAYBE it was a few weeks he stayed here . . . or a few nights. I don't always remember everything these days. But he was here, had to have been," Pete said, his voice sounding strong, clear where his recollection was admittedly hazy. Darren suggested that the older man might be tired — or *confused* — and patted his knee.

Pete swatted it away, vexed at being treated like an overtired child.

"Naw, I remember them two."

According to Pete, Darren's parents had met at Lincoln High School in Coldspring, the only colored secondary school in San Jacinto County. Duke was two years ahead of Bell, and though he knew of her, had seen her around, something happened in his final year when Bell was bumped up two grades in English, and they were suddenly in the same class together. Duke liked the looks of her, always had, he'd confessed to her older brother, the only Callis brother to properly grill his little sister's suitor. She was slim with sharp features, had skin the color of burned butter, and when she threw her head back laughing, the length of her neck was leonine and strong. But it was when he heard her talk, really *talk* — when he got to be in her presence for at least an hour a day, five days a week, in English class — that he felt his world start to tilt on its axis. It was the sweet, flute-like sound of her voice but also the no-nonsense way she talked about Steinbeck, a cat she claimed knew a thing or two about the real world, knew what it meant to be poor. "And we were," Pete said. "Dirt poor." No land, neither of his parents with more than a third-grade education because *their* parents had been sharecroppers and had them in the corn and cotton fields by age eight, everybody taking a row, so the family wouldn't end each year upside down. Hard work that never led anywhere, except to a third generation that by then didn't see the point of it. His brothers had all turned to a life of petty crime to get by, and as their mama's and daddy's bodies gave out after years of hard labor, with no safety net or savings, they too felt a rigged system no longer deserved or even demanded their respect. Pete's brothers — Cleveland, John David, and Dwayne — started fencing and selling stolen goods to get by.

"Duke come from money, far as we was concerned," Pete said.

But Bell never hid where she come from, he added.

In fact, when Duke took to asking could he walk her home after school, "she made a point to have him walk her all the way up to our raggedy door." And Duke didn't act like it fazed him at all. In fact, since he'd grown up in fields himself, picking cotton on land his people *owned,* mind you, he had tremendous respect for Bell's parents, would never have faulted them for their fatigue, as he knew what farming did to a body, could imagine what it did to a soul if you were losing money faster than you had time left on the planet. Duke walking Bell home started to stretch into long afternoons of the two of them talking on her back porch, which looked out on a patch of dirt and an outhouse. She lit up his mind, he'd said, made him think a little differently about the way he'd been raised, the gifts he'd been given unearned, made him want to share his bounty. "Plus, my God, she's pretty, man," Duke told Pete. She was a shot of light right to the center of his soul. She'd lit a fire in him. "You'd have to ask her what made her fall in with Duke," Pete said, looking up at Darren in the dark. "I just seem to remember he was there one day, and they was each all the other would ever talk about. I don't know that I ever seen two young people fall in love that hard. And that's what it was, Darren. Your parents were very much in love. Despite what all you mighta heard." He meant from the two men who'd raised Darren, Clayton especially.

"That girl, she ain't the one," Clayton had told his younger brother about Bell.

Pete said he never did understand why Clayton was so dead set against two kids in love. Darren didn't know either, had always been told or assumed it had to do with Clayton's natural snootiness and wanting to keep his baby brother away from the air of lawlessness that surrounded Bell's family. But it also wasn't lost on Darren that around this exact time, Clayton was losing his beloved Naomi to his brother William. Perhaps trying to keep Duke and Bell apart was as much petty as it was principled; perhaps it galled him to see another brother so happy in love. He very nearly forbade his baby brother to see Bell anymore, especially when Duke started talking about marrying her.

That wouldn't keep him out of Vietnam, Clayton reportedly said.

Clayton had ordered Duke to put school first.

"The country was at war and still trying to live up to the promise of its creed, or however King put it," Pete said, his voice slowing, his whole posture sinking a little in the chair. He seemed fatigued, Darren thought, worn out from the effort of putting words in a pattern, lining them up in the right order. "The whole country was a mess, and it was . . . it was . . ." He searched for the word he wanted and seemed disappointed to only come up with *hard*. He shook his head. "It was a hard time, Darren, hard to feel a sense of optimism." Darren leaned against the railing with his arms crossed, feeling a strange echo in the senti-ment, in the despair over a country at war with itself. He wondered what those kids marching for civil rights, marching against Vietnam, would have made of the country today. Wondered which wounded the soul more, living in a country that had *never* kept any of its promises or seeing America's capacity for good catch wind and fly for a while, only to come crashing back down. He thought to ask Pete but noticed his uncle had started to nod off in his chair. The sight of it tugged at Darren, made him feel protective of the older man. He moved the cigarettes off his leg and nudged Pete gently, waking him and offering him a hand. The older man gripped Darren's arm so hard it felt like he'd hit bone. His left side was still strong. He used it to get himself upright and together they shuffle-stepped into the small house, where Bell was indeed on the couch, lying on her side, where she had already fallen asleep.

She looked sweet in her pink robe, harmless, just somebody's aging mother.

Pete must have felt he owed Darren the rest of the story. Bits of it came out in dribs and drabs as Darren walked him to his bedroom, the one closest to the living room: Duke driving to Nacogdoches every chance he could ("Wasn't trying to keep 'em apart, I promise, son," he said. "Couldn't have even if I had tried"); Bell finding out she was preg-nant a few weeks after graduation; Duke enrolling at SFA to be closer to her.

This last bit called into question the entire story Pete had told him tonight.

It was a fiction woven from tangled wires in his uncle Pete's brain.

It couldn't be true. No Mathews man of that generation had ever attended Stephen F. Austin University. Not when there was Prairie View, not when there was Texas Southern in Houston. If you were going to be the first wave to integrate an institution, let it at least be the University of Texas for your troubles. Duke Mathews had been a PV man, that much Darren was sure of. He was reminded of his mother's warning: Pete's mind came and went. He was tired and weak, almost tripping as his slipper snagged on the metal bar batting down the seam in the carpet in the doorway to his room. Darren helped him to his bed. This close, he could see Pete's eyes more clearly, the red veins and the cataract in his left eye. The sadness in both. "Don't tell your mama we talked on it. She don't like to speak about him." Darren pulled the blankets to cover Pete's chest then leaned down and laid a soft kiss on his uncle's forehead, surprising them both. Pete smiled, already drifting off again.

"Just like Duke," he said, turning on his side.

Darren turned off the bedside lamp and left the room.

In the end, he took the other bedroom, his mother's.

She had stacked Sera's things in a corner of the room, a thin sheet of wax paper between each layer, clearing the way for him to lie down, which he did, deciding only then that he would sleep here tonight. He was exhausted, for one. And he hadn't had a drink all day. It was a fragile peace he held to tightly as he fell into a hard sleep.

He woke early, dry-mouthed and confused. Wrong bed, wrong room, and outside it was dark, the world covered in the blue-black of predawn.

He needed water.

He needed to stand, to test his legs.

He needed to check that this hadn't all been a dream.

He threw back the layer of quilts he didn't remember covering himself with last night, swung out of bed in his socks, and found his boots lined up next to the bedpost. This, too, the removal of his boots, he didn't remember from the night before. And for the first time in weeks, there was no reason to blame drink for a black hole in his memory. Which left open the possibility that his mother had at some point in the night come in and covered him up with quilts, had labored to remove his boots so that he might be more comfortable. He heard no sounds on the other side of the bedroom door, smelled nothing from the kitchen to suggest that anyone else was awake. He glanced at his phone. It was just coming on five in the morning. And he'd missed two calls during the night. Greg and Randie. Greg, a night owl, had told Darren to call back at any time, his voice high and pitched with excitement at the idea that Darren wanted to talk to him. Randie had declined to leave a voicemail, but his heart soared at the idea that she had reached out too. He wanted to call her back, needed to hear her voice. There was so much to tell her: the drive to Nacogdoches, the investigation into the whereabouts of Sera Fuller, the fact that he wasn't about to let it go, even in the face of a grave reprimand from his former boss. He remembered Wilson's words about the grand jury debating his fate. This he wanted to tell Randie too. The earlier times that DA Vaughn had attempted to indict him, Darren had laid his head in Randie's lap, asking her to hold the weight of his prayers, desperate pleas she thought unnecessary because she didn't know — no one did — just how guilty he was. How he had lied.

He slipped on his boots to go outside.

He didn't want to make the call inside his mother's house.

Outside, Lanana Street was dark. The lone streetlamp had done its nightly duty, had clocked out before the sun had officially risen. To the east, the horizon was a deep purple, like the skin of a bitter plum. Darren walked down the concrete steps, heading toward his Chevy, liking the idea of the privacy the cab would give him, the deep quiet.

But something stopped him.

In the early-morning darkness, he noticed a snake of smoke curling out of the tailpipe of a small pickup truck on the street. Darren could just make out the sunny yellow of the Thornhill logo, the company name an almost deep orange in this light. Darren heard the engine humming, as the truck idled, saw the silhouette of a body behind the wheel, someone who had been waiting outside the house for who knew how long. Hadn't he seen Thornhill police last night? Or had he dreamed that? Either way, he was sure this was a Thornhill vehicle parked fifty feet from his mother's house. It was some coincidence — a thing he'd been trained to distrust on principle. But this was a truck, not a squad car. Despite the logo, it felt civilian.

Joseph Fuller popped into his mind. His anger.

The way the older man had looked at him disparagingly. Asking if Darren was a cop. A *vigilante cop,* Darren now heard in Fuller's question. The one with a public target on his back. He remembered his lawyers' warning: *All it takes is one idiot with a gun.*

Even to his own mind, he sounded paranoid. But the truck was real. It was idling right in front of him at such an angle that it was possible the driver hadn't seen him emerge from the house. Darren ducked back inside to grab his pistol, which had slept beside him on the other side of his mother's bed. As he slunk back toward the front door, he heard his mother stirring on the couch.

She sat up, still in her pink robe. "Darren?"

He ignored her as he went back out, the Colt held low on his right side so as not to alarm her. But she'd seen the gun. "Darren?" Fear rose her voice to a high pitch. He shushed her and made a motion for her to stay put. "Please, Mama," he said.

Back outside, he crept down the front walk to the street.

As he stepped off the curb, he angled his body toward the Thornhill truck, moving in a crouched position, just as the interior light in the cab clicked on, sharpening the outline of the person behind the wheel. It was a man, all right, but something was off. In a split second, Darren's brain was trying to process. The posture, the hair, color or texture, something in his gut told him not to lift his gun. *Don't shoot.* He heard the words out loud, coming not from him but the slim Latino kid he'd seen at Thornhill.

The kid raised his arms.

In his right hand, the flag of his surrender was a blue shirt.

13.

SOMEHOW, PETE slept through all this, was still in his room when Darren brought Rey inside. The name was short for Reynaldo, after a father he couldn't remember, he'd said. Darren stared at him, hit with a wave of fellow feeling, something in the boy's eyes that was familiar to Darren, reflecting some part of himself. He didn't know his dad either. But he wouldn't let that soften his vigilance, his natural suspicion of a kid who'd shown up at the house with a T-shirt he'd been driving around with in his truck. A *bloody* T-shirt. The truck that wasn't his, he said. He'd taken it from his stepdad, and, looking at the watch on his left wrist, he said he needed to get it back soon, before Artie's shift ended. His hands hadn't stopped shaking since he'd been made to sit in the dining room. Darren kept his .45 on the table, pointed in Rey's general direction. He had sent his mother into the kitchen for a grocery bag. "Paper," he said. "It has to be paper." And another pair of those gloves from last night. He didn't want to further contaminate the shirt, which was blue and had the Thornhill logo on it. Bell returned from the kitchen with a Brookshire Brothers grocery bag and a face that was a flat, ashen gray. She set it in front of him along with a pair of the black vinyl gloves.

"Darren, what the hell is going on?"

"I heard you're a Texas Ranger," Rey said. "That's what Benny said."

"Sera's brother?" Darren remembered the young boy.

Pudgy and anxious, worried about his sister too.

"How did you find me?" he asked the kid.

"Followed you yesterday." He picked at the cuticle on the thumb of his left hand with his forefinger. "Watched the policemen walk you to your truck same time as Benny come running out, bragging as he does about the important people coming to his house, a Ranger this time," Rey said. "I just grabbed my stepdad's truck and took off."

He'd followed the squad cars, actually, shaking in fear then as he was now.

Rey had been too afraid to approach him last night, and anyway he'd had to get the truck back to his stepdad. But he'd been up all night, thinking that Darren might be the sign he'd been waiting for. "I didn't know who else . . . I didn't know what else to do."

He'd had the shirt for two weeks, had found it out in the woods the Sunday following Labor Day weekend. "And how do you know it's hers?" Darren said.

"I just do," Rey said with a kind of intimate certainty that moved Darren.

The kid looked scared, truly scared. But not of the gun or the two people hovering over him at the table, one of whom was law enforcement. In fact, he'd sought Darren out *because* he believed something had happened to his friend. He was shaking with it, what his presence here meant. That he was frightened enough for Sera to steal his stepfather's truck and chase down a man just because he thought he might be able to help. He was thin, so thin, in that way of boys before puberty or vanity hits, before they naturally puff up with hormones. He had a faint goatee and a square jaw, and you could have told Darren he was fifteen or twenty-one, and he would have believed you.

"Nineteen," Rey said when Darren asked him point-blank.

He and Sera had met during their sophomore year at the high school, when she'd transferred from a school in Houston. Her family had had a rough run of it before Thornhill. She'd never said so explicitly, but he got the impression that they'd been homeless for a while, before the family landed a spot at Thornhill. "Lot of medical bills, she said," Rey told them, adding that he always got the sense that she felt kind of guilty about that, like it was her fault, her family's financial situation. He knew she had a condition for which she had to take great care. He knew she was sometimes in sudden pain that laid her out for days, sometimes weeks. He knew she had more appointments at the Thornhill medical facility than other folks. But she was strong — "Tried to be," Rey said. "College was a big deal, something she never thought she'd get to do, and she pushed back when her dad wanted her to get a business degree." He scratched at the thin hair along his chin. "She's been thinking she wants to do something with medicine."

"Yeah, how do they get along?" Darren said. "Sera and her dad."

"Okay, I guess. She looks up to him in a lot of ways, for the things he's done for her family. Benny always says she's a daddy's girl, but they're different, you know."

He grew quiet, thinking of what else he wanted to say.

Softly, he added, "He's just really strict with her."

"Like with clothes and curfews and stuff?" Darren said, wondering what influence the father of a college student could still possibly have over his adult child.

"More like the kind of people he wanted her to be around." Rey pressed his lips together, not quite biting his tongue, but close, as he tried to think of how he wanted to say this. "Mr. Fuller, he doesn't always have a lot of nice things to say about people who look like us." He gestured between himself and Darren. Brown and black folks. "It's not their fault, he says, that they've been brainwashed to think of all the things they *can't* do, because politicians, a lot of them are invested in 'keeping black folks begging.'"

"The shirt?" Bell cut in, pulling their talk back to the most pressing issue.

"It was just left in the woods," Rey said.

He showed Darren a weird tear in the shirt along the neckline, the fabric jagged and frayed. And there had been beer bottles he'd found in the same area.

"Sera didn't drink," he said with a certainty that felt forced. He'd already told Darren that Sera's college life had been a wedge between them, that Rey didn't know anything about her life as a student. But in all the time she'd been at SFA, in all the time they'd been friends, he said, she had never ghosted him like this. She hadn't been responding to any of his texts. And he hadn't seen her at the Fuller house next door since Labor Day weekend, when they'd been together in the Angelina National Forest, at the exact spot in the wooded area where he'd found the shirt a week later.

"Hmph," Bell said, a pincer-like expression on her face.

She'd grown irritable since Rey arrived. Even though his presence here was further proof that her instincts had been right about Sera — that something was very wrong — it had irrationally put her in a bad mood. Maybe because it was Rey who now held her son's undivided attention. She openly bristled when Darren asked her to retrieve the girl's things from the other room, sent on a lowly errand, no longer the center of the story. "You've had this shirt for *two weeks* now," Darren said, raising his voice at Rey, "and you didn't say anything to anyone? Why didn't you call the police?"

Rey got visibly upset, stammering his words. "I just, I don't know. I didn't know what to . . ." He looked Darren up and down, taking in his brown skin, deciding what it might mean for what he was about to say. "I'm not even supposed to be there, man."

He was the only one in his family who had no papers.

His kid brother had been born here in the States, Virginia, in fact.

His mother, who had left Mexico with Rey after his father died, when he was still a toddler, had remarried a citizen but was still two years away from turning a green card into something no one could touch or tear to pieces. That left Rey. And the rules of Thornhill had changed in the six years since his mother and stepfather had come to work and live there. The families they'd come in with had been undocumented or mixed status, but they were all gone now. His family was the last of that original group. The work was hard. Chicken *and* pork processing, it turned out, the animals being brought in on trucks from a back entrance, never the front. People were frequently injured on the job or got sick from the working conditions. And they left, sometimes packing up in the middle of the night, gone by the time the sun came up.

By the new rules, which had started last year, there was no job for Rey at the plant. He needed documents to work and, according to these same new rules, live in Thornhill. Everyone had to be here legally from now on. So he was living doubly outside of the rules, in a rainbow of shadows, hiding within his country and within his town. His mother was worried sick over what would become of him. Stress on top of chronic poor health, diabetes worsened by twelve-hour shifts deboning and preparing chicken carcasses all day, her hands slick with blood and bile, head aching from the smell none of them were able to get out of their clothes, even though Rey had never stepped foot in the plant. "I was going to leave, start over somewhere I wouldn't be a burden on my mom, but then I found the shirt, and I couldn't go without knowing where Sera was or if anything happened to her. I didn't think I could tell the Thornhill police when I'm not even supposed to be living there anymore, and I was too scared to call a sheriff or somebody." He gestured toward Darren's brown skin, a look of hope in his eyes. "I never seen a Texas Ranger in person before, just something on TV one time. I didn't know they could look like you." Darren nodded. He wanted to tell the kid there were Rangers who looked like *Rey* too. He was reminded that it mattered, to be protected by a color or a cadence of speech that you associated with safety, the color of a father's arms, maybe, or the tenor of an auntie calling you in for the night.

Bell returned with Sera's belongings. She placed them carefully on the dining-room table—after shoving aside a stack of bills, paperback books, and a drugstore set of watercolors—and nearly swatted Rey's hand away, as she would a child reaching for a jar of candy, when he went to touch them. But Darren said, "Mama," in such a way that she backed off. Rey looked over the hair products and toiletries and balled-up clothes. He frowned for a while at the bottle of pills, his eyebrows knotting into a look of confusion. Then his eyes landed on the flip phone. "It's hers," he said softly, followed by a sound that rolled up from the back of his throat and escaped as the start of a sob. "This was in the trash?" He'd been calling and texting it for days.

The phone, Rey said, was Thornhill-issued, three per family. He and his brother shared one just like it. Bell perked up despite herself. "They give y'all cell phones?"

Rey asked about her schoolwork—were there notebooks, binders, anything he could have or take a look at? There was a particular project he'd helped Sera with, a school paper she'd written about the benefits of living in their town, and he was curious if she'd ever turned it in, how it had come out. He stared expectantly at Darren, who shot his mother a look, realizing she hadn't brought out *all* of Sera's things. Bell clearly didn't trust the boy, who had very quietly started to cry, twin streams of tears down his cheeks. He'd seen the photographs by now. And he ran his fingers over the vibrant green of the pin oaks and tall pines, taking special care with a picture of Sera, her brown face turned up to the sun. "I took this," Rey said softly. He looked up, first at Bell and then at Darren. "This is where I found her shirt," he said. "By the mill." Darren leaned over his shoulder as he saw in the photo of Sera what he hadn't before, that behind clinging vines were the remains of a structure. An ancient thing that once you spotted you couldn't unsee. This touch of humanity that had marked the woods forever.

"Show me," Darren said.

He would, he said.

He promised.

But right now, he had to get the truck back to his stepdad. He knew a back way into the town and worried that the longer he waited, the more he risked being caught. They ran shifts at the plant around the clock, he said, glancing at his watch. He needed to get the truck to his stepdad by the time he got home from his six p.m.–to–six a.m. shift, the same one as Joseph Fuller next door. Rey's stepdad, Artie—his name at Thornhill; he was Art or Arturo at home—had a second job on a ground-maintenance crew for the town for which he was given the use of the small pickup truck parked outside. And because there were lots of events happening in the town lately, VIP types coming through, it had been stressed to Rey's stepfather and his crew to make sure that the grass and hedges were freshly clipped and the planted flowers, daffodils and petunias, were misted with a mixture of water, sugar, and a pinch of witch hazel to keep them looking dew-kissed and standing at attention. There'd been a lot of outsiders passing through Thornhill over the past few months. "What kind of outsiders?" Darren asked. Rich ones, Rey said. The cars were big, often black with tinted windows, a style that television had taught him to associate with rappers and NBA stars and CEOs. "They go in and out of the high-rise building at the front of the town." Thornhill headquarters, he said.

"Plus, sometimes they tour the houses, showing us off . . . well, not me, of course, not our family." There were often surprise visits to the Fuller household next door, people in those fancy cars coming to take a look, to see how the workers lived. With *la jefa* around all the time, Rey said, he had been trying to lay low the past two weeks until he could figure out what to do about the bloody shirt.

"Who?"

But Rey insisted he had to go. He was already coming out of his chair.

He asked again about taking Sera's school notebooks as he wiped at his wet eyes with the back of his hand, then said he really had to leave. He would show Darren the place in the woods, he would. He promised again. He just couldn't do it right now. He gave Darren his cell phone number and then rushed out before he could be stopped.

"You just gon' let him go?"

Bell was in his ear as soon as the boy was gone. Darren saw the truck's lights come on through the front window a second before Rey pulled away from the curb. "How do you know he didn't have something to do with that girl getting hurt?"

"I don't," Darren said.

There was something squirrelly about the kid, it was true.

But he didn't set off the kind of alarm bells in Darren that Joseph Fuller had, or Kelsey, the Rho Beta chapter president, for that matter.

He felt there was some piece to Rey's story that had not been divulged; he couldn't understand why the kid was going on and on about wanting Sera's schoolwork and her notebooks, for one. But there was also a tenderness in the way he spoke about Sera that Darren recognized as care and affection, maybe even love. That was mostly what he saw: love and fear. Rey was scared for her.

He told his mother to get dressed.

And reminded her they were on their own with this, without the weight of the Texas Rangers—worse still, they were actively blocked by Wilson's warning. Darren acting in any official capacity, when he was a man with no badge, would only provide the district attorney in San Jacinto County with more damning evidence against him.

To find Sera, they had only each other.

"Go to work this morning like nothing is wrong. Smile and nod and all that business you were doing yesterday. But, Mama, look...see if you can get in that girl's room. Sera's. I trust you can come up with a lie about why you might need to get inside." As he said it, he wondered why she hadn't done this from the beginning—if there might be evidence in her bedroom that they would have at their disposal now.

Darren was heading to the campus. They had her schedule, after all. He wanted to visit her classes from the last week anyone ever saw her...he didn't want to say *alive*. But the word hung between him and Bell nonetheless, the fear that they might be too late, if not today then tomorrow or the next day. If they didn't move fast enough. It was why they needed Greg, who was already on his way. Darren hoped the former FBI agent could get Sera's cell phone—*and* the bloody shirt—processed and mined for any information that might help. Darren knew it would take hard evidence to make Wilson and the Texas Rangers believe Sera Fuller was missing.

★   ★   ★

Despite the assertions of the two Rho Beta Zeta girls that she had moved out of the sorority house on the fourteenth of this month, Darren trusted only the visit from campus police the day before as the last known sighting of Sera Fuller. Which meant, according to her class schedule, her last class would have been the Wednesday before.

It was an intro to economics course, located in the Dugas building in the center of campus. Despite the quaint Victorian-style lampposts along the walkway to its front doors, Dugas looked very much like a suburban office building someone had plopped in the middle of the campus. The same warm sienna–colored brick as the rest of the campus structures but with sharp, hard angles and a pressing flatness in its facade. Inside, low-pile industrial carpeting and fluorescent lights contributed to a feeling that Stephen F. Austin University was not so much committed to the business of learning as they were to the learning of *business*. Though technically in a liberal arts building, Darren felt a seriousness of purpose here, the plan for where an SFA degree should lead: a good-paying job in the public or private sector with health insurance and a 401(k).

According to everything they'd found, it didn't appear that Sera had declared a major yet, and Darren wondered what she imagined for her future, one very likely foreshortened by her condition. A glance at her classes suggested an interest in medicine, as Rey had said. There were courses in public health and a microbiology class whose title alone was beyond Darren's understanding of the field. All together, they spoke of a young woman using her college education to make sense of the hand she'd been dealt, confronting head-on a blood disease that would require constant care for the rest of her life. It touched Darren to think of Sera wrestling with a legacy she hadn't asked for, trying to make her own sense of the why and how of her fate, the caprice of human genetics.

He arrived at the economics lecture two minutes before the end of the session, slipping through the door in the back and into a hard plastic chair in the last row. He glanced around the room, hoping to see Sera packing up like the other students were, that this whole thing might still prove to be some wild misunderstanding. In the front of the classroom, the professor, a white woman who was barely older than the students she taught, did a double take when she saw him enter. She tripped over her next few sentences, having to repeat three times the reading assignment for the following class, so startled was she to see a strange man enter her lecture hall. Her shoulders tensed as students started filing out of the room, two of whom also shot looks at Darren on their way out. Both were black, an athletic-looking girl in a Lumberjacks school hoodie and a tall, lanky young man whose fade was in need of a touch-up. They were the only two black students in the whole class.

When the room thinned out, Darren approached the front of the lecture hall, where Rose-Marie Hammel was sliding papers into a pristine leather satchel, so smooth and un-scuffed as to give Darren the impression that this was maybe her first year as a university professor. She looked at him from behind curtain bangs wispy and thin, strands of her brown hair catching in her eyelashes as she blinked repeatedly and told him, before he could even introduce himself, that she had office hours to get to. He gave his name in a way he hoped conveyed both authority and due deference, hoping the combination would be a stand-in for the missing honorific *Texas Ranger* that would normally open doors, command obedience and prompt compliance. "I'd like to speak with you about a student of yours," he said. "Sera Fuller. She's in this class."

He looked around the now empty classroom.

"I mean, usually," he added. "I didn't see her here today."

Outside, he could hear voices muffled by the carpeted hallway, laughter, and the ring of a cell phone. "When was the last time she attended your lecture, Ms. Hammel?"

"Stein."

"Excuse me?"

"It's *Professor*. And it's *Stein*. I got married earlier this month," she said, lifting the strap of the leather satchel onto her shoulder. She was wearing what looked like a homemade sweater or maybe it was vintage. It was dotted with kelly-green pills, like little trees sprouting all over her torso. "The university sent out word of the name change." She pressed the body of her bag against her chest, using it almost as a shield against someone she took as an interloper—or else he would have known about her name change. "So I'm not sure who you are or what this is, but—"

"Darren Mathews, ma'am. I'm concerned about a student of yours—"

"Are you from the town?" Professor Stein said.

The question surprised Darren. "Thornhill?"

That he rattled off the name so quickly, she took as confirmation.

She grew more rigid, further unnerved by his presence in her classroom. She immediately started for the door of the lecture hall. "I have to get to my office." She sounded, if not frightened, then wary and disturbed. Darren followed closely behind, mindful of his height, of towering over her. He didn't want to make her any more uncomfortable than she already was.

"Has someone from Thornhill contacted you about Sera?"

"I'm sorry, but like I said, I have office hours," she said. "Please."

Together they passed over the threshold of the door to the hallway, just a few steps between them. She picked up speed and made it out of the building's front door and onto the campus. Moving so fast that Darren would have had to break into a sprint to catch up to her . . . and then what? Grab her by the arm? Manhandle a white female professor in broad daylight? He stopped on a dime, halting his pursuit right outside the doors of the Dugas liberal arts building, where the two black students he'd seen inside were talking. They too had been in Sera's economics class.

Darren introduced himself and pulled from his pocket the picture of Sera in the woods, her face angled up to the sun. But, still, you could tell it was her.

The boy — Mehki, he told Darren his name was — turned up his nose in a faint sneer, said, "What are you asking about her ass for?"

The girl — Ella, she said — elbowed the boy in the ribs. "Why you say it like that?"

Mehki said Sera was phony and "weird," newly coming around to the Black Student Caucus meetings even though she pledged a white sorority, lived all the way out on Steen Drive. He had never seen her at an Alpha party, Kappa, or Omega Psi Phi, not a step show or pregame tailgates, none of the black social events on campus. "But here she come around, suddenly wanting to attend meetings, asking about maybe becoming an officer," he said, pursing his lips. "I swear I thought she was a plant."

"Fool, what?"

Ella rolled her eyes.

Then she stepped to the side as two Latino students walked between them to enter the building. "Don't listen to his paranoid ass," she told Darren. "It's been some drama on the other side of Trump, but that's been every-damn-where. Conservative groups on campus were making noise, talking ugly, trying to get us kicked off campus for not allowing whites. But the school supports the caucus. They've backed our play.

We are a safe space. Of course Sera was welcome. And not that she has to defend herself, 'cause blackness don't gotta look one type of way, but she's only living at the Rho Beta house, only pledged them because her daddy made her do it, she said."

"Her father?" Darren asked.

Ella nodded, running a long fingernail through the part between two of her burgundy-colored braids. "It made her mad, the fact that he wouldn't let her pledge a black sorority. They had some words about it, she told me. I got the feeling she grew up pretty sheltered, with a daddy who turned up his nose at a lot of black culture. One of them that want to be loved by white folks more than they want to be equal to them."

"Just say Trump supporter," Mehki said.

"Sera didn't even know there was such a thing as black sororities till she got on campus," Ella said. "She didn't learn about the Black Student Caucus until this year. I get the sense that her eyes were opening to a lot of things, that she was breaking away from her parents a little bit. It's some kids here who ain't had a lot of life experience."

Darren started to ask if Ella knew Sera was sick, that she had sickle cell.

But he felt protective of her.

If she hadn't mentioned it, it wasn't for him to tell.

"And when was the last time either of you saw her?"

"You some kind of a cop?" Mehki said with nearly as much contempt as Joseph had asked the same question for an entirely different set of political reasons. But the suspicion of a cop's motives held in both men.

"And what do you care?" Ella asked Mehki. "Said you ain't like her anyway."

"He's just asking a whole lot of questions."

"About someone you ain't said more than two words to." She held up a hand in the general direction of Mehki's face, which was pockmarked with razor bumps. For all their bluster, there was an underlying playfulness between the two students, and Darren wondered briefly about the true nature of their relationship, if they were dating.

Ella turned back to Darren. "She hasn't been in class in over a week."

Mehki made a face. "She drop the class or something?"

Ella's expression likewise shifted. Darren watched a flicker in her eyes, a new consideration of this whole conversation that she had entered into with so little inquiry of her own. Was Darren a cop? And if so, what exactly did that mean?

"Wait, is she okay?"

In the back pocket of his jeans, Darren felt his cell phone buzz. It was a text from Greg. They'd earlier agreed to meet at the house on Lanana Street at a quarter to eleven, and he was close, he said. Darren needed to get him Sera's phone and the bloody shirt. He thanked the two students for talking to him without answering Ella's question.

Because he did not know if Sera Fuller was okay.

Greg was close. But somehow still late.

Darren would wait, grateful for the help. Greg had been alerted that in addition to him breaking into the girl's phone, Darren now wanted a DNA test run on Sera's shirt. He wanted to confirm the blood was hers beyond a shadow of a doubt. If he was going to do something crazy, like go over his lieutenant's head all the way up to Austin in order to get help, he would need to know for sure. Greg took this in stride, asking only the obvious: How could they confirm it was Sera's blood when they didn't have any other genetic material of hers as a sample? Darren smiled to himself, remembering his mother's obsession with the girl's hair. They had a brush. They had a sample, he told Greg, who had already contacted a friend who worked in the FBI's resident agency in

Lufkin, just twenty miles south down Highway 59. While he waited on his uncle's front porch for Greg to arrive, he thought about his visit to campus, how the mention of Thornhill had spooked Sera's professor and shut down any willingness to talk to Darren at all. He pulled out his phone to look up everything he could about Thornhill.

It had a website . . . sort of.

The home page was a picture of a white family seated before an abundant table set in a field of the greenest, most obedient grass, each blade on its tippy toes. The mother in this tableau was standing as she set a plate of plump grilled chicken next to a platter of buttered corn on the table, which also held pork chops, burgers and hot dogs, two pitchers of lemonade, and a salad with fat tomato quarters as red and lush as painted lips. Everything on the table was shining, winking in the sunlight. The members of the family—a dad, two boys, and a girl—all had perfect rows of white teeth. They were all attractive in a regular-folk kind of way, in that they didn't look like people who belonged on TV. They could be your neighbors. They could be you.

Well, not me, Darren thought.

Just as a clever bit of animation morphed the white family into a black one.

Clean fades on the kids, pressed shorts, a mother wearing a belted dress. The food was the same, though this family drank pink lemonade. Their teeth were just as white. The camera's angle on the family widened so that Darren could see the black family's Craftsman-style home in the background. Just then the image morphed to show a Latino family, whose table had a plate of corn tortillas, and they drank soda instead of lemonade. The family changed to South Asian next, with their bowls of rice and glasses of milky iced tea. The faces of the families kept changing as the camera lifted to give a bird's-eye view of the entire town of Thornhill, including the industrial buildings behind the steel gates Darren had seen at the back of the town. He recognized the twin smokestacks, the cozy home-meets-industry vibe that was the Thornhill logo, as the image showed men and women heading off to work in their Thornhill coveralls. A tagline popped on-screen: Work Where You Live, Love Where You Work. A Job at Thornhill Means Never Going Without — Food, Medical Care, and Your Child's Education. Here, You're Family. And We Take Care of Our Family.

There was an About page . . . kind of.

When Darren clicked on it for more information, the image of the original white family from the home page filled the screen below a simple banner: Thornhill Is One of the Newest and Largest Suppliers of Pork and Poultry Products. Suppliers to whom, it didn't say. There were no brand names listed, nothing that he might choose from a refrigerated shelf at the Brookshire Brothers in town and trace back to the processing facility in the town of Thornhill. And that was practically it for the whole website. A home page, an About page, and one labeled simply Apply. Darren clicked on it. It was a basic form. You could leave your name, an email address, and a cell phone number. But you could not know from this website the exact job you would be applying for. It was odd, all of it. There was no mailing address on the website, no listing of a CEO or president, not even an 800 number. Darren opened a new browser window and ran a wider search using the company's name, which yielded very little.

Clicking his way down a Thornhill-search rabbit hole led him to the Facebook page for *Society Texas* magazine, a publication Darren hadn't known existed until this very second. It was a story covering the wedding of Carey-Ann Thorn and Ethan Jacob "E.J." Hill. Darren stared at photos of the lavish wedding as his brain ticked over the names. Thorn. And Hill. Married together. A wedding portrait of the bride and groom showed a man with reddish-brown hair in his sixties and a younger woman with a head of glossy gray hair. The color seemed an affect. Darren wouldn't put her within six months of forty. The gray was to let the world know that even though she had enough money to run every wrinkle on her face out of town, she was a grown woman who didn't suffer fools. And yet the gray was a foil for her sharp features, her cutting expression. It softened her. She could be the later-in-life mother of a sprightly toddler.

Thornhill was not a publicly traded company. Nor could he find any lawsuits associated with the corporation. No trademark filings or patents. According to the Texas Secretary of State website, which listed contacts for every corporate entity in the state, the only way to get in touch with Thornhill was through a law firm. Thomlinson, Ratford, Morris, and Mulligan, which had offices in Austin, Dallas, Chicago, and Washington, DC. The firm did its fair share of "public policy law," which was another way of saying they were government lobbyists. One of its biggest clients was a coalition of manufacturers in the U.S., for which the firm had secured a favorable piece of national legislation in DC, according to a few articles in the *Dallas Morning News* back in 2010. Darren was opening a new browser page to google more about the firm or the Thorn-Hills themselves when he heard a car engine approach, one that purred too smoothly to belong to any of the aging vehicles that regularly passed on this block. Darren looked up just in time to see Greg Heglund getting out of a late-model BMW.

14.

THE THREE years since he'd left the Bureau had apparently been good to Greg.

It had almost been that long since Greg and Darren had last seen each other.

Oh, there'd been texts here and there, birthday voicemails, neither willing to go totally radio silent. When Greg had heard through the grapevine—the vine holding a single grape named Lisa—that Darren's uncle Clayton had had open-heart surgery last year, Greg had made contact, only to find out that Darren was not in fact bedside at St. David's in Austin, had, in fact, never left the farmhouse in Camilla. Darren had been getting regular updates from Clayton's wife, Naomi, and once he was assured Clayton was in recovery, that he would live, Darren had resumed not speaking to his uncle. Darren was angered by Clayton's extreme disappointment over the breakup of Darren's marriage, pressing his nephew to make right "the best thing that ever happened to you." He had gone so far as to call Darren a tomfool for cutting ties with Lisa for some ol' gal he didn't really know. It was, in Clayton's opinion, an even stupider decision than quitting law school years ago to become a

Texas Ranger — which only stoked Darren's grief over the death of his uncle William. The man he most admired, in whose footsteps he had set his life's path. Darren hadn't wanted to talk to Greg then or since. About Clayton or his marriage. He had pointedly dodged any attempt at an airing of grievances between them. Mostly because he didn't have any. Not deep down, not when you got past his ego. Greg and Lisa fucking and not telling him about it was so low on his list of reasons he and his wife didn't work out that it wasn't worth getting too agitated about, not when he could just pour another glass of Jim Beam. But as he was now into his second full day without drinking, without that sloppy skirt around his feelings, he said, "You should have just told me, man." Greg stopped in his tracks at the base of the porch stairs, one foot on the first step, one still in the marshy grass. He was in ropers — something Darren had never seen Greg wear — jeans, and a sweater that Darren took for cashmere. It was a heathered charcoal gray. It lightened Greg's green eyes, drew attention to the feathered lines around them. He looked older than Darren now.

"That's it," Darren added. "That's all of it."

Greg did not advance, did not move at all, as if he wasn't sure that either of them was ready for him to come closer. He scratched at the stubble on his chin, a patch of gray. "I wanted to," he said. "All these years ... I wanted to say something, brought it up to Lisa many times, but she always said it would only hurt you over something that wasn't anything real. It happened only once, and every year put more distance between it and your marriage. Not that I'm trying to put it all on Lisa."

"But it sure is convenient," Darren said.

He didn't even mean it as a dig. He knew Lisa to be headstrong and particularly adept at getting someone with an opposing view to bend to her will. It was the reason that, of the three of them, she was the only one who'd become a successful lawyer.

"She cared about you. We both did. *Do*."

"Which is why you should have just told me."

Truth had always been one of the core emotional principles of their friendship.

Greg, treading gently, asked, "Would you still have married her if I had?"

Darren sighed, not exactly proud of his answer. "I probably would have."

At the time, he'd never thought any woman would love him besides Lisa.

His own mother had seemed fifty-fifty on the whole deal herself.

It had cost them nearly five grand in couples therapy for him to say that sentence, another six sessions to admit this was a wound he'd been carrying for too long and was likely why he'd gone through with a marriage that had holes in it before it even started. Greg, feeling no outright rejection coming from Darren, finally walked up the steps, slowly, as if testing the weight of their friendship, wondering would it hold.

"You look good."

"You look old," Darren said, and Greg threw his head back with a laugh.

There was love in it. Relief.

Hope too.

Theirs was a mixed-race friendship that was as real and deep as any true brotherhood, and their previous fights had had more to do with the ways the world around them often put a viselike pressure on their relationship, when pinpricks of mistrust ate at them over the ways that, despite their bond, they would always see the world differently. It had happened in Hopetown years ago, when Greg had had to reckon his privilege with the way it often and with great irony interfered with his best intentions for doing right by black folks. Greg was his boy, but he had racial baggage like everybody else. Even the ones who were awake now to the problems of race in this country still had sleep in their eyes, were still walking on wobbly legs they didn't know how to use. But white people interested in justice in this country were sitting on a kind of superpower — if they would learn how to wear the cape, if they would learn how to fly high over the swampy morass of their own self-pity and shame. *You really want to help, then time to put on your big-girl panties, your big-boy britches,* Darren had told Greg many times. *Learn to tolerate your feelings about y'all's part in America's ugly history. And then get to work.* The race problem lay at white folks' feet; it lay in their willingness to talk to their cousins, their friends and coworkers, to call out their bosses, even people on the street, when they did or said something racist. Darren and Greg's friendship had endured so many heated discussions about America's race problem that a long-ago romantic entanglement was almost welcome in its banality. And anyway, as Darren told Greg now, he hadn't been a saint either. There had been other girls when he was at the University of Chicago. Greg asked if Lisa knew, and Darren said, "She does now." He stood so he could properly greet Greg. "That's the beauty of a good divorce. The purge. We left it all on the conference-room table in her lawyer's office on Milam."

They embraced, Greg holding the hug a beat longer than Darren.

Then he pulled back and said, "So if you haven't been mad this whole time, that means you've been avoiding me for no good reason. You had me sweating, man."

Greg asked him to ride with him to the FBI's office in Lufkin. They could catch up on the drive. Darren told him he didn't think it was a good idea, which required explaining that he'd turned in his badge and that he was maybe being indicted, for real this time, and law enforcement agencies in the area had been warned off dealing with him. Greg's brows knotted over news of Darren quitting. Darren caught a fleeting look of judgment, Darren's decision falling on the wrong side of Greg's idea of right and wrong.

"What?" Darren asked, feeling truly defensive for the first time since he'd made the decision.

Greg threw up his arms innocently. "Just doesn't sound like you is all. You always said your uncle William said never stop fighting."

The nobility is in the fight, in all things.

Words Darren had set his life by.

"What about 'Put on your big-boy britches and get to work'?" Greg said.

"My God, you have a knack for missing the point of every god-damned thing."

Greg didn't immediately relent. Instead, he let Darren sit in the silence following his words, knowing that somewhere deep down it was still eating at Darren — that he hadn't toughed it out like his uncle, who was a Texas Ranger until his last dying breath.

"I'm tired, Greg," Darren said. "Can you even understand the kind of tired I'm talking about, how the marrow in my bones aches from years and years of this shit, the decades and centuries we been in this fight? My DNA is tired, Greg."

"You know who isn't tired?" his friend said. "Donald Trump. That motherfucker pops up every morning looking for something else he can fuck up, some other angle on this presidency thing, who he hasn't grifted yet. And you know who else isn't tired? The fucking Aryan Brotherhood of Texas, the Patriot Front, and the Proud Boys, the needle-dicked fools who worship him, who think he's going to change white folks' fortunes, when a Mexican or black person has never been the reason they can't afford health care, that they can't get a decent job, that this country has no fucking safety net for anybody, black, white, brown, or purple." Darren reminded Greg that he hated that purple shit, white people's hyperbole run amok. There are no purple people up late at night wrestling with the future of the country or their place in it. Still, Greg said, "He's stoking their anger. These guys are out somewhere plotting to kill people like you, D."

"Fuck you, Greg," he said, hearing a catch in his throat. "I spent my career going after guys like that." And it hadn't changed a thing.

"And so you just quit?"

Darren turned from Greg's gaze.

"I'm just saying, it's all hands on deck out here, man."

"Says the guy who just rode up here in the Beemer he got from working at a high-end law firm." Greg had become a highly paid white-collar investigator at a large nationwide law firm. It had nothing to do with the public sector or the work he'd done at the FBI, where he'd dreamed of being a modern-day Robert Kennedy, a liberal lion at the head of any fight for civil rights. Darren didn't think he had his history quite right, but either way, clocking in for a white-shoe firm (or black 'gators — this was Texas, after all) wasn't a perch from which he had a right to judge Darren about anything. And anyway, they were wasting time. Darren reminded Greg that there was a girl in trouble, and they needed information on the phone and her bloody shirt as soon as possible. Darren asked if he was still willing to help. "Only if you ride with me," Greg said.

15.

IT WAS total silence for the first few miles, not even the hum of music on the radio to soften the static in the air between them. Darren realized too late how angry he was, how much he wanted to chuck all of this and go home and drown himself in drink. He missed the farmhouse, missed the sweetness of the dewy midmorning air. The sun would be clearing the tops of the pines that ringed the property right about now. He could keep his glass wet, boots up on the porch railing, watching birds fly, trying to guess a yellow warbler from a goldfinch. Instead, he was trapped in an eighty-thousand-dollar car with a man whose friendship it pained him to admit he'd missed. His blood hot over the guilt trip Greg had no business trying to lay at Darren's feet. But he loved him because Greg was always honest, even when it didn't sound pretty, even when his views might embarrass him if challenged. That was the other thing. He took it. Greg *listened* when he got pushback on things.

Darren respected the hell out of him for it.

"I left the Bureau after Comey was fired because I didn't even know what the hell we were supposed to be doing anymore, the top law enforcement agency in the country just watching folks in the White House bend the law this way and that, pushing it to its breaking point. So I'm sorry, man. I am a fucking hypocrite. I just...I don't know. I worry that if we all just walk away, what are we doing? Just handing the whole thing over to them, letting them trash the whole country?"

The car fell quiet again, each man conceding he didn't have the answer.

Greg shot a glance at Darren, a question in his raised eyebrows. *We good, man?*

Darren didn't answer directly. Instead, he ran his hand over the car's lush detailing, tracing the wood grain with his fingertips and half expecting them to come away smelling of lemon oil polish. "Nice ride," he said, looking at his friend, acknowledging they were all of them just doing the best they could in what he'd told Wilson were unimaginable times. Still, he appreciated Greg's apology.

"You ever heard of a company called Thornhill?" Darren said, changing the subject. They had passed the town sitting primly off Highway 59 a few miles back. "Some kind of live-work deal," he added.

"I don't know about that, but I'm pretty sure that's E. J. Hill's company."

"Yeah, who is that?"

"Baby of the Hill family, used to be in timber before they sold to Georgia-Pacific. I know 'cause the Bureau did some background work for the FTC before the deal could go through," Greg said as he put on his blinker, trying to pass a sluggish eighteen-wheeler.

"Naw, Thornhill is meatpacking or some shit."

"Yeah, he got married and changed direction, I guess."

As they approached the outskirts of Lufkin, Darren pulled out his phone to again check the Facebook page for *Society Texas,* the lavish photo spread of the nuptials of Carey-Ann Thorn and Ethan Jacob

"E.J." Hill. The post was from the spring of 2012. Seven years ago. The year before Rey and his family, along with other undocumented and mixed-status families, had moved to Thornhill to live and work, have their medical care paid for, their children educated, and get three free cell phones per family.

"Weird company," Darren said. "I couldn't find a whole lot about them online, not even a real mailing address for the business, just a link to a law firm out of Austin."

The steady sound of Greg's blinker echoed in the otherwise silent car.

Darren looked out at the town of Lufkin, a veritable metropolis compared to Jefferson, the last time Greg and Darren had been in a car together. Off Angelina Street, Greg turned onto Townsend. "Thomlinson, Ratford, Morris, and Mulligan," Darren said as Greg pulled into the parking lot for the FBI's resident agency.

"That's a lobbying firm," Greg said.

"I know," Darren said. "Weird to have them as the public agent of the company. It's like they're just putting it out there that the business has some agenda to push. It's so nakedly political, so obvious that they're trying to game the system in some way."

Greg found a parking spot near the back.

"No one cares, D," he said, turning off the car. "Shame died in the last century. And anyway, Hill and Thorn are political players. They donate big money to candidates in Texas and other states as well. They funded a few runs for Congress."

"Republican? Democrat?"

Greg shot him a look. "Aren't you adorable? The new game is to play the spread."

"Hmph."

Darren looked through the windshield at the eighties-modern hulk of a building that housed this offshoot of the Federal Bureau of

Investigation as Greg unbuckled his seat belt and exited the car. He motioned for Darren to join him. In the air seeping in through the driver's-side door, Darren smelled rain coming. He looked outside and saw gray clouds moving in. He told Greg it was better if he stayed behind, that it was smarter for everyone if he wasn't officially on the record distributing evidence to the FBI. Greg said *none* of this would be on the record. He was hoping his buddy Nathan could do all this on the low. Hack into the phone and call a lab tech Nathan was dating to see if the guy could get DNA from the blood on the shirt without leaving a paper trail. That one was going to be hard, but Nathan's paramour was apparently smitten enough to try. Greg grabbed the two bags holding the phone and bloody shirt and left Darren alone in the Beemer. He heard a roll of thunder. It shook the ground beneath him.

There was a good-sized Texas storm coming, and again Darren felt an impulse to flee, to watch sheets of rain roll over the back lawn behind his house, all twelve acres of it, to watch droplets of it dance in the wind, washing everything clean. He could get gorgeously drunk, make an art of it. It would be so easy to slide back to life before he ever learned that Bell was sober. He reminded himself of the reason he was here, that his mother's clearheaded thinking had led to a search for a missing student.

He opened his phone and got back to work.

In no time, he confirmed that both Carey-Ann Thorn and E. J. Hill, as private citizens, were bipartisan contributors to our nation's two political parties as well as many candidates for state and local office, and at least one political action committee, a super PAC called KAW, for Keep America Working. Its stated aim was a bipartisan approach to improving the lives of American workers. The super PAC donated to political candidates on both sides of the aisle. Maybe American workers were a meeting ground of sorts. Next, he googled Carey-Ann and E.J., trying to piece together a story about their partnership. Both the love match and the birth of a new kind of industry.

E. J. Hill's people had been in the timber business going back well over a century. In the early wildcat days of the timber game — cut first and ask forgiveness later — what was then the Hill Lumber Company had carved up the now protected land in the Angelina National Forest for years. They built their own sawmills and processing plants, which led to the creation of mill towns for their workers. Each company town consisted of housing for workers and their families, plus schools, a general store and commissary, churches, two gathering halls, and even a small hotel. These towns were strategically placed near forestland where the cutting was done or near the mills where raw timber was turned into an extremely profitable commodity, wood for building a nation on the rise. He found a photo online, so sepia-toned it looked as if the image had been burned. It was a picture of one hundred or so employees of the Hill Lumber Company in 1905. White and black workers were segregated and standing apart from one another, everyone gathered in front of the company store. The Hill Lumber Company paid partial wages in tokens that could be spent at the general store in town. These were self-contained communities in which lumber workers were meant to want for nothing. Darren found more photos of families standing on the front porches of their Hill company homes, sturdy, A-frame clapboard houses, as narrow as a balsam fir. The families were well dressed, the women in clean cotton dresses, in cuts that copied the Edwardian fashions of the day, the men with tobacco-stained teeth and scuffed work boots, but everyone looking well fed and seemingly happy. Mill towns disappeared sometime around the Great Depression, and as the timber industry dwindled down to just a few big players in Texas, the Hill family gobbled up smaller outfits, buying up companies left and right. In the 1970s, it was *this* outfit, Darren put together, that had employed his uncle Pete and thousands of other men at a mill in Nacogdoches, where Pete had swept floors for years, working his way up to janitorial supervisor. Then, in the 2000s, the owners of what was then called Hill Lumber Holdings sold their company to an even bigger conglomerate and got out of the business altogether—but not before E. J. Hill carved out a pocket of his family's land along Highway 59 in the deal, land he'd held on to for reasons it appears no one in his family or in the larger business community fully understood. And at the time, maybe E. J. Hill didn't either.

He had long been considered one of Texas's most eligible bachelors, which seemed to be more about his last name than anything. He was something of a dilettante, with no clear role in his family's company. He was not an officer, nor was he an innovator. *And of what, anyway?* People had been cutting down trees for millennia. What new could be invented or added to the process? He seemed to resent being perceived as dead weight on the company's bottom line, and in interviews, he was often cagey or downright evasive about what exactly he was being paid to do. Instead, he diverted reporters' attention to whatever was the reason for his current interview or glossy-magazine profile: the purchase of a Triple-A baseball team, followed by a winery in Texas hill country; the dabbling in conservative politics, including a failed run for Congress as a Republican in 2012; and the announcement of his engagement to Carey-Ann Thorn.

Carey-Ann Thorn was also the scion of a dynastic family in Texas manufacturing. And Texas Democratic politics—with at least one senator in the family tree, two assemblymen, and a lieutenant governor going back to the beginning of the state. Thorn Family Farms had been in business since shortly after Texas joined the Union, in 1845. They were chicken farmers out of Longview, a large operation that grew so steadily that as they neared the turn of the century, they were supplying poultry to restaurants and wholesalers and butchers all across the eastern part of the state and into Louisiana. They were one of the first in the chicken business to build their own processing plants, a game-changer for the industry, taking the whole operation from egg to chicken to shrink-wrapped three-piece package — thighs, legs, and breast — conveniently sold in a refrigerated shelf at your grocer's. By the 1980s, they were the top supplier to several fast-food chains, having perfected an all-white-meat nugget, and soon they branched out into pork processing too. Carey-Ann had worked for her father's company since she graduated from SMU, where she'd been an active member of that campus's chapter of the Rho Beta Zeta sorority. She had been the keynote speaker at the sorority's centennial celebration in Savannah last year and was currently a board trustee of the national organization.

Interesting, Darren thought.

Carey-Ann Thorn was the baby of the family *and* a woman, and even though she was smarter than both of her older brothers, as she had cheekily suggested in a *Texas Monthly* profile for the one-hundred-and-fiftieth anniversary of Thorn Family Farms, she was passed over for CEO when her father retired. She made an announcement on her Instagram page that she would be leaving the company at once.

Some reports said E. J. Hill and Carey-Ann Thorn had met on a golf course in the Caymans; some said it was in an Austin night-club; some said it was at a private party after a Luke Bryan concert at the Houston Livestock Show and Rodeo the year Milquetoast Mitt Romney lost the election and set off a bloodlust in the Republican Party — Romney, whose lack of any measurable charisma or true point of view E.J. always blamed for his own loss as a down-ticket Republican congressional candidate that year. No matter the theories and rumors about how E. J. Hill and Carey-Ann Thorn met, their courtship was always written about with an aura of fate and endless fascination. Two heirs of Texas industry royalty get married just as they're both, for different reasons, on the outs with the companies under whose banners they were born.

Carey-Ann Thorn. And E. J. Hill.

Marrying not just two political loyalties but also two industries.

And so Thornhill was born, Darren surmised.

A town that was a stone's throw from the Angelina National Forest, the old hunting grounds of Hill Lumber Holdings, né the Hill Lumber Company. A town that was built around a meat-processing plant where residents worked. A town that gave every appearance of being a twenty-first-century version of an old mill town.

It was raining by the time Greg dropped Darren back at his uncle's house. On the porch, he thanked Greg for his time, to which Greg, reacting to Darren's formal tone, said, "Come on." He held out a hand and they shook in a way that bled into a hug, Greg again holding it longer than Darren, who fought an impulse to pull away and let himself be held. He was nearly embarrassed by how much weight it took off him, not just to be held, but to be *held up*. He had to admit that it felt nice. After, Greg patted him on the back and said he would get him news about the phone or DNA off the shirt as soon as possible. Whichever came in first. "It was good to see you, man," he said.

Darren smiled and said, "You too."

As Greg climbed back into his BMW, he nodded to the house. Bell's home and where Darren had spent last night. "How's that going?"

"Weird," Darren said.

Before adding, "Pete says he knew my dad, and my mom might have gone to high school or something out here?" The muscles in his shoulders lifted in a half-hearted shrug. He wasn't yet sure he believed much of what he'd heard from his mother, a known liar, or his uncle, whose age and condition were messing with his body and mind.

Darren watched his friend drive off but hesitated before going in the house.

It made his mouth water to think of how easy it would be to slip off and get a little taste of something, get a bottle tiny enough to nestle in his shirt pocket, like a baby bird he was nursing. He was just feeling for the keys to his truck when his mother's blue Nissan came tearing up Lanana Street, hours before she was supposed to be off work, and pulled into what counted for Pete's driveway, two parallel ruts in the grass just to the right of the house. She was getting out of the car before she'd even turned the engine all the way off. She stepped out into the rain with a thin plastic grocery bag tied around her head, moving so fast, Darren thought she might slip on the wet grass. "What are you doing home already?" he said as he came down off the porch to offer her a hand. She grabbed hold of his wrist instead, squeezing tight, as she told him matter-of-factly, "I got fired."

"What?"

"But listen, don't worry about that none," she said, pulling his wrist toward her car as *he* tried to steer her toward the house, the two engaged in a cross between a do-si-do and an all-out tug-of-war. Bell's eyes widened as she tried to wrest his full attention to hear what she was about to say. "I talked to her," she said, smiling widely.

Darren felt something lift behind his breastbone. *Hope.*

"Sera?"

Bell shook her head. *Not Sera.*

But she *had* found a link to the missing student.

"That Michelle girl ... the one I thought might have left the note under Sera's door, the note we found that was checking on her after what happened 'last night.' Remember?"

"Wait, did you get into Sera's room?"

She shook her head and explained. "Kelsey caught me trying to get in there and said they were gon' have to let me go." It was said so casually that Darren felt that her excitement about finding Michelle was dulling a coming pain, when the realization that she'd lost her job would hit her hard. For now, she was too proud of herself. She had gotten to Michelle before Kelsey realized Bell was in the building. "I saw the girl, only one I ever heard called Michelle. And since nearly everybody else on her floor was away on campus, I got a feeling she might talk. I been seeing her since the end of her junior year, when she waited and waited until all the other girls moved their stuff out for summer break, so no one would see her dad loading up her things in an old plumbing truck. Wasn't even his. It was borrowed from the man he worked for part-time. She always seemed all right to me. Kind. Sometimes you gotta be careful with white folks who ain't got much of nothing. Either they get it, how it's about eight different ways we're both getting screwed in this country, or they're sure *you're* the reason they ain't got shit, or as much shit as they think they *should* have, and they hate you for it."

"Mama." Darren tried pulling his mother by the elbow to get her into the house and out of the rain. But she pulled him right back. "Naw, we gotta go. I got us a lead."

16.

THERE WAS a party Labor Day weekend, Michelle had told Bell. The first big one of the semester and the first exchange with Rho Beta Zeta's brother fraternity for the year, Pi Xi. It was going to be out at "the Pound," what the frat called their compound tucked behind a wall of pines off Highway 59, south of the campus.

"A bunch of us were going," Michelle had told Bell. "I remember Sera didn't want to go. I don't know if she wasn't feeling well — that was a thing with her sometimes, with that thing or whatever she has — or if she wanted to study, but Kelsey said she had to go." The rain had slowed and the worn-down wipers on his mother's Nissan squeaked with every motion, sounding like a braying donkey in distress. They were heading south on 59 now, Bell driving at speeds Darren wouldn't have advised even if it weren't raining. From her perch behind the driver's seat, Bell told him, "Michelle said that Kelsey stayed on that girl, monitoring her closely. Fit checks and telling her how to wear her hair. Apparently, Kelsey even got all the girls to pitch in and get her a flat iron for Christmas last year, not understanding that wasn't gon' do a damn thing for that girl's hair. I mean, if it had been a hot comb or if they'd just let her wear it natural —"

"Mama!" Darren slammed his hand against the dash as she inched too close to the business end of an eighteen-wheeler hauling dozens of bales of hay, bits of straw flying loose, as if he could stop the car with the force of his fear. The gesture tickled her.

"Boy, I been driving since before your balls dropped."

She put on her blinker and edged over into the passing lane on the left and got back to her story. She still hadn't told him where they were going, was too caught up with a perverse excitement she couldn't hide. They'd argued before getting in her car about *whose* case this was. While they waited for Greg to work his FBI contacts, Darren had wanted to stick near the house on Lanana Street in the hopes that Rey would return any of the texts he'd sent him or just arrive back at the house unannounced. He still wanted Rey to show them where he'd found the bloody shirt, another vital part of the investigation. But Bell was now adamant that what Michelle had told her changed everything and insisted she was in charge. She reminded Darren, "It wouldn't be no case if I hadn't come calling for you," as if Sera were missing only because Bell had noticed it, because she'd spoken up about it. Darren privately groused about what he'd set in motion by deputizing his mother to poke around the sorority house. But hell if she hadn't hit a jackpot. And she believed she should have earned Darren's trust.

"Sera didn't fit in, is what I'm trying to tell you I got out of talking to Michelle." Which to Darren had seemed obvious from the start, confirmed for him after her classmate Ella revealed that joining Rho Beta Zeta hadn't even been Sera's idea.

Sera was pressured into going to the Labor Day party, into a lot of things around the house. Socials and committee meetings, several times a week. Sera was studious and didn't want to do all that. Would just flat out tell Kelsey no, Michelle told Bell. And it drove Kelsey crazy that the girl wouldn't follow the rules, and that weekend she put her foot down. Kelsey said Sera had to go to the first RBZ–Pi Xi party of the year.

Bell finally shut off the windshield wipers as the rain stopped.

She was so quietly thrilled to have him hanging on her every word, so proud of herself to have brought valuable information to her son, the Ranger. As Bell switched lanes again, she took him back to the night of the party, what Michelle knew about it and what had led the senior to slip a note under Sera's door to see if she was okay the day after. Bell told Darren, "There had been a lot of drinking, like it is with most of these kids' parties nowadays. My time, maybe you'd sneak one or two beers. Your daddy and me, we never needed nothing to drink to have a good time. He was only at SFA a month or two, but he took me to a couple of parties with the few other black students enrolled back then, and we had a good time. But I ain't really start drinking until he was gone. I got through nine months clean with you."

What was she talking about?

His father had never been at Stephen F. Austin.

"No," Darren said. "Duke went to Prairie View, like his brothers."

"Well, he did," Bell said. "Until he didn't."

Darren had heard Pete say something about Duke being at SFA, but he assumed Pete had it wrong, was confused about the history. But here was his mother, her voice as clear as her name, saying his father had been a student at Stephen F. Austin University. He stamped his boot into the floorboard. "No. Duke, my dad, he went to PV and then got sent to Vietnam, near the end of the war—" It was the story he'd always been told, but even as the words poured out now, he felt a strong wind blow through the holes in it. How *had* Duke Mathews ended up in Vietnam if he was in school and surely up for a draft deferment? Randie had posed the same question, but Darren hadn't been able to take it in, had simply pushed away any details that didn't fit what his uncles had told him about his dad. Bell gripped the steering wheel and clenched her teeth. It stoked her pique with the men who had raised her son. Every detail of Darren's life story that she had to explain to him was another poor mark in her assessment of William's and Clayton's parenting. "I thought you knew some of this," she said. "Would have thought your uncles had told you at least a little about how you came into this world." She sighed and shook her lowered head. "Found out I was pregnant with you just two weeks after I graduated from high school, whole life in front of me. Your daddy transferred to SFA that fall so he could be here when you came. I'd get in as much school as I could till you was born. We'd set our schedules around taking care of you. Don't know why they thought we didn't have a plan."

She was having this argument with his uncles, men who had spurned her after Duke's death, but she was also angry with Darren for favoring their version of events.

"I don't believe you," he said.

Bell cut her eyes at him. She looked hurt, flushed with irritation.

"Why, Darren? *Why* would I lie about this?"

Stunned that she could even make her mouth form the question, he said, "I don't know, Bell. Why do you lie about everything?"

She swallowed hard, and then in a near whisper she said, "Not everything."

They were, after all, chasing a lead about a missing girl that Bell Callis had most certainly not lied about, as evidenced by her son in her car with her now. And then, as if to prove her point, she slowed at the highway median, turning left across the two lanes heading north on 59 and steering her car onto a narrow, unpaved road behind a wall of pines and sugar maples, some of whose leaves had blushed to a ruddy red, the edges lit in a burning gold. She kept her gaze locked in front of her as they drove deeper into a wooded area. It was hard to understand where the dirt road was taking them as they ventured further into tangled thicket. Darren fidgeted in the car, feeling overheated and trapped inside the cramped space, his knees up near his armpits. Finally, the road deposited them in front of an enormous, multi-winged property in an English Tudor style, a structure that reminded Darren of the fairy tales his grandmother had read to him as a child. The house had two Greek letters, each over three feet tall, above the front door.

It was the Pi Xi fraternity.

Though the house was impressive, the parking lot was unfinished. It was a rough circle of dirt and gravel on which Darren might have thought twice about parking the late-model Cadillac Escalades, the BMWs, and the eighty-thousand-dollar trucks. Oh, there was a Kia here and there, but for the most part the residents of the Pi Xi house had a little change in their pockets. Darren heard music now, coming from the house. The hypnotic bass of rap, plus voices from around the back of the house, laughter and splashing water. Darren caught a whiff of chlorine in the air. The Pi Xi house had a pool somewhere on its sprawling acreage. Bell tucked her Nissan inside a stand of cedar oaks far enough at the edge of the parking lot that they had a clear view of the front door of the fraternity but also cover from the hanging branches, which swung low and wet over the car, making for a decent stakeout spot, Bell proposed.

"Stake out what, exactly?" Darren asked.

"The party was here, Michelle said. And Kelsey's boyfriend lives here."

Bell shut off the engine and picked up the story that she'd heard earlier.

"Michelle said Sera had a lot to drink that night, more than she'd ever seen Sera drink before. In fact, Michelle said she wasn't sure she'd *ever* seen her drink. She knew the girl took medicine, knew Sera was sometimes so tired she missed class for days. She told Sera she shouldn't do anything she wasn't comfortable with." Here, Michelle had gotten up and closed the door to her room so they wouldn't be overheard.

Michelle had told Bell, "I took a drink right out of Sera's hand."

She'd looked at Bell, who was standing awkwardly just inside the closed door of Michelle's room, never having been inside one of the girls' rooms without a specific task in mind, trash to take out, a feather duster to run over the baseboards and the girls' desks. Michelle seemed to sense Bell wasn't totally comfortable and she wanted Bell to know she wasn't like the other girls. "I come out of Crockett," she'd said, speaking of a poor town west of Lufkin. She was trying to make Bell understand something about herself, was trying to imply some fellow feeling—where money, or lack thereof, might cut across the racial divide, might stitch their circumstances closer together than others'. "My dad's a part-time plumber. His biggest dream is to get a job down at the prison in Huntsville. Not saying there's anything wrong with it, but you get into a sorority like this and meet girls like Kelsey Piper, whose family knows people, who can have just about any job she wants when she walks out of here, and you just hope some of that rubs off. The dues to be here and all that money, that's what you're really paying for—someone out there to give you a real shot at cutting to the front of the line once we graduate out of here, someone to offer something more than what my daddy could, which is, what, answering phones at Coonskin Plumbers." She let out a low sigh, looked at Bell, and said, a forlorn note in her voice, "Yes, ma'am, that's what it's called. *Coons* for short." She wore an apology on her face. "I want something better than that, better than what all I come from and the way folks there act and talk about certain people. Not all of us voted for Trump. It's just easier not to get into it with the folks who did."

A pickup truck pulled into the parking lot in front of Bell and Darren, finding a spot closer to the front door. Bell fell silent for a moment, holding her breath as she watched two young men climb out carrying tattered backpacks. She studied them, squinting, as if that would bring them into greater focus. "That's not him," she said.

"Kelsey's boyfriend?"

Bell nodded. "I got his name and pulled it up on Facebook."

She fished her cell phone out of her back pocket, turning its cracked screen to Darren. She was showing him a photo of a white man in his early twenties with dark blond hair in a mullet-ish cut. His name was Brendan, and his eyes were a deep brown. They were too small for a face that was swollen with beer or 'roids or cheeseburgers or a cocktail of all three. According to his page, he was a senior and a running back for the Lumberjacks, Stephen F. Austin's football team. Darren felt a distant guilt about deciding that he hated the kid on sight. He looked like an asshole.

"And why would Michelle share all this with you?" he said.

"'Cause she feels like something weird went down at that Labor Day party."

She told Bell that at one point during the party she actually grabbed Sera by the hand and tried to get her to go back with her to the sorority house because Sera was so drunk. But Kelsey intervened.

Beyond the pine tops, a snatch of blue sky could finally be seen, suggesting the worst of the rain was over. It had come through, made a great show, and was now winding down, a break before the next sudden storm. Texas weather was like a conjure woman's magic, like that of a bored sorceress playing tricks for fun. Darren craned his neck to see the top window of the frat house, an attic eye looking out. He could have sworn he saw the curtain move. He wondered distantly if they were being watched. It sounded crazy, even to his overly suspicious mind, and yet he couldn't shake the feeling that there were eyes on them. As he stared at the window, Bell turned to him. "Michelle got a feeling that Kelsey was setting up something between her boyfriend and Sera. It was a game of hers, letting girls she didn't like think they had a chance with Brendan and then pulling the rug out when a girl got herself into a compromising position so Kelsey could publicly accuse the girl of trying to steal her boyfriend. Michelle had heard stories that it had gone too far a few times, Brendan actually having sex with these girls, and Kelsey would still find a way to twist it and blame them, using it as ammunition against them. Well, Kelsey wanted Sera out of the house, out of the sorority, and Michelle had a feeling she was going to try some shit."

"And Michelle didn't do anything to stop Kelsey?" Darren asked.

"Said she didn't feel like dealing with Kelsey's bullshit. Or pissing her off. She must have told me nine different ways that Kelsey is connected, someone she might need when she's an alum, which was her whole reason for pledging in the first place."

Bell reached past her son to the glove compartment. Inside was a half-full bag of cherry sours, the generic kind the Dollar General sold in bags with a crimped piece of chipboard stapled at the top. She popped a few in her mouth, then offered to pour some in his hand. He accepted them for the gift they were, knocking them back and feeling sugar shoot through his blood before he even swallowed. "I want to know what happened that night," Bell said. "Michelle never saw Sera come home, didn't see her leave her room Sunday or on Labor Day. And she never got a response to her note."

Darren tongued the globs of gooey red sugar stuck in his back teeth.

"So, what is your plan here?" he said, gesturing to the frat house. "Corner this kid, the boyfriend —"

"And ask him what happened."

He wasn't sure it would work, wasn't sure that it mattered. Rey still hadn't returned any of his texts, and it would be a while before he heard anything from Greg. And he wouldn't be able to get Iris Fuller alone until Joseph's shift started this evening. This was as good a lead as any. "I know it," Bell said, reminding him this was her case too.

And so they waited, watching frat boys arrive and leave, arrive and leave, none of them Brendan, none with quite the same almost-mullet. The same puddle-brown eyes. Darren also kept an eye on the top-floor window with the twitchy curtain.

Bell smoked and ate cherry sours.

"I'm sorry," he said about her losing the job.

He knew she needed it. She waved him off with the cigarette in her hand. Still, he saw a dimness in her eyes, felt tension creep into her posture, a distant sadness.

They passed the next twenty minutes or so in silence. Bell sitting up a few times to take a closer look at some of the young men going in or out of the Pi Xi compound.

After a while, Bell turned on the radio. Aretha Franklin was singing "Bridge over Troubled Water," a favorite of Darren's, but still he reached over and snapped it off. They needed all their senses sharp. Bell turned it back on, the volume so low it was more a memory than a song. The car was messy: a pile of laundry, including a sheet dotted with watercolor stains, was spilling from the back seat onto the armrest between them. It turned out that all those paintings of Zion Hill Baptist Church inside Pete's house were Bell's, a hobby she'd picked up. A little music and a set of paints, she said, and a night could pass without a drink. The church, its divine grace, held a special place in her heart. "The day I found out I was pregnant, I went in there and prayed."

Darren heard a catch in her voice, a rare display of raw emotion.

Her throat was thick with it. "And again after your father died. I went back to Zion Hill and sat in a rear pew by myself, and I tried to think what it would mean for the little thing I was carrying in me. If Duke was really gone, what then? And hard as it is to say, if I'm telling the truth on it, I wasn't sure I wanted it. I wanted a clean break. I didn't think I could take a reminder of Duke pulling at me for the rest of my life, needing me, my body, tugging at it. I didn't think I could take it without him."

Darren turned as best as he could in the front seat, his long legs straining.

He stared at his mother, who looked both abashed and relieved, as if she'd burped up something sudden and sour and now her stomach could settle itself.

The thing was out.

Darren knew, though, didn't he?

Wasn't this the pain he'd carried his whole life?

"You didn't want me."

It was no longer a question but a statement of fact.

Bell turned to her son, burrowed her dark eyes into his. "Darren..."

She just as quickly looked away, unable to hold the stark intimacy.

She stared out the windshield and then suddenly sat up straighter.

"It's him, Darren." She pointed in the direction of the front door where the kid from the Facebook profile was indeed walking up to the Pi Xi house. Brendan.

She agreed to let Darren take the lead as they approached the front door of the fraternity. He was still unsure that this would bear any fruit, was still not wholly convinced that the kid would talk to them, let alone tell them anything that would be a direct line to finding Sera Fuller. This thought had barely settled in his mind when the door of the frat opened and a young man in khaki shorts and flip-flops and no shirt emerged, nipples hairy and pink as a piglet. Darren wondered how he'd known to stop them at the threshold. He then remembered the window on the top floor, his feeling that they were being watched. The young man, a kid, really, said, "You guys can't just come up here like this." Something in the slope of his shoulders was off, the right one sitting lower than the left. It was then that Darren saw the gun, a Glock as big as the kid's forearm. It hung down at his side, explaining why one half of his body dragged toward the ground, why he had the loping appearance of a baby Bigfoot, a monster who didn't know his own strength, who hadn't yet grown into the power of his body.

Bell called out her son's name, a ragged, terrified whisper.

Darren raised a hand in surrender just as the young man raised the Glock and pointed it at Darren's head.

All it takes is one idiot with a gun.

An evergreen statement in Texas, apparently.

Darren felt a rush of adrenaline at the same time as a bone-deep weariness that nearly sank him. How had this day started with him nearly killing one nineteen-year-old and arrived at him now maybe seconds away from being shot by another one with a nine-millimeter? It was madness, he thought, this loose gunplay — even as his palms itched for the Colt .45 at his side. Until he remembered he was without a badge, here without permission or an invitation. They were within their rights, by state law, to kill him if they felt afraid. Darren raised both arms then and nodded at his mother to do the same.

The kid took a step toward them. He had a blocky face, puffy with drink, a condition Darren recognized. The boy had either been drinking late into the night or was still drunk right now. He narrowed his eyes at them and said, "What are you, like, her parents or something?" His speech was thick as paste. "That Rho Beta chick."

A voice bellowed from inside the fraternity house. "Jackson!" It was a warning from Brendan, who was now standing behind his frat brother in the doorway. "Dude, they could be her lawyers or something."

Darren, maybe. Bell was still in her Cheery Clean Maids smock.

Both of them arms up in front of a drunk child, an armed drunk child.

He would give anything to rewind this day, the past year while he was at it.

"Well, they can't just come up here like this," the kid with the gun, Jackson, said.

His neck flushed a deep pink color. He was angry, full of raw indignation.

Darren could feel his mother's body shaking beside him. The scene had now drawn a couple of other frat boys. They stood just inside the Pi Xi house, behind Brendan, whose hands, Darren noticed, were swollen and covered in bruises, like two overripe plums on the end of his arms. There were bruises on his biceps too. And was that a scabbed-over cut on the side of his temple? Jackson said, "Fuck if we're getting kicked off campus over some shit that did not fucking happen, dude."

"I didn't do anything to that girl," Brendan said to Darren. "Nothing."

"The whole thing was a goof." Jackson had spit in the corners of his mouth. "Leaving the house, that was *her* idea, by the way. She drug us out in the middle of a fucking national forest, wanted to show us something in the fucking woods. I mean, she was in on the whole thing. And nothing happened anyway. We were just fucking around," he said, jerking his head in Brendan's direction. Darren made a quick decision.

"Run," he whispered to his mother.

Then, in one swift move, he grabbed Jackson's wrist, the one above the hand that held the Glock, whipped his arm behind his back, and headbutted the boy. He heard a pop like the sound of two billiard balls colliding. The boy stumbled and fell on the front steps. Darren disarmed him as Jackson sank to his knees, holding his head.

Once the gun was in Darren's hand, it took over, blotting out reason.

He aimed it at the young men, adrenaline tearing through every muscle in his body. His own head was throbbing. He wondered absently if he'd broken skin. The fraternity brothers gathered on the steps around Jackson, who was moaning in pain. One of them whipped out a cell phone, and Darren was ashamed to admit his first thought was fear that they would film him, when it was just as likely, more dangerous even, that they were calling the sheriff's department. He remembered Wilson's warning not to do anything stupid while a grand jury was deciding his fate.

Too late, he thought as he backed away from the front door, still leveling the nine-millimeter at the young men. He no longer wanted it in his hands, but he was afraid to give it back to them, boys who were in high school a few years ago. Just as he was afraid, if cops were on their way, to be in possession of a stolen weapon. Without a badge, could he convince law enforcement that he was harmless? Across the lot, Bell had the car running. Darren moved toward it quickly, hopping into the passenger side. They fled the scene, flying down the tree-lined road, the mud-dappled car bumping over potholes and pockets of rain. Darren carefully ejected the magazine clip from the handgun and then threw them both out of the car window and into the piney woods.

17.

He had a headache and acid-hot adrenaline running through his veins.

Bell had yet to release her iron, double-fisted grip on the steering wheel, even after they'd made it back onto Highway 59 without further incident. She was jumpy and nervous and, something he'd never seen before: scared. And disappointed by the turns this case had taken. When she'd first reached out to her son about Sera Fuller, she thought she was asking a man who had the heft of the Texas Rangers behind his name. She had no idea it was going to lead to this kind of ham-fisted carrying-on, she said. Else she might have saved them both the bother. She seemed angry that he had no badge on him, no real power, an irony that she failed to appreciate in her current state.

She could hardly steady her breathing.

For all her tough talk of having grown up with rough and rowdy brothers with a taste for lawbreaking, having a gun pulled on her by a boy whose behind she might have cleaned up after, if she still had a job, had rattled the tiny, fragile thing inside her rib cage. Darren told her to turn off the highway, and a few minutes later they pulled into an RV park off 59, stopping between a white-and-black teardrop model trailer and a wooden shack that had a painted sign that read MAIN OFFICE. Darren looked at his mother and said, "You were right." He served himself a large plate of crow and ate it cold. Everything that had happened at the Pi Xi house made clear that something significant had gone down at the party or an after-party someplace in the national forest — the one where Rey had taken those pictures, likely, where he said he'd found her bloody shirt — an event so potentially violent and violating that those boys thought lawyers might show up at any moment, that they could very possibly get kicked out of school.

He took a deep breath and went over the bits and pieces they'd picked up from the frat boys and from what Michelle had told Bell earlier. "Sera had too much to drink," he said. "And who knows how her medication interacted with alcohol. Michelle reported that she wasn't in her right mind. And she was worried enough about Kelsey's predatory behavior, a pattern she had of using her boyfriend as a tool to hurt girls she didn't like, that she tried to get Sera to leave the party and go back to the Rho Beta house."

He ran through the possibilities of what this all meant.

But came back over and over to the possibility of sexual assault.

"You were right, Mama."

"Darren."

"Sounds like something went down out there. And it led to Sera threatening to tell on Brendan, on the frat, maybe Kelsey too. I can imagine Kelsey launching some kind of campaign to get her off this idea, which is maybe where the bullying came in. But we need to get to Rey somehow, get him to show us where he found the —"

"Darren," Bell said. She'd grown plaintive, soft-spoken, and pensive as she looked out the window at the countryside. "About what I said earlier..."

Did she want him to make a show of her being right, make a song out of it?

"I see it now," he said. "How the party might tie into what happened to Sera. I mean, who knows if this Brendan kid and Kelsey tried to exact some kind of revenge—"

"What I said...about not wanting you." She was still shaking from the brush with deadly violence. It made her confessional, somber and penitent.

"What more is there to say?"

"I didn't mean it the way it came out, son."

He wanted to snatch the *son* from her lips.

"You didn't want me. I think that's pretty clear."

"It's not that simple, Darren."

He chanced a glance in her direction, saw the pain on her face, the regret.

"But it's what you said."

"I said that's the way I felt when I sat in that church on that one day. But I had you, son, and like I said, I didn't take a drink for nine full months with you inside me."

Which was quite literally the least she could have done, he said.

"No, Darren, you ain't got no idea how hard that was. I was gon' have to drop out of school, first in my family to step foot on a college campus. But I was sick all the time, up all night, your little butt turning my body inside out. And without Duke, I got scared. He was the one who held up my dreams with me. I was good at math. I had an eye on getting a government job maybe. But without Duke cheering me on, I was just a poor girl, knocked up and alone."

The air in the car had grown stuffy. The sun had come out after the rain, and it was warming every inch inside the Nissan, puffing up the air with the smell of the dirty laundry. Darren pressed on the button to let down his window, enough times that Bell got the hint and turned over the car's engine so Darren could roll down his window. The air was thick outside too, but the smell was sweeter. Pine and damp earth, plus the cedar chips arranged around the steps to the front door of the teardrop model trailer. The RV park had set out a few potted plants, a half dozen red petunias.

"What changed your mind?" Darren said softly, dipping a toe in dark waters.

He thought of the watercolors in the halls of his uncle Pete's house, the prayers Bell had put down on paper. Zion Hill Baptist, a warm, sticky morning in 1973. It was hard to picture his mother as a young girl, a teen, but the paintings caught something, a hang in the light, a moment suspended in time. She could go left, or she could go right.

"I got used to carrying you," she said. "It was like having a little piece of Duke with me while I was studying, trying to get as much school-work done as I could before I got too big. And I talked to you, and it seemed like you became like a friend, kind of, keeping me company, making me think I hadn't dreamt up my time with Duke. That we had been something real. It had all been real. Somebody had loved me once."

She took a breath and looked out the driver's-side window, eyes tilted up toward passing clouds, new and weighty and gray. Darren contemplated the wisdom and folly these pines and their ancestors had seen over centuries. "And he did love me, Darren, he did." She shot a glance at him and there were tears in her eyes, making them glassy with emotion and tender feeling. It changed her countenance, made her beautiful in a way he'd never seen. She bit her lip and then smiled at some private memory.

Darren felt a shiver run up his spine, felt something ride in on the air coming in through the car window. The car felt more crowded suddenly, and he was too embarrassed by the hoodoo of it to admit to himself what he was thinking: that his father had joined them in this little blue Nissan. It was crazy, and yet it felt true.

He grew heated again. His mother was hiding behind a dead man.

"He wasn't alive. But you were," he said. "Why did *you* give me up?"

Bell pinched her lips together. Darren saw her eyebrows knit, a look of pain or shame washing over her face. She lifted her eyes so that they met his and then, without a hint of apology in her voice, she said matter-of-factly, "Let me ask you something, Darren. Have you ever wanted for anything? Missed a meal? Didn't you go to a fancy private school in Houston? Didn't they pay for a place for you to stay out there? College. Law school. Everything in this world I might have wanted for myself one day. Well...we both couldn't have had it." The bitterness he'd known from his mother his whole life had crept back into her voice, crusted over the dulcet kindness of the past few days. "It was you or me, and I felt I owed it to Duke to at least give his son a shot at the kind of life he would have given you had he lived. I gave you life, yes, but I also gave you *a* life."

Darren sat for a second, listening to the whoosh of cars on Highway 59 behind them, feeling the car shake just the tiniest bit whenever an eighteen-wheeler went past. He was running her story through his mind, panning for bullshit. "But you didn't do none of that stuff no way," he said. "You gave me over to Clayton and William and then proceeded to do absolutely none of the shit you said you wanted to do with your life."

"I told you, I ain't have Duke around to make me think I could."

"You could have taken me back then. You could have raised me."

"I told you, Darren, I didn't have nothing for you," Bell said. "You had a good life with your uncles. They raised you to be a good man, full of your own faults, sure, but none that you ought to be too ashamed of. Ought to be proud of what you did being raised up under them."

She sniffed a little and looked out her window again.

"What did you want for, son, really?"

Darren ran his hand across his face, before leaning his elbow on the open window's door frame. He let out a doleful sigh that caught both of them by surprise. "The fact that you can't imagine the answer to that question is ultimately the reason why you're right," he told his mother. "I *was* better off without you."

He thought he saw her flinch just the tiniest bit, as if blocking a blow.

She nodded, accepting his flat and somewhat final assessment.

"Let's go," he said suddenly, his voice hardening.

Bell started to turn the car on, forgetting the engine was already running. It let out a cry of distress, the starter squealing in protest. She told him to roll up his window and put on his seat belt. He bristled over her giving him any commands. Just because she was right about the frat party didn't mean she was in charge here. He felt a foundational need to let her know *he* was in control now. Darren told her that the plans had shifted. They would go to Thornhill. They needed to get to Rey. And Darren needed Bell's help getting him inside a town that had, with great force, already removed him from their municipality. Fine, she said, but she wanted it done quick. Having revealed so fragile a part of herself, she was now petulant, at the edge of anger. With pursed lips, she reminded him she needed to get on the job hunt soon. There was a clear accusation in her tone, a suggestion that it was Darren's fault that she was now out of work. As if she'd forgotten the whole reason Darren Mathews was even in Nacogdoches was because she'd come to him about a young woman in trouble. Or maybe she *hadn't* forgotten, and therein lay her true grievance with him: that her son had come only because someone else needed him. He hadn't come for *her*. These past three years, like the whole of his life, he'd just made clear, he had been better off without her. They had circled back to the original wound, his birth and her feelings about it, the pain his life stoked in her. "I told you I couldn't handle it, what all I'd lost."

"What *you* lost, right."

Bell finally wrenched her body around in the driver's seat and looked at her son.

"You don't understand. I blamed myself for it. If he hadn't been in Nacogdoches trying to see after me, maybe Duke would have lived, might still be alive right now."

He felt the mechanics of her manipulation, the play for self-pity.

It enraged him.

"What does Duke in Nacogdoches have to do with it? He died in Vietnam."

"Darren," Bell said, as slow and gentle as any parent might be with a difficult truth, with words that might shock their child. "Your father was never in Vietnam."

18.

SHE TOLD her version of it in a straight line for the first time, certainly the first time she'd ever told any of it for Darren's benefit, a son who hadn't asked the questions she'd been dying to answer since she met him when he was eight years old. Met him for the second time, that is. She'd had a good twenty hours with him after he was born, wrapped in her arms after Gracie, a midwife out to Camilla, had delivered him in her parents' front room. The room was close and damp, the air bitter with the musk of blood and shit and piss and other fluids she didn't realize, despite half a semester in college, could come out of a body in one sitting. She'd held her boy in her arms, seated near the front window, letting a beam of sun warm his little face, skin as brown and smooth as cocoa pudding. She wanted to nibble every inch of him. Her mother hollered to get the baby out of the sun, *'fore you blind the boy good.* "But you hadn't even opened your little eyes yet, hadn't even seen your mama. We just held each other close, you in my arms, your hand wrapped around my pinkie finger. We stayed like that for almost a whole day before your uncles got word of the birth, that their baby brother had a son. And then here they come, pointing out what I already knew. That I didn't have no money, no help with the baby. Pete was on shift work at the plant back in Nacogdoches and rarely home. My other brothers was in and out of jail, and my own mama, your gran, was in and out of touch with the real world. She liked a drink too. And the Mathews men, your uncles, come around and said Duke would have wanted better for the boy, and honestly, looking around my parents' little shack, knowing how far I was from how I thought this was all gon' go, I couldn't argue with either one of them."

"The war, Mama," Darren said, pressing her back to the topic.

"He had a deferral."

"Because he was a student at Prairie View, that's what Clayton said."

Bell nodded. She followed it with a sigh that seemed to steam-press all the air out of her lungs, deflating her completely. "But then I got pregnant. The two of us had been finding ways to see each other his freshman year at PV and my senior year at Nacogdoches High School," she said. "He had a little Mercury Comet he used to drive up from Waller County on weekends. And, sure enough, I come up with a baby in me right after my high-school graduation, even though I was planning on going to college that fall."

"Were you scared to tell him?"

Bell gave him a rueful smile because of all he didn't know about his daddy.

"No," she said. "He drove up when I did, and we sat on that porch at Petey's house, and he said, 'Well, lil' Bell, what are we going to do, then? We can marry here in Nacogdoches, where we got at least one of your people. Or we can go back home and get married in San Jacinto County with all our families. Either way, looks like we 'bout to make ourselves a home somewhere. May not be nice as we want it right off the bat, but I promise you, girl, we get through this rough part, we finish school and all that, and we gon' make a life together. Me, you, and that little one in there,' he said."

Duke was rubbing her feet, even though she wasn't even hardly showing then, didn't know yet the kind of aches that would take up residence in all corners of her body. "But he was gentle like that, your daddy," she said. He'd leaned down and kissed her toes, and by the following morning, he had enrolled in Stephen F. Austin to start his sophomore year in the English department that fall. "He moved into Pete's with us."

"English?" Darren had never heard this before. It was, frankly, unbelievable to him. The whole story had the gauzy feel of a fairy tale, scenes washed over in pastels rather than the sharp edges of real life. Darren once more wondered what decades of hard drinking had done to his mother's mind. Could he honestly trust a single thing that was coming out of her mouth? "He was studying English?"

"Wanted to be a professor, he said. Boy loved, loved to read."

Not history or law or sociology or political science, the academic paths that had been chosen by the other Mathews men, studies that led to careers in law *and* law enforcement. His father, Duke, had supposedly charted a course that led to a study of art, that built a life around the pleasure in it, of a good story. Books and a quiet life of the mind. How then had Duke fared in the grand debates in the Mathews home between William's faith in American laws' capacity to bend toward justice and Clayton's certainty that nobody had time to wait for that sickle to curve in just the right way not to cut your head off? Was Duke's answer a passage from James Baldwin's *No Name in the Street*? With books, had his father escaped Darren's fate of growing up feeling forever trapped between his uncles' two different versions of being black in America? One built on our native optimism, a natural tendency to see and believe in our ability to make beauty out of almost anything, and the other built on base pragmatism, on recognizing the limits of our grace in the face of folks who double down on their cruelty at every turn. Because to let up on the whip, this many centuries in, even if only for a minute, was to leave time enough to consider how the whip came to be in your hand, to ponder your continued grip on it, how it still benefited you.

"But if he enrolled in SFA," Darren said, still trying to get to how Duke coming to Nacogdoches had anything to do with whether he had served in Vietnam, which is what his uncles had told Darren any time he asked—admittedly fewer and fewer times as he got older. It was easier in some ways for his father to stay shrouded in history. "He would have still been eligible for deferment. Is that what you're saying? That because Duke had a student deferment, when he got called up to go, he had an out?"

"He *had* an out," Bell said. "But something went wrong when he transferred from Prairie View to go to school out here. You have to remember, shit was just done county by county back then, wasn't no computer or nothing to make a system out of it, to make it fair. When his number come up, a letter showed up at the farmhouse in Camilla..." At the mention of the home in which he had been raised, Darren felt his skin flush, felt something turning over inside him. He got an image of his uncles finding the letter from the United States government telling their baby brother to report to service. Did they still have the letter? In a hatbox somewhere? In the leather trunk where his grandmother had kept her quilting supplies and family photo albums and two tattered Bibles, one from her side of the family and one from his grandfather's ancestors? There were marriage licenses in there, maybe even the original deed to the property. Why had his uncles not sat him down and gone through every inch of the thing, why hadn't they told him more about his father? Why hadn't he asked?

"I will go to my grave believing the draft board in Nacogdoches County was up to some funny business, somebody claiming they couldn't find the right paperwork saying he'd properly transferred to a new school. I remember he spent a few days running between here and his home county and even down to Waller where Prairie View is, anything to fix what was clearly just some kind of clerical error. But in the end, they told him they had no record of a deferment, and he would have to report for duty. And that way somebody else's boy didn't have to go. Draft board playing slick."

"So he *did* serve in Vietnam," Darren said. They were back where they'd started.

"No," Bell said. And here a bittersweet smile came through, lifting her eyes as if they were on a string. The smile was quivery and unsure of itself. "He wouldn't go. Said it wasn't his war, and he wouldn't follow any law that would make him leave his child. They could come get him if they wanted to try. But he'd made up his mind."

She looked at Darren, proud of this next bit. "He told them he was a conscientious objector, wasn't gon' fool with the violence they were asking of him."

This is where she lost him.

Because there was just no way.

In all the political discussions he and his uncles had had around the kitchen table, a Lucky Strike burning in an ashtray and Solomon Burke on the hi-fi, there was no way Clayton would ever have shut up about his baby brother refusing to put his life on the line for a war that benefited not a single soul on the shores of the United States of America, a nation that could just barely be bothered with fortifying its own democracy. He would have been too proud. It would have been his forever trump card to play with his twin, William, who had volunteered to serve in a very different "Vietnam conflict" when he turned eighteen, who believed in the power of service. It took a certain courage to love your way into this country's goings-on, to find a passion to mend what was broken. No, it was impossible, Darren thought, that he wouldn't have heard that not only did his father *not* die in Vietnam, but he had also blatantly broken the law on principle. William would have been heartbroken, Clayton elated.

"No," Darren said, rolling up his window now, signaling an end to this. "I don't believe you." He didn't know what she was trying to pull, what she thought this story might gain her, or if there was simple pleasure in holding up a narrative contrary to what his uncles had told him. It felt spiteful. And petty. *She'd* brought up the church. Deciding his fate on a wooden bench in the back.

There was a ruthlessness to telling all this to him now. He just didn't know yet what her play was, why, this late in the game, she would introduce a new story about his father. And he didn't want to know. He felt the bricks being laid inside, walling off this whole line of inquiry, stopping himself from asking the questions that lingered, the pieces in this he still didn't understand. If his father hadn't gone to Vietnam, if he chose to believe any of what his mother was saying, then how did Duke Mathews die? And if she was telling the truth, did that mean his uncles, the men who had raised him, had deceived him his whole life? *There was just no way.* "I don't believe any of this," he said, shaking his head against all that this would mean if this tale was true. Opening that door would only lead to him drinking himself into a stupor this very night. He didn't have time for this. Sera Fuller didn't have time.

19.

It was Darren's idea to make it seem like Bell was entering Thornhill alone. He'd already been escorted out of the town, and he worried his face might raise a red flag to security. Bell, on the other hand, was on record as a prospective resident. And precisely because she still had an open application to live and work at Thornhill, she wasn't a fan of this whole idea. She didn't want him ruining this for her, her one big chance, didn't want this to go left in a way that reflected poorly on her. Darren, who'd laid himself out flat in the back seat, or as flat as his six-foot-one frame would go in the back of the Nissan, and was presently hiding and sweating under a mound of her and Pete's dirty laundry, assured her he had no desire to drag this on any longer than necessary, gently chastising her for her inability to put her own needs aside for the sake of finding Sera Fuller. "Ain't about me," she said. "This about taking care of Petey." This time, he heard no recrimination in her voice, neither a plea for Darren's pity nor a demand for his love. In the silence, there was just the fact of where her life had deposited her at sixty-two. It would change their lives to get a job and a place to stay out there, she said. Get Petey's medical bills covered. Thornhill was a dream, her whole plan for taking care of Pete, as the two of them aged. "You ain't got no kids, ain't never known what it is to be responsible for another person, but me and Pete, we struggling, son. A job at this place would mean free housing, maybe free medical care for the both of us. It's a wait list there a mile long. I'm sixty-three this year, Darren. My mama gone. Daddy too. One of my brothers died locked up in Huntsville, another's body give out before fifty-five. It's luck that Petey made it this long before a stroke got him. Neither one of us getting any younger, and we only got each other. And when he goes . . . I'll be alone. I need this, Darren." She didn't want him messing this up for her.

If they got pulled over or in any kind of trouble, she assured him that she wouldn't claim him as her son or even a man she'd ever seen before. She was prepared to holler and carry on and say that Darren had forced himself into her car to get into Thornhill. "I'm serious too," she said, speaking loudly so he could hear her beneath the mounds of musty fabric as they approached the gates. Inside his hot and dark cocoon, he couldn't even lift a hand to wipe the sweat from his brow without upsetting the careful con he'd arranged in the back seat, without Bell having to pull over and reposition the dirty laundry and paint-dappled sheets on top of him. So he lay perfectly still with his *own* worries about his potential future, years ahead spent alone. He thought of Randie and the proposal that never was. He remembered that he'd never returned her call and felt a sharp panic that he might never hold her again.

He heard the click of her turn signal and then Bell's voice again, softer now.

"I put in a good eight, ten years at Thornhill, if my body can handle it, and I could put some money away, some real savings in our pockets for the first time, a nest egg of some kind. If Petey went first, I'd be all right, maybe. I've been thinking about it a lot, my last years. Somebody like me, not a lot of education, not a lot of money —"

And then they were turning into Thornhill, and she saw something that snatched the train of words right out of her mouth. She let out a low hum of curiosity. "What?" Darren said. "What is it?" It was killing him that he couldn't sit up and see for himself.

"It's just a lot of cars out here, that's all," Bell said.

"What kind of cars?"

"I'm behind one at the security gate, a black SUV. But it's some other ones on up ahead too. Look like they heading to the high-rise over here. Company offices, I guess."

Darren remembered Rey's description of black SUVs coming around Thornhill lately. The kid had reached for context and come up with rappers and NBA players and CEOs. He remembered Rey's story of people frequently touring the homes in Thornhill, and he wondered if these moneyed types were potential investors in the company.

"Ma'am?" Darren heard a male voice say as Bell rolled down her window.

They hadn't gone over a cover story. Not being with Darren Mathews had seemed like half the battle of getting back inside the town with no trouble. But when Bell started talking to the guard, she lied with such ease and finesse of execution that Darren felt something close to awe. For the first time in his life, he was thankful for not having a normal mother, one whose pastimes might have included knitting rather than artful dodging. He heard the cheer in her voice as she reached into her purse for her identification. Could picture which of her smiles she had on display: the one that favored her left side, a half smile that was coy and maybe the tiniest bit flirtatious. "Here to see the Fuller people," Bell said. "They my cousins — well, *she* is. Me and him, we don't always get along, not since he brought chitlins to my house last Easter and dumped 'em in my sink to clean. You might already see my name in the system," she said. "I come through a couple of months ago for a preliminary interview. I don't suppose you know anything about my application?" It was a foolish and tacky question but all the more believable for the eager and hopeful way that she delivered it. Because there was truth in it, her naked desperation, her faith in a place like Thornhill.

Throwing off the paint-splattered sheets and dirty clothes brought back the smell of the town, the rot beneath the scent of damp pine and cedar. A hundred yards past the security kiosk at the entrance to the town, Bell had told him he was in the clear, and he'd come up gulping for air, nearly gagging when he smelled the sickly sweet-and-sour smell of decay, edged with a whiff of something burning, all of it puffing out of the smokestacks up ahead. From the back seat, he finally witnessed what Bell had been talking about. There were indeed quite a number of black SUVs with windows tinted a shade that would be illegal on a Texas highway, something that for Darren brought to mind not the cars of CEOs or potential investors but rather government-issued security vehicles. Several were turning onto the street that led to the company headquarters. Were these the outside visitors to Thornhill that Rey had spoken of?

It was another question to ask Rey when they saw him.

From the back seat, he told his mother, "Keep driving."

Darren directed her to Rey's house, which was next door to the Fullers', while he tried to think of how they could steal away the young man without drawing any undue attention, since Rey wasn't even supposed to *be* in Thornhill anymore. But as soon as they turned onto Juniper Lane, something else stole his attention entirely.

It was the hair he noticed first.

A shock of silver that Darren realized, as the car drew closer, was as much ash blond, almost white, as it was gray. It was cut in a bob that curled softly toward her chin. He stared at the wholly unexpected sight of Thornhill's corporate matriarch, Carey-Ann Thorn, sitting on the Fullers' front porch, the centerpiece of a scene that seemed a re-creation of the one on Thornhill's website, as if they'd stumbled into a commercial. It was an odd sensation, and Darren wondered what in the world they had come across. A set of farmhouse patio furniture had materialized since yesterday, arranged exactly like the advertised images of al fresco family dining, down to the pitcher of lemonade on the table. Darren told Bell to park at the curb between the Fuller house and Rey's, where a black Mercedes sedan was idling. The same darkly tinted windows, the appearance of executive import. On the Fullers' porch, Joseph was sitting beside Carey-Ann at the head of the barn-style table. He wore an ill-fitting suit that was a strange brownish-green color. To his left was a man Darren recognized as E. J. Hill, and beside him sat a jowly older man in a dark gray suit and a red tie that had tiny sailboats on it. He looked up as Iris came out of the house carrying a tray of chicken-salad sandwiches. She set a plate in front of her husband and then each of their guests.

Darren noticed Carey-Ann didn't touch hers.

He got out of the car and started toward the Fullers' front porch.

Behind him, he heard Bell hiss, "Thought we was talking to the boy." She nodded to the house he'd told her was Rey's. But Darren's attention had been diverted to whatever was going on at the Fuller house: the CEO of Thornhill in front of him, talking to Sera's parents. He told his mother, "Stay in the car." Bell ignored him, of course, following behind him as he approached the Fullers' front porch, where Darren could hear Carey-Ann holding court, speaking with company pride about the Fullers.

"They are one of our success stories, a model family."

She looked over at Joseph, and as if on cue, he nodded to the man in the red sailboat tie. "We've been really happy here," Joseph said. "We're living proof that most folks want to work, want to earn their keep, know that a man expecting a handout will never earn the world's respect. You put us on that stage at your fundraiser thing, and we will preach the gospel of Thornhill. I'm ready to tell our story."

He looked across the porch to his wife. "Very happy here," he said. "Huh, Iris?" Then he patted his thigh, an affectionate call or a quiet command: *Come.*

Iris dutifully set down her tray, walked to the end of the table where her husband was sitting, and perched herself on his lap. He wrapped his arms around her and smiled. She smiled too, Darren noticed as he walked up the porch steps, but hers never made it up to her eyes. They were as full of quiet woe as when he'd first met her.

Darren mounted the porch steps. "Well, what do we have here?"

Every head turned in his direction.

E. J. Hill glanced across the table at his wife, whose eyes narrowed ever so slightly before she held up a hand to him, suggesting that whatever this was, she had it under control. She turned and gave Darren a smile that could cut glass.

The man with the red sailboat tie was perspiring at his hairline. He dabbed it with a handkerchief, waiting for his hosts to explain this new presence. "Carey-Ann?"

"This is Darren Mathews," she said, leveling her eyes on him.

She wanted Darren to know there were no surprises in her town. It had the intended effect. Despite himself, Darren was momentarily caught off guard by hearing his name out of her mouth. Carey-Ann Thorn knew who he was. "And yet," he said, "we've never had the pleasure of meeting." He held out a hand in greeting.

Like the food, she refused to touch it.

The two locked eyes across the porch, and Darren sensed her making quick calculations, deciding how to play this intrusion, what it would cost her to reveal that his presence was not a part of whatever script was playing out here. There was a courtship going on, Darren concluded from the way she sat tall and tautly attuned to the man in the sailboat tie. *An investor?* Darren wondered again, though instinct told him something else was afoot. Carey-Ann seemed to decide it was not in her best interest to make a fuss over this interruption. She smiled broadly, as if welcoming a late but invited guest. She wore a pantsuit of an expensive bouclé fabric that rode the line between business and leisure wear. She might have just come from a boardroom or a high tea. "Would you like to have a seat, Mr. Mathews?" she asked.

Bell, in her Cheery Clean Maids smock, crested the top step of the porch too.

Carey-Ann blinked a few times, reworking her earlier calculations. How the hell was she going to spin this? Darren saw her poise briefly falter. The man in the sailboat tie was clearly flummoxed by the new arrivals in Wranglers and working-class garb.

"I'm sorry, who is this?" he said.

"He's a Texas Ranger," Sera's younger brother, Benny, said. Darren hadn't seen the boy in a back corner of the porch, playing a game on his Thornhill-issued phone.

"Former, I understand," Carey-Ann said.

Again, she cut her eyes at Darren. She wanted him to know he had no power here, would continue to move freely through Thornhill only on her say-so. It chilled him a little that news of his presence in the town had made it all the way to the top of the Thornhill corporation, that they'd done their due diligence, asking questions about him.

"I'm a concerned citizen, that's all," he said. "How *is* your daughter, Mr. Fuller?"

"Fine."

"You keep saying that, but no one can seem to find where she—"

"She's a sophomore up at Stephen F. Austin," Joseph said to the man in the red sailboat tie, jumping back into what sounded like a sales pitch. "That's all Thornhill, Miss Carey-Ann's doing. Sera's been real happy up at the university—"

"Except she wasn't, was she?" Darren said. "At least not about being forced to join a sorority she didn't want to be a part of. Isn't that right, Mr. Fuller?"

"*I* made the call to get Sera a coveted spot in a prestigious sorority," Carey-Ann broke in. "It is well understood that women in institutions of higher learning fare better with a support system of a chosen family of sisters. I wanted that for Sera. I found it enormously helpful when I was an undergraduate at SMU. It is a part of my success story. And when Joseph raised the idea of Sera being in the Rho Beta sisterhood, I was flattered and readily agreed. Because Thornhill is invested in Sera's success."

The words were delivered with such sincerity that, for a moment, Darren worried that his cynicism, home-brewed over years of living in a culture of double-dealing and dishonesty, was clouding his judgment, that his distaste for Joseph Fuller bled into a blanket distrust for Thornhill and a near instant dislike of Carey-Ann Thorn.

To the man in the red sailboat tie, she flawlessly worked all of this into what was now, to Darren, *clearly* a sales pitch. "We put people to work here, we support families, we educate the next generation," she said. "This family didn't ask for the circumstances that brought them to Thornhill, but this company, this unique community, has a way of doing business that puts families first. The Fullers know this intimately."

"But where is she?" Darren said, repeating out loud a refrain in his mind. "Where is your daughter, Mr. Fuller? Because no one seems to have seen her at school or her sorority. What's more, Ms. Thorn, why has Thornhill Police tried to stop inquiries into the whereabouts of one of your residents?"

"I told you, she's at school," Joseph said firmly.

"What's this about police?" the man with the sailboat tie said, sitting up in his chair. E. J. Hill set his phone down on the table and shot Carey-Ann a look. *Wrap this up.*

"You know, I think it's about time for your shift, Joseph," Carey-Ann said. She smiled placidly and stood to signify the end of the meeting. Joseph stood too, so quickly that he nearly knocked Iris to the floor, as if he'd forgotten his wife was sitting on his lap. "I thought I might meet with some of the others," Joseph said, smoothing his shirt.

Darren kept going. "The thing is, though, campus police has no record of Sera living anywhere but the sorority house, and those girls said she—"

"Sweet girl, Sera," Carey-Ann said, turning to smile at Iris. "I can only imagine what it's like with kids in college. Can't ever get a hold of them half the time."

She looked at the man in the red tie and added, "She's a busy girl."

"I still want to speak at the KAW fundraiser in a few days," Joseph said.

E. J. Hill looked at his wife and ever so slightly shook his head. *Absolutely not.*

Darren kept an eye on Iris through all of this. She wore the same look of unease that she'd had the day before when Darren first asked about her child. He felt again a desperate need to talk to her alone, away from her husband. By now, the man in the red sailboat tie was shaking Iris's and Joseph's hands as he prepared to leave. He paused long enough to smile at Benny. From his pocket, he pulled out a tiny toy construction hat and offered it to the boy: "Just a small little thing

my office gives to smart young fellows like yourself." Benny palmed it
while his parents said goodbye to Carey-Ann. E. J. Hill was already on
the front lawn, heading for a second black car on the street, a Cadillac
that had newly arrived for him and his wife.

Joseph followed Carey-Ann down his porch steps.

He still wanted to "help with the whole thing," get his story out
there to folks.

"Best way you can help Thornhill now is to put on your uniform and
clock in."

Carey-Ann patted his shoulder and then joined E.J. in the Cadillac.
The man in the red sailboat tie was already in the Mercedes with his
driver. The two cars pulled away from the curb and rode off down Juniper Lane. Joseph, his tie thickly knotted and hanging too high above
his belly, grabbed a nearby bicycle that was leaned against a tree. Iris
let out a huff as she brushed past Bell and Darren on the porch and
down the steps to her husband. She grabbed one of her husband's arms
and said, "Don't go down there, Joseph. They already picked another
family. Leave it alone. Just go on to work."

"I come too far with this thing—"

"They don't want you—"

"*We've* come too—"

"They don't want us anymore," Iris said. "Don't go where you're not
wanted."

She was pleading with him in a way that made not only Darren
uncomfortable but also Benny, who was watching from the porch,
watching Iris appeal to Joseph's pride by wounding it. It seemed to
embarrass the boy. The suit, the way his father was awkwardly squat-
ting on a kid's bicycle. "Dad," his son said softly. People were watching.
A few neighbors at the bus stop. A young mother who had come out
of her house with a toddler on her hip. On the grass, Iris had a grip on

Joseph's arm, which he shook off roughly. Iris's eyebrows knit together. She looked confused and hurt, Darren thought. She watched as he took off on the yellow bike, going past the communal park, past the bus stop. He made a right turn onto Hill Street, the main road that led to the churches and the medical center, the schools, and the offices of Thornhill Industries.

Iris watched him pedal away on the too-small bike.

Then she turned back to her house, her jaw tight. Darren thought he saw exasperation rippling through her entire body. His eyes followed her as she came up the porch steps, took her son by the hand, and entered the house, the door to which hung open for a few seconds. This was their chance to get Iris alone, he thought. Darren turned to look for his mother but didn't see Bell anywhere. He felt a moment of panic and a pang of guilt over the fact that he'd so easily dropped her from his consciousness, that he hadn't been paying attention to where she was in the world.

Then he heard his mother's voice coming from *inside* the Fuller house.

"And these shelves, they're all built-in? They come with the place just like this?"

She'd slipped past him and already let herself in, was already asking questions about Thornhill's housing and amenities before she'd even given Iris her name.

20.

DARREN THOUGHT the only way to gain Iris's trust was by telling the unfettered truth. Yes, he had been a Texas Ranger for over a decade. But he'd recently voluntarily turned in his badge because he had a hard time coloring inside the lines of white folks' ideas of justice for people like them, he said, gesturing between himself and Iris. They were sitting at the kitchen table on a banquette that was decorated with yellow throw pillows. Benny was in the living room, which they could see from here. He was in the same position as he'd been in when Darren had first seen him — on his stomach, playing and watching cartoons. Meanwhile, Bell was moving around the perimeter of the living room, calculating square footage in her mind and running her hands along the walls to gauge if they were plaster or drywall. Having been in her and his uncle Pete's place, Darren understood the allure of the Fullers' bungalow: rich wood floors, braided rugs, sconces, and a staircase to a small second floor, those built-in bookshelves, plus a dishwasher in the kitchen. Bell quietly oohed and aahed as she surveyed the home, which Iris, Darren noticed, tolerated without a word. Iris's spirit seemed coiled in on itself, radiating a quiet but intense heat. She kept clasping and unclasping her hands, her gaze unfocused, her mind a million miles away.

"Ma'am," Darren said.

Iris looked at him as if she had no recollection of inviting him into her home. She glanced at Bell and frowned at both of them. Darren was aware his frank honesty could backfire—for all he knew, Iris Fuller didn't trust him any more than her husband did.

"When was the last time you saw your daughter, Ms. Fuller?" he said.

Iris sighed, and Darren thought she might be stalling.

"You said you *were* a Texas Ranger?"

"*Was*, yes," he said. "You don't owe me nothing, don't have to answer me none."

Iris didn't say anything right away. She twisted her hands together again and glanced into the living room at her son. Darren couldn't easily place Iris's age. Her skin was smooth and deep in color. There were no feathered lines around her eyes, no creases around her bow-shaped mouth. But there was a whole ocean of lines across her forehead, waves that rose and fell with her many unspoken trials and worries.

"I'm trying to find your daughter. I believe she's missing."

She shivered at the word *missing*. Her right hand gripped the edge of the kitchen table, but she shook her head. "She's at school," she said, repeating a comforting script.

"I found some of her things," Bell said. "What started all this."

She had stopped her covetous inspection and was standing in the kitchen, leaning on a countertop. "I work at the sorority house, and a few days ago now, I found a bunch of her things thrown out in the dumpster behind the building."

Iris sat up a little straighter at the same time as some unseen force of gravity pulled at her shoulders and all the muscles in her face. She seemed to both rise and sink as Bell went on. "I come to Darren because I hadn't seen the girl in a while. Something didn't sit right in my soul about the whole thing. So I went to him."

Iris's eyes shot between the two of them, running through questions in her mind.

To Bell, she said, "That your boy?"

"Don't know 'bout a 'boy,' big as he is, but yes, ma'am, this is my son."

For some reason, this made Iris cry, the tears springing up so fast they caught all of them by surprise. Iris brushed them away before they even had a chance to fall, to truly announce themselves. Then she wiped her hands on her apron and asked if they wanted coffee. Not waiting for an answer, she stood as if to go to the cabinet but then sank again onto the banquette, unable this time to keep tears from flowing freely.

"I'll make some," Bell said, nodding to let Iris know there was no need to hold back on their account; she was free to fall apart in her own home. She started opening and closing cabinet doors, hunting for a tin of Folgers. This prompted Iris to stand, finally. She opened the cabinet just to the right of Bell and pulled out not coffee grounds but a fifth of brandy. She uncapped it and took a quick look into the living room to make sure that Benny was still engrossed in his cartoons, then took a long swallow, nearly a three-count. She then held out the bottle to Bell, who froze.

Darren recognized the panic she felt; the same stab of longing had grabbed him at the base of the throat. Bell's eyes pinched into two question marks, turning to seek out her son's gaze for help. Couldn't they? Just a lil' taste? It was the weakest he'd seen his mother since her professed sobriety.

"No, thank you," Darren said, even though he could taste the sweetness of the brandy, the warmth. He did it for his mother, who had more days than him, who had more to lose. "Don't mean any disrespect, Mrs. Fuller, but we won't be drinking."

Talk of coffee forgotten, Iris walked the bottle of brandy back to the kitchen table.

"I haven't seen her in a few weeks. It's not like her not to call, but I know she's busy with school, and I want to give her that little piece of freedom. She's had a few health setbacks recently, but that's to be expected with her condition, and we've been trying to let her manage her own health, grow up some. I would just feel better if I laid eyes on her or knew that she was taking care of herself."

Darren tried to gauge when or if to bring up the bloody shirt.

It could be days before he would know for certain if it was Sera's blood.

He didn't want to scare her unnecessarily, but he did want to sound an alarm.

Because he could sense Iris trying hard to chalk up her obvious anxiety to being a nervous mom who was just missing her kid, trying so hard *not* to entertain the terror that something had gone wrong, had kept Sera from calling. "There've been text messages. I believe my husband already told you that." She looked down when she said it, worrying the stitches on her apron pocket, one corner that wasn't batted down well. She fiddled with a growing hole in the pocket, as Darren leaned across the table. Up close, he could see that its wood grain was fake, a heavy-duty plastic.

He spoke gently. "And these are messages *you've* seen, Iris?"

She took a deep breath, let it out in a huff, a show of impatience.

She resented Darren for pressing, for making her prove something.

"Benny, bring me my cell phone, hear?"

While they waited, Darren asked her, "Are you and your daughter close?"

"What kind of question is that?" She had found solace in her righteous anger, and she was holding on to it for dear life. "She's my daughter, of course we're close."

Bell, who knew a thing or two about the gap between the relationship you wanted to have with your kid and the one you ended up with, piped up, "And she woulda told you if something was wrong at school, if she got into some trouble?"

"Sera's a good girl, and she's doing well in school, better than we expected. College, that was something we hadn't dared dream Sera would get in this lifetime."

"I meant if some trouble found her," Bell said. "She talk about those Rho Beta girls, the way they treat her? What'd y'all talk about that last day you saw her?"

Darren shot his mother a look: *Slow down.*

Iris looked weary, confused as to what Bell was talking about, even confused as to how these two people had gotten inside her kitchen, the heart of her house.

"She ever mention them being mean to her, pulling some tricks on her —"

Darren asked if that was why Sera had moved out of the sorority house.

Iris looked up at him in a way that made his heart sink for her. It was obvious she hadn't heard this before — that her daughter had reportedly moved out of the sorority house. Her body gave an involuntary jolt, a tiny earthquake that charged the air in the room. Then, indignant, she nodded to imply that of course she knew. The more Darren asked questions that suggested Iris didn't know what was going on in her daughter's life, the more it made her double down on the idea that nothing was amiss. In Joseph's absence, she clung to the very assurances she'd seemed to doubt before.

As Benny approached with his mother's cell phone, she said, "She came home to do some laundry, and she hung out with Rey a little that day," she said, nodding her head in the direction of the next-door neighbors' house. "We watched some TV while we folded clothes, and she said she had to get back to campus. There was a party she had to go to." Darren and Bell shot each other a look. Was Iris saying she hadn't spoken to her daughter since the weekend of the Pi Xi party? She looked up and seemed to sense the question. "She's sent the texts, of course," Iris said as she looked down at her cell phone, scrolling through its multicolored apps. This phone was identical to the one Bell had found in the trash. The one that was dead. As he thought about how he was going to break that news to her, he asked, "The company gives those out, right?"

"It's part of the employment package, yes."

A cell service plan, a computer and free Wi-Fi. These were just some of the benefits that came with living and working at Thornhill, along with K–12 schools, medical care, and a grocery and dry goods store all inside these gates. It was all included. Joseph, she said, worked at the plant. Iris worked at a childcare facility they had inside the community center. Benny, having deposited his mother's phone, made his way back to his spot in front of the wide-screen television — also included; Bell had made sure to inquire.

"Like I was saying, there have been text messages, to her father for sure, I know. I think Benny got one too. If you give me a second, I can find the last text message she sent me —"

"On a Thornhill phone," Darren said.

"Her phone, yes."

"An account you don't pay for, that's maintained by your employer."

"I'm not sure I understand what you're saying."

"I'm merely repeating back what you've told me," Darren said, treading lightly, as he'd had to do with victims' families in the past, revealing the obvious as gently as he could. "You're telling me that your last contact with your daughter is on a cell phone that is owned and maintained by your employer, the same employer who insists that your daughter is not missing—proof of which only exists in these texts to your family on, again, a company-issued cell phone." Darren noticed a few beads of sweat had sprung up along Iris's hairline. The worry lines on her forehead rose and fell.

"Are you suggesting that Thornhill is lying to our family?"

The word *lying* came out of her mouth, not his.

That was important, he knew.

She was getting closer to accepting that something was off here.

"I am stating the obvious fact that if they wanted to lie to you, they could. They could send text messages as if they were from your daughter." Iris shook her head at Darren, at this whole conversation she wanted so badly to find utterly absurd.

"But why would they do that?" she said.

"I don't know, but for reasons I don't understand, Thornhill doesn't seem to want the Rangers or any other police around here looking into your daughter's disappearance. They told me to stand down, insisted that she isn't missing—"

"My daughter is not missing." She continued scrolling through her phone, looking for something that she was realizing in real time wasn't there. Her eyes dropped to her lap for a second, then she looked up at both of them, a pinched expression on her face. "It must have been on Joseph's phone," she said. "But I know I saw the texts. I wouldn't go *weeks* without some contact from my child. Sera has been in touch."

"We found her phone," Bell said.

Darren kicked her ankle under the table. There was a rhythm to this, a way you had to take someone by the hand and walk them up to the truth right in front of them.

But Bell swatted back at Darren's arm. "She needs to know."

"What do you mean, you found her phone?" Iris said.

"It was in the trash with some other things, battery drained all the way down."

Iris glared at Bell. "Show me."

This was why Darren wished his mother had simply followed his lead.

To Iris, he said, "We don't have her belongings with us."

"Then I don't believe you," she said, crossing her arms tightly, her jaw set tight, her chin jutting out. Darren could practically feel molecules in the air rearranging themselves, could feel the force of Iris's will, rejecting this entire conversation. "Why would Thornhill try to make us believe that our daughter is safe if she isn't?"

"You tell me," Darren said. "Tell me what you really know about this place."

"This 'place,'" she said, her tone mocking what she took for Darren's poorly concealed distaste for the town of Thornhill. "This place saved my daughter's life."

21.

SHE SHOWED them pictures. Not from a photo album, but ones she kept, of all places, in a kitchen drawer. They were grouped in stacks, each collection in its own plastic sandwich bag. Sera two months old, then twelve years old, then eight, all mixed together. The same for another set. Darren couldn't make sense of Iris's classification system, why certain images had been cataloged together, but it made sense to a mother's heart, and Iris wanted them to know her child, and to see her as an attentive and devoted mother who'd loved her way through more than her fair share of troubles.

"Sometimes I sit up at night thinking about the pain she was in before she could even talk, before she could tell us what was wrong, where it hurt, nights she would cry for hours and hours, and there wasn't a thing I could do to calm her down. That brandy," she said, nodding at the bottle. "I sent Joseph out for that when she was six months old, when we thought maybe she just had a bad case of teething. They said sickle cell when she was born, but she didn't have symptoms for months, and I guess I just wanted to believe the doctors had figured it wrong. And here I had aunties and grannies on Joseph's side telling us to run a little of this over her gums. Lord, I liked to have that baby drunk, much as I was trying to get that brandy to calm her."

She ran her finger over a photo of Sera as a new-ish-born baby, spindly arms and legs in white pajamas with red and yellow hearts all over them, but cheeks as puffed up as rising bread in the oven. The eyes were Iris's, wide and a deep, almost black brown. They made Darren think of bits of coal, flecks of mica within. There was a sparkle within Sera, a depth to her spirit. "I lay up at night worrying about all the days I didn't know what it was, all the days she was looking to her mama to make it right, and I let her down because I didn't know any better. Sometimes Joseph was the only one could get her to stop howling. It was pain still, you could hear her whimper, but in his arms, she would quiet some, find some peace. She's a daddy's girl since she was born. I think of how that got down in her somewhere, a feeling that she couldn't count on her mama. I worry that something like that sticks with a child, a stain you can't wash away."

"Naw, don't do that," Bell said. She reached across the table and patted Iris's hand. "You can't carry that blame. It'll kill you. Don't do that to yourself now."

Iris looked up, her gaze traveling from Bell to Darren and back, sensing a story between mother and son, hearing in Bell's voice a wisdom born of experience. Darren felt the pain in his mother's voice. He tried to catch her eye, but she avoided looking at him. From another bag of photos, Iris pulled out a photo of a toddler Sera. "This was the year things started to get really bad. She was barely three years old. No sickle cell on either of our sides that anyone could tell us, going back years and years. And then here it just popped up in my child. It was hard, damn hard. But we adjusted, did what we had to, got to the best doctors in Houston, which are some of the best out there. It was scary, sure it was. But it was relief in it too, to know what was wrong with our baby, what made her hurt so much."

Luck had it that Joseph had a good job at the time. He was a foreman for a company building homes in Texas and Louisiana. The family — "It was just the three of us back then" — was under his health plan, and they got Sera on the best meds that were available. It wasn't an easy life and she had "spells," episodes where nearly every inch of her body hurt. She had to miss school sometimes, but her life was as normal as it could be. "And we were proud of that," Iris said. "Joseph, oh, it made Joseph feel good that he could take care of us, that he could get Sera everything she needed." Iris didn't work. It wasn't that she hadn't worked before or didn't want to, but Joseph could be traditional in his thinking, "and I think he liked the idea of being a man whose wife didn't have to work, always believed in men taking care of things, resting a family on his shoulders." She thought it made him feel like the men he saw on television when he was growing up, men who made everything possible for the people in their lives. It seemed to fit the image of himself as a man of substance. It was the yardstick by which he measured his life, and if that meant comparing yourself to white folks, more times than not, well, it only made Joseph satisfied that he was in the game.

He was measuring up, doing better than some of them, actually.

He was running three or four project sites when the bottom fell out of the economy, taking with it any firm foundation beneath their feet. First, they lost the home in the suburbs they had stretched themselves to buy. And then Joseph lost his job with the construction company. They were downsizing, and the men who'd been at the company longer would simply manage more build sites. Joseph was out.

"It messed with his mind," Iris said.

He'd lost jobs before, but they'd finally been on an upward trajectory as a family. Owned a home, had Sera's condition under control, and Joseph had thought he might move up within the company; it was a place that had not cared that he hadn't finished college, long as he was smart, long as he knew about hard work. "I was pregnant with Benny by then, and everything just started to feel like a rock down a hill, gaining speed, us losing things faster and faster every day until our new reality was just a bunch of sad days strung together that we didn't hardly recognize."

She looked down and only then noticed that Bell was holding her hand.

She didn't like that, the condolence in the gesture.

The Fullers were not ones for pity.

Iris gently moved her hand away, folding it with her other one in her lap.

They eventually lost their health insurance, she told them. They cycled through a series of apartments they couldn't keep, while Joseph tried to find work. Iris too. But someone had to be with Sera during the many weeks she missed school. Without health insurance, they were having a hard time keeping Sera on her medication, even with Iris forgoing prenatal care so they could spend everything they had on keeping Sera well. They got on a treadmill of sorts, always running, but somehow slipping farther and farther back. They began making emergency room visits when Sera fell ill and was in so much pain in her limbs that she would scream her throat raw. Those bills caught up to them, and after wearing out the welcome of a few friends who would let a pregnant woman and an ill child sleep on their floor, they were homeless for a while and living out of a used van that Joseph had traded in his pickup truck for, a loss of a work vehicle but a gain in real estate, the only kind they could claim anymore. By then, Obama was installed in the Oval Office and there was talk about a health-care plan, a way folks wouldn't go under over a twist of fate, a curl in their DNA that lay in wait.

Bell had her hand on a bag of photos, the top image Sera and her baby brother. Darren might have put them at eleven and two years old. They were on a beach—Galveston, Darren would guess by the grayish color of the sand—and Sera was as thin as ever, with her arm around her chubby little brother. There were dark circles under the girl's eyes and her neck bulged with swollen lymph nodes. But there was a smile.

There was that light in her eyes still.

"May I?" Bell said, reaching for the picture to get a closer look. Iris's babies.

Then she looked at Darren to make sure he didn't think she was overstepping.

He was touched by this, and by her interest in the photos of Iris's kids.

He was reminded that this had all started with his mother's care. She was an enigma to him, his mother, a cipher. He thought back to the story of his father, her version of events, Duke as a man who put his child above following the law, felt it tugging at him. If Bell had been telling the truth about Sera Fuller, was she also telling the truth about his father? The idea threatened to undo him.

"Obamacare is when it went really wrong for us," Iris said.

Darren realized he'd lost the thread of the conversation.

Bell was now looking through a whole stack of photos of Benny and Sera growing year by year, and Iris was smiling at the images of her children, but she was again wringing her hands in her lap. "They passed that law and then it wasn't really no hope for people like us to get help, people with burdens that are no fault of our own."

Darren glanced into the living room, remembering the photos he'd seen in there.

Joseph at a MAGA rally.

He didn't want to open an ideological debate, didn't want to do anything that might close Iris's mind or stop her from talking. Before she'd pulled out the photographs, he'd gotten her to concede that the only texts she'd seen from her daughter had been on Joseph's phone, which was right now on his person and therefore not something that Darren could verify. Iris was still deep in her defense of Thornhill, precisely because of the hell their family had gone through before they'd found their way here. Still, Darren felt protective of the former president. "I think the whole point of Obamacare was to get help for people exactly like you. Access to quality care, not being able to lock y'all out of coverage because Sera has a preexisting condition."

"But we couldn't afford it, the whole business of the exchange," Iris said. "It was this big promise and yet we were going deeper into debt every year and Sera falling further and further behind in school because we were trying to ration her medication."

"I struggled too," Bell said, setting down a photo of Sera in a homemade Tiana costume for Halloween, a rubber frog like you might find in a bait-and-tackle shop glued onto the shoulder of a pale green nightgown. "Before I got this latest job. But that's Abbott doing that mess. It's Texas that played funny with the way the whole deal rolled out in the state, making it harder for poor folks to get help with health coverage."

It was true, Darren thought.

It was his beloved state that had let down folks like Joseph and Iris Fuller.

Texas had failed Sera.

"Joseph feels like he used us to get elected but wouldn't let us stand tall, live with dignity like white folks do," Iris said. "That he wanted to be the only one folks see as special and make the rest of us black folks feel like we're just a drain on the system."

Darren couldn't remember a single Obama speech that had said any of this.

But it was the lived experience of this family, led by a patriarch who appeared to have his own need to feel special, to feel important in this world — which started with at the very least being able to keep your family healthy, well fed, with a place to live.

Joseph was sensitive to Republican messaging about Democrats making working folks feel they weren't as good as other people. Academics and pundits on television, folks with degrees from states Joseph had never been to. When, out of curiosity, he went to a rally for the Republicans' 2016 presidential candidate, he'd felt seen as a black man, appreciated even. He talked to people at that rally and other rallies he went to after that, men who wanted to hear what he had to say. "They put him on stage in Fort Worth," Iris said. "He told his story of what Obamacare had done to our family."

Greg Abbott, Darren thought.

What Greg Abbott *did to your family.*

"That's where he met E. J. Hill."

"The timber guy?" Bell said.

Darren nodded. "He used to be, yes."

Bell made a face.

That's who her brother had worked for, she said, before he got laid off when Hill Lumber Holdings sold to some outfit out of Georgia that had business all over the world. She shook her head at the memory of it. "Lost his health coverage then, was going without for years, not getting regular checkups and then he up and has a stroke." Bell said it in a way that blamed the Hill family and their company for her brother's stroke.

Which was absurd. Or not. In a country where you got only the kind of health care your employer thought you deserved . . . or you paid through the nose.

"Same Hill that's running this place, you realize that, right?" Darren told Bell.

She looked around the Fullers' well-appointed home, trying to reconcile her dislike for the Hill family with the potential she saw for herself in a town like Thornhill.

"Yeah, but they figured it out now, how to take care of folks," Bell said.

Iris told them, "It was meeting Carey-Ann that changed everything. She invited us to be a part of a new way of living and working, where everything our family needed would be taken care of. She's concerned about people, families being protected. She knows most of the people in town by name. Joseph got a job. I'd have to find some kind of work. It's a condition of living here, that every adult has a job."

"If you have papers," Darren muttered.

He remembered Rey's story of the families without full citizenship who'd been in the community before the Fullers. They'd been the town's first residents. And then, according to Rey, these families had suddenly gotten sick and left. "Has your family had any health problems?" Darren asked Iris. "I mean, beyond Sera's sickle cell? My understanding is there's been some concern about the working conditions making folks sick, whatever's in the air out here, what y'all are being exposed to."

Iris crinkled her brow, the lines on her forehead rearranging themselves vertically above the bridge of her nose. She seemed confused by the question and maybe just the tiniest bit frightened. Was there something in the air that could make them sick? Would she end up with *two* kids in and out of doctors' offices? She involuntarily coughed. It was the power of suggestion, surely. But it embarrassed her, the momentary lack of faith in the religion of Thornhill. "Our family has thrived here," she said. "Especially Sera. She was able to start a new medication earlier this year that's the best she's been on, and it's the strongest she's ever been, the closest she's ever had to a normal life, especially for a young woman. We've started to let her manage her own health care, go to the doctor on her own. And it's what allowed her to go to college. Thornhill helped with that too, paying for Stephen F. Austin. That was Ms. Carey-Ann's idea to make education a part of the Thornhill experience. She's a remarkable woman."

"We found her medication in the trash too," Bell said.

"What?" Iris said.

"Lenarix," Darren said. "My mother found a bottle of pills."

Iris scrunched her face, confused. *"Pills?"*

"Prescribed by a doctor out of Thornhill," Bell said.

"So wherever your daughter is," Darren said, "she doesn't have her medicine."

Iris let out a short, sharp gasp, then covered her mouth with her hand. Panic had finally found her, actual fear. "Oh no," she said, moaning to herself as she fumbled with her cell phone. "Oh, Sera, my baby, my baby, oh no." She accidentally dropped the phone on the floor and cursed under her breath as she got up and crossed the room to a yellow wall phone connected to a land line. As she lifted the receiver, they all heard Benny's voice. "Mom." He had entered the kitchen. He was leaning against the doorjamb and was playing with the toy construction hat from the man with the red sailboat tie. Flustered, Iris raised her voice when she told her son, "Go to your room."

"But there are police outside."

"Police?" Bell said, her voice rising with alarm.

Darren put a calming hand on his mother's forearm. He had been expecting this ever since the run-in with Carey-Ann Thorn and E. J. Hill. The town's police force was likely here to again escort him off the premises. He asked Iris about a back door. She shook her head. There wasn't one. Your life here was a shared community with your fellow workers. There were no private backyards and therefore no need for back doors.

There was a banging at the front of the house.

A frazzled Iris hung up the phone and marched toward her door. Darren reached for her arm and looked directly into her very dark, very worried eyes.

"I'm going to find your daughter," he said.

She pushed past him into the living room and to the front door beyond.

"What's going on?" Benny said.

Darren tried on a reassuring smile, then noticed the boy still had the tiny plastic construction hat in his hand. "Can I see that?" he asked; it was out of his mouth before he even knew why he'd asked. It was hunger for any information that might shed some light on this town and what the meeting with the man with the sailboat tie had really been about. Benny handed it over. It was then that he heard Bell call his name, heard a haunting in it. "Darren." She had a view into the living room and the front of the house from where she was now standing beside the kitchen table. Iris had opened the front door, and where Darren had expected to see the blue of Thornhill PD uniforms, he saw instead the pale, chalky brown of the San Jacinto County sheriff's deputies' uniform.

Vaughn, Darren thought.

Bell tried to catch his eye. "I'm sorry," she said.

There were two deputies, a man young enough to get carded buying beer and a woman deep in her thirties. She was the one who held handcuffs. As he realized what was about to happen, his knees gave, enough that he might have collapsed if he hadn't reached for the nearest hand. His mother's. She looked gutted. "I'm sorry, son."

He looked into her eyes, trying to make sense of why she kept saying this, a word she'd offered so seldom in his whole life, and now she couldn't stop saying it. *Sorry.*

He flashed back to her surprise arrival in San Jacinto County when he'd feared she'd testified to the grand jury. If she said she was sorry again, he might actually vomit.

"What did you do?" he asked his mother.

The female deputy said, "Darren Mathews, you're under arrest for obstruction of justice in a felony homicide."

"What did you *do,* Mama?"

The deputies shoved his arms behind his back.

He felt a deep pinch in the nerves of his right shoulder. The cuffs were tight, but surprisingly light. He should have known this. But he'd never worn them, had never had a hand press his head down to keep it from banging on the door frame as he was shoved in the back of a squad car. Iris and Benny had come out on the front porch to witness. Neighbors on Juniper Lane watched as Bell ran after the car, beating a palm against the trunk. As the deputies pulled away from the curb, Darren's mother howled.

Part Four

22.

HE KNEW enough not to speak during the ride south.

He hadn't said a word for an hour, not even to ask them to roll down a window, to beg for some way to breathe in the stuffy back seat, which was closed off by plexiglass. The air was thick in the back of the squad car, weighty and still, save for his own hot breath, which he had been counting at a steady clip to keep his nerves even. It was a trick his uncles had taught him when he was a boy, a way to still his mind when he was blind with fear. And he *was* afraid. Terribly so. If an hour in the back of a squad car riding through his beloved East Texas, among the tall, regal pines, made him feel like he could hardly breathe, how would he fare a day, a month, a year in a Texas prison, the birthplace and breeding ground of the Aryan Brotherhood of Texas? He was at one thousand and thirty-two inhales; he was running a separate counter of every third exhale, anything to keep his mind occupied, to carry it far away from the trap he'd found himself in, a trap he could, in this moment, admit he'd laid for himself. His mother had only found the gun that killed Ronnie "Redrum" Malvo, had only begun her black-mail campaign against him because Darren had let the .38 lie hidden on his property. Because he'd thought he was protecting Mack, putting a black man's freedom over "justice" as the State of Texas recognized it. Somewhere beneath the swampy surface of his pain over what his mother had done to him — turning over the gun to Frank Vaughn, the district attorney of San Jacinto County, and, it sure as hell seemed, testifying in front of the grand jury that indicted him — was a willingness to tell a painful truth. He had done this to himself.

His neck was damp with sweat, a sharp line of it running down his back, as the three of them rode in silence, the deputies having likewise decided that talking now wouldn't do either of them any favors. The less Darren Mathews knew, the better.

They passed snow-cone stands and abandoned gas stations. A trailer with a sign advertising homemade armadillo sausage. The winding driveway to a horse ranch, mere yards from a semicircle of trailers rusting in dirt. He wondered if this was one of the last times for a while that he'd see this stretch of Highway 59, its humble grace, the beauty in its contradictions. Outside the town of Corrigan, they passed a café with dusty colored bulbs lining the A-frame of its clapboard structure, faded to a dull gray. The place made him think of the day he'd walked into Geneva Sweet's Sweets in Lark. He could almost taste her fried pies, the peach that made your knees buckle. He thought of the bell on the door and the day that brought Randie into his life. He hadn't called her back. She would have no idea what had happened to him. This scared him as much as anything, that he had yet to give her a clearheaded apology, that his disrespect would linger between them, that she might slip through his fingers for good.

He was booked and fingerprinted, photographed, and had his pockets stripped. They let him keep on his street clothes, let him wear his boots on the filthy floor of the jail, but he knew better than to be lulled into thinking this might mean an arraignment was coming quickly. A small, poor county like this one saw a judge one or two times a week, at best. Darren had understood from the time they cuffed his wrists that he could be in here for a while. He asked to call his lawyers, the first he'd spoken since he'd left Thornhill. His voice croaked on the words. He cleared his throat, stamped down his nerves, and made the demand again. The intake officer said Darren would get his turn, even though Darren was the only man or woman in booking, even though there was no great rush of folks trying to get at the lone pay phone in the front room.

They put him in a cell by himself, a blessing and a curse.

It was the moment he began to dry out for real.

He'd gone days without a drink, sure. But fueled by spite, by a need to prove that his mother was no better than him, to cede her no higher ground. And there had been the adrenaline inherent in working any case, even one as unofficial as this one. Now he was alone, truly alone, his boots sticking to a floor that smelled of urine and something else sharp and sour that he couldn't name, the air hot and damp. Down the hallway outside of his cell stood a slow, oscillating fan that mercifully hit one corner of his cell every forty seconds, so he parked himself on the very edge of the metal bench affixed to the painted brick wall, where he could feel the fan's intermittent blessings.

Back against the wall, he sat and waited for what he knew was coming.

It wasn't like he hadn't tried to quit before. There had been a time when he and Randie first started getting serious. There had been a time around Bill King's pro forma trial for the murder of Ronnie Malvo (because of the confession Darren had horse-traded out of him). And, of course, in the madness of the past three years, he'd woken many a night, bolted straight up in bed in a cold sweat, nights he swore he saw his uncle William sitting at the foot of his bed, always delivering the same message from the other side: *You know you can't drink him out of office, right?* He'd tap Darren's ankle and say, *You can't right a sinking ship in* retreat, *son.* Some part of him knew, had known for a while, that his drinking was slowly killing the one thing he trusted about himself: his ability to hope. It was a precious legacy he'd inherited from generations of Mathews men and women. Sure, hope was too often offered instead of real change, a cheap placeholder for a better day. But it also kept people alive. You couldn't grow a tomato, a sweet pepper, or a peach without hope. You had to believe the land you were on could bear fruit to bother trying. You had to have vision to eat.

He didn't realize he'd nodded off until he opened his eyes to total darkness.

The lights in this part of the jail had been cut off.

The slow buzzing of the fan, the little rattle it made when it turned in a new direction, was gone. Someone had turned it off. The heat made Darren's stomach turn. His throat was dry, and his head felt heavy and untethered at the same time. It was so quiet that he heard Frank Vaughn breathing before his eyes adjusted and he saw the district attorney of San Jacinto County sitting across from him in his cell. He thought he might be hallucinating, like seeing his uncle at the foot of his bed.

The DA's presence here, like this, broke several state laws.

Vaughn knew it, and he knew Darren knew it too.

The audacity of it stirred him, woke an instinct to fight back, to play outside the bounds of propriety as well. He felt a strange and dangerous kind of freedom here in this dark room, alone with Frank Vaughn. The DA sat in a straight-backed chair, his legs comfortably crossed. He'd filled out over the years, grown fat living off the drippings of America's latest madness, its toe-dip into dystopia, fascism under the guise of a return to better days, nostalgia as a slow, magnolia-scented death. He was clean-shaven and wearing glasses with square frames. "Your lawyers have been informed, Mathews, don't you worry about that. And I pulled some strings to get a district judge out here to arraign you in the morning. One night here, that ain't so bad."

He shifted in his chair, and in the dark, Darren caught a flash of the man's white teeth, thought he saw the makings of a smile. "Of course, as far as your stint in state prison, well, I doubt it'll be as comfortable as this," Vaughn said.

"You don't have a case," Darren said. He'd been *Miranda'*d, but he also didn't care. This was cynical and foolhardy, he said. The murder case on which the obstruction charge rested had been adjudicated, which was one of the reasons this gamble of trying to indict Darren had never paid off before. "Bill King confessed to killing Malvo."

"You mean the man you visited just days before King signed an affidavit saying he'd killed a man there was no evidence he'd ever even *met?*" His smile spread in the dark. "That's right. I've got the visitors' log from Telford Unit. I know you two talked."

Darren's head came off the brick wall. He sat up a little. This was new.

In all their work around the case, all his lawyers' conference calls and meetings in the years that Frank Vaughn had been trying to get Darren to stand trial, no one had ever brought up the visit Darren had made to Bill King that led to King's coerced confession. Because Darren hadn't told them. He hadn't told a soul on earth what he'd done. It was just him and Bill "Big Kill" King, who'd agreed to confess for his own reasons. But now, would his lawyers have to address this in a court of law, in front of an East Texas jury, folks who could smell horseshit from two counties over? "His kid was missing," Darren said, trying on an argument for court. "He was feeling penitent. There were marks on his soul he wanted cleared in his lifetime. He'd renounced the ABT." That was the reason he confessed, Darren was trying to convince the DA.

"That's one way of looking at it," Vaughn said. "The other is you playing fast and loose on some agenda ain't got a thing to do with doing right by Ronnie Malvo."

"I could say the same about you. Quite a leap from DA of a tiny county in Texas to representing the whole of the Eighth District in DC. Bet it takes a lot of noise for anybody to remember your name. This trial ought to get you a few rounds on Fox TV."

"And CNN," Vaughn said. "MSNBC. Story like this, and I may make one of the late-night shows. *The Daily Show,* one of them. I'll fundraise off this for a year."

"That gun doesn't have my prints on it," Darren said. "You don't have enough."

Vaughn gave a little shrug. Maybe he did, maybe he didn't.

Darren wondered again how deeply his mother was tied to this. Had she anonymously dropped the gun at the sheriff's department's door, wiped clean as a newborn baby's bottom, as she'd told him? Or had she fed Vaughn a story that would nail her only son? In the dark cell, whose blackness was graying, as Darren's eyes continued to adjust, Vaughn uncrossed his legs and stretched them out in front of him. There was a forced casualness in the gesture that made Darren sit up even straighter.

Vaughn cleared his throat lightly and said, "What were you doing in Thornhill?"

Darren didn't speak right away. One, he was shocked to hear Vaughn mention a town and a company that were not in his district—as a county prosecutor or a wannabe congressman. Two, he suspected his silence would be useful. Because sure enough, after a few seconds passed, Vaughn seemed to feel pressure to broach the topic of why he was asking. He crossed his legs again and said, "Where we arrested you..."

Vaughn waited for him to fill in the rest.

Darren was too curious now to waste a bit of awkward silence.

There was a new restlessness in Vaughn, a twitchiness in his limbs. He shifted a few times in his chair, which creaked softly. "The folks out there appreciate your concern for one of their families," he said, "but there's no story there, Mathews."

"Folks." Darren finally spoke. "You mean the cops who wouldn't help?"

Vaughn smiled again. This time it felt pinched, his lips pressed together.

"This is coming from higher than that."

Carey-Ann Thorn's face popped into Darren's mind.

And then he understood. "How much are they giving you?"

He took a second look at Vaughn's suit, its clean stitching and the sharp fit through his shoulders. He glanced down at boots made of buffalo leather smooth as apple butter. Someone had had him replace his Timex with something Swiss and shiny, someone who knew they had to pretty a hog before taking it to market. Yes, someone was pouring in money to turn this country lawyer into a United States congressman.

"Carey-Ann Thorn and E. J. Hill?" Darren said. "How much have they contributed to your congressional race?"

Vaughn set the soles of his boots on the floor and pressed his hands into his knees.

"I got Judge Pickens here at eight in the morning tomorrow," Vaughn said as he stood, looking at Darren as if they were colleagues in this, a piece of business that couldn't be helped. "Oughta lay your head down for an hour or two at least."

He started for the cell door, calling for a deputy as he went. Within a few seconds, one of the sheriff's men led the DA away, leaving Darren alone in a cell that suddenly felt pitch-black again. He leaned his head against the wall. His throat was thick and scratchy, as if a nest of leaves were clotted at the back of his mouth. He called out for a glass of water. None was forthcoming, but about five minutes later, he heard the oscillating fan start up again, and, despite himself, he was deeply grateful.

23.

His LAWYERS spirited him from the jail at a quarter to seven. They had a change of clothes and offered to give him privacy in the attorney-client meeting room in the courthouse, but Darren told them not to bother. He didn't want to waste time. He wanted to talk about the arraignment, yes, but he also wanted any news about Sera Fuller. Without mentioning Frank Vaughn's visit last night, he asked if there'd been a break in the case. Could they check with Thornhill PD or the Nacogdoches sheriff's department? Or even call her parents? Had they heard if she'd been found? He was tucking a white button-down into a pair of black slacks that were not his size. His lawyers, Justin Adler and Nelson Azarian, asked him to stop pacing and have a seat.

They were a little spooked by the fact that Vaughn had pulled it off, gotten an indictment on his fourth fucking try. Even though they'd warned Darren for months that this could happen, they wondered aloud what had changed, if there was some new evidence that swung this grand jury. Darren wondered too: Had his mother testified for the grand jury or was Bill King Vaughn's new ace? He did not mention the visitors' log at Telford Unit. There was in his conversation with

Vaughn last night an indication that he was maybe reopening the Ronnie Malvo homicide case. In fact, a conviction in an obstruction case against Darren almost demanded it.

Darren knew shame was a useless emotion when dealing with your lawyers, but it was why he couldn't bring himself to admit, maybe especially to them, men of the law themselves, that he'd coerced a confession. He was every dirty cop, and he just couldn't say the words out loud. Justin and Nelson were too focused on the arraignment anyway, busy crafting rebukes about the time it took for them to be informed of their client's arrest and that Darren hadn't been given a chance to call them himself. Darren told them to take their feet off the gas a little. Vaughn had this county under his thumb. "They'll just say I fell asleep or that Vaughn and the judge wanted to settle on a court date before they bothered y'all all the way down in Houston." He told them their best bet was to talk up his roots in the community, the fact that his family had been in this county since they were enslaved. If he was gon' run, it would have been a long time ago. "That means something around here." White, black, whatever. "Tell them this is my home." He still didn't mention Vaughn's visit to his cell last night. He wouldn't unless he had to — if Vaughn reopened the Malvo investigation, which might mean several convictions hanging over him. The thought made him lightheaded. He was now nearly four days without a drop of alcohol, and he bit his cheek against the want. Chewed on himself like a wounded animal trying to break from a trap. One day at a time was an ocean to cross. He would only survive this mess by taking it one breath at a time.

The arraignment was surprisingly swift.

Judge Pickens seemed vaguely put out and sweaty beneath his robe. The room was warm and empty, only half of the overhead lights turned on. Darren's was the only case on the docket, and it indeed seemed that Vaughn had dragged the judge in on an off day just for this. Pickens waved Vaughn through his argument for a stiff bail, then listened rather attentively to Darren's lawyers use Darren's own argument that he be released on his own recognizance, adding with a flourish that he was both a respected member of the community and a man of the law. "A Texas Ranger."

"Former," Darren said.

"What's that?" Pickens said.

"Former Texas Ranger."

His lawyers glanced his way, twin expressions of confusion on their faces.

Had he not told them he'd quit? The past week had started in a daze of alcohol, losing Randie and Sera Fuller and chasing down leads with his mother. *His mother.* He felt a flush all over his body. He counted the next five breaths and declined to say more.

Still, the judge let him go, as his was not a violent crime and he had no record.

He was free to leave.

Darren turned and saw Greg sitting alone in the gallery.

The real show was outside, where Frank Vaughn was making a statement to several camera crews by the time Darren walked out of the courthouse. It seemed the stunt of pulling a district judge out of a hat had had everything to do with Vaughn getting this "win" for himself in the press as soon as possible. Stringers for Fox and Newsmax and two others Darren didn't recognize at a glance. He heard the words *vigilante* and *menace* and some bit about there being no place in America for a man, black or white, who decided he was above the law. *That's rich,* Darren thought as he considered the state of the country. He followed

Greg toward the parking lot, where, miracle of miracles, his truck was sitting tall. He had a quick conference with his attorneys, during which Darren promised to be at their Houston offices as soon as possible. They'd again advised him to take precautions regarding his safety, as demonizing Darren publicly was part of Vaughn's strategy. Then, he and Greg were finally alone, and Darren learned how Greg had found out about his arrest.

From Bell, of all people.

He'd gone by the house on Lanana Street when Darren stopped returning his calls. He'd introduced himself to her as a friend of Darren's, which Bell had accepted without further inquiry. "Vaughn got him," she'd said.

"She used his name?" Darren asked.

He was behind the wheel of his Chevy, Greg riding shotgun. He bit at his cheek again when Greg nodded. This spoke to an intimacy between them, Bell and the DA of San Jacinto County, a familiarity that he added to his internal list of circumstantial evidence that his mother had testified before the grand jury that had indicted him. He gripped the steering wheel as he turned onto State Highway 150, heading for the farmhouse in Camilla. Greg had been calling Darren nonstop because he'd gotten some big news. "You finally got something off her cell phone?" Darren asked hopefully.

Greg shook his head. "DNA."

"What?" Darren was surprised the lab had come through that fast. "You found a match?"

"Not yet, but the blood isn't Sera's."

"How can you be so sure?"

"The DNA was male, Darren."

"Huh," Darren said, pressing the back of his head against the seat, thinking.

"They'll keep looking for a match, but I thought you'd want to know as soon as I did," Greg said. He shot Darren a look from the passenger seat, gauging his reaction and tensing over something else he was gathering the courage to say. "Darren—"

"The boy," Darren said, remembering the marks on Brendan's body, the particularly nasty injury on his skull. Head wounds often bled in copious amounts, the scalp rich with tributaries of the heart. "She could have fought back," he said, telling Greg the story of the night at the frat house and an after-party in the Texas woods. "He pulls some shit," he said. "He makes a pass at Sera, with Kelsey's permission or participation, a rough game that goes too far. She grabs the nearest rock or drift of wood and hits Brendan in the head with it. He grabs the shirt to stanch the bleed—"

"Darren—"

"Don't know why he would have left it behind, but it sounds like they were all drunk and treating the woods like some kind of a trash can—"

"D," Greg said. "Can I ask you something, man?...Is it possible you've read this thing all wrong? I mean, yeah, those frat turds sound like assholes, the sorority girls too, but is it possible Sera is smart enough to have gotten out of both situations? Maybe she just went home, and her parents don't owe you any kind of an explanation."

"Why did her dad say she was at school, then?"

"Don't know, man, but it's their kid. And Sera is an adult in the eyes of the law." Greg looked at his friend, turning his entire body in the truck's cab. "I'd be a shit friend if I didn't remind you that this all started with your mother. Your mother, Darren. The reason I just picked your ass up out of lockup. There is no proof that girl is hurt. It's not her blood. We don't know that anything happened to her at all—"

"Her mother, man," Darren said because Greg's doubt was sowing seeds, was making him question his own judgment, his lens on this whole case, if that's what it was, the surreal haze over the days since Bell walked back into his life. "When I said she didn't have her meds . . . I'm telling you that woman doesn't know where her kid is."

"And I'm telling you, you got a hell of a row to hoe in front of you. Maybe you need to drop this and focus on getting ready for your trial. You turned in your badge . . . it ain't your problem anymore, D. Get right with what's in front of you."

By now, Darren was pulling down the red dirt road that led up to his house.

He threw the truck into park, red clay dust swirling right outside his window.

His head was an absolute mess.

He turned to Greg and said, "Need you to do something for me."

His mind was spinning from a night in lockup; the threat of a conviction, maybe two; his mother uttering Frank Vaughn's name, the same woman who had sent him down a rabbit hole searching for Sera Fuller, who Greg, like Wilson, was now suggesting was possibly not missing at all, that Darren had again fallen victim to his mother's manipulation or delusion or both. But why then was Frank Vaughn so curious about the fact that Darren was asking after the girl — Vaughn, who had a connection to Carey-Ann Thorn and E. J. Hill? And why had Thornhill been attempting to block Darren's inquiries into Sera's whereabouts? His head hurt from the swirl of confusion, the lingering questions. It was a lot to process, and he didn't want to have anything in the house that might make all this go down easier. He asked Greg to go in first and search every inch of the place, to be sure not a drop of liquor remained.

He would wait in the truck for the all-clear.

With the window down and a damp breeze blowing through the

truck's cab, he sat staring at the house where he'd been raised. To keep from biting a hole through his cheek while he waited, he opened the glove box and pulled out the plastic bag of his belongings that had been returned to him right before the arraignment, what he'd had on him when he'd been arrested. His pistol and a wallet, charcoal gray, the leather worn at the corners. His watch, which he took from the bag and returned to his wrist. And his cell phone. Plus the tiny construction hat he'd gotten from Benny. He now noticed that there were words printed across the front of the plastic toy. *Sutton Fielder.* The name sounded familiar. A quick search on his phone told him Fielder was a United States senator from Maryland. He was chair of the Senate Committee on Health, Education, Labor, and Pensions. This was who had met with the Fullers about their experience at Thornhill. Carey-Ann's "model family." Mom, dad, two kids, one in college, thriving enough to belong to a posh sorority. It made for a pretty picture of what Thornhill had to offer its employees. Hell, his own mother was sold on the place.

"You're cool," Greg called out from the front porch.

Inside, Greg asked if Lisa knew about the arrest.

Darren was filling an old jelly jar at the kitchen sink. He shook his head. Calling Lisa meant her telling Clayton, and he didn't want to deal with his uncle right now.

"You guys still aren't talking?" Greg asked.

"He's unhappy about the divorce," Darren reminded him.

It was that—Clayton's judgment. But now it was the other thing too, this business about his father and Vietnam, new questions about how he'd died. His mother had sprinkled poison on the story he'd always been told, a trail of it leading all the way back to his uncles. And it left a burning inside, a low fire at the base of his sternum that he didn't know how to put out. He didn't trust her version of events, but hearing them had left him feeling newly unsteady, as if the foundation of the house he stood in had cracked. He lifted the jar of water to his lips and drank in large gulps. It tasted dewy, like drops off morning grass. It tasted of home and briefly cooled his fevered fears.

He refilled the jar at the sink, needing something in his hands.

Then he pushed out thoughts of his mother and turned to Greg.

"Carey-Ann Thorn and E. J. Hill," Darren said. "I think they might be giving money to Frank Vaughn's congressional campaign."

"Easy enough to find out."

Turned out it wasn't just Frank Vaughn. It was congressional candidates in Virginia and Utah, Washington and Maine. It was men and women up for Senate seats in Mississippi, New Mexico, and South Carolina. Nebraska and Iowa. Several of whom were on the same Health, Education, Labor, and Pensions Committee as Sutton Fielder.

"Stacking the deck," Greg muttered as they both stared at Darren's laptop.

"Yeah."

The question was why.

After Greg left, promising to call him with any information on Sera's cell phone as soon as he had it, Darren sat on his back porch. The view of the low rolling hills, golden green this time of year, was a blessing after a night in county jail. He set his boots on the porch railing and looked up more about Sutton Fielder. Had the Thorn-Hills donated to him as well?

Not directly, it appeared.

But the super PAC they gave money to, Keep America Working, had made contributions to Fielder's campaign in 2016. The political action committee was also donating to the campaign of every candidate that Carey-Ann Thorn and E. J. Hill were backing, including Frank Vaughn, running for the Eighth District of Texas.

Stacking the deck.

His phone rang, vibrating on the railing in front of him, scooting like a June bug.

Darren grabbed it quickly before it fell off the edge.

He answered without looking at the screen.

Randie's voice cut through him like a warm knife through butter.

24.

BECAUSE HE hadn't returned her call, she'd worried endlessly over him, had booked a ticket to come back, but when he didn't call her again, she wondered if he still wanted her. "Around," she quickly added, to dampen the weight of the question that she'd hung in the air. It fluttered in the swirl of silence between them.

"I want you around," Darren said softly, feeling an exquisite ache in his chest, hot and sharp, a pang that almost sang to him. "Randie, I want you always. In every day, in every way. I want to make a home with you, girl. Texas, Chicago, wherever the hell you are right now—"

"Photo shoot in Marfa."

He heard the smile in her voice before Marfa registered. She hadn't left the state, then. Instead, she'd taken a job that kept her tethered to him. It gave him the courage to say, "I want to marry you, Randie." He heard and felt the throaty gasp on the other end of the line, and for a moment he didn't know if it was shock or disgust or glee. He took a deep breath himself and told her he knew he'd fucked up. It was the liquor, but that wasn't his excuse, because there was none. Not for the way he'd spoken to her. He'd been ugly, cruel even. And he'd had enough days now to consider the ways in which he'd too greatly owned the narrative of his life: as a boy, and then a man, unworthy of love because his own mother hadn't wanted him, couldn't be bothered to raise him.

"I haven't had a drink in a week. Four days, actually," he corrected, because he didn't want to start whatever might be repaired with half-truths.

"Okay," she said, a thinness in her tone. Darren couldn't tell if it meant she didn't believe him or that she thought this was business he needed to handle on his own and not for her sake. She would require no check-ins. She wasn't interested in being his minder. "If you feel good," she said. *That's all I need* sat in the air behind it.

"You really scared me, Darren. I thought to call Lisa again, but I don't know, much as I wanted to make sure you were okay out there, I wanted us to work through some of this on our own." She sighed. "Darren, what's between you and me, that's ours." Her impulse to erect a sacred wall between the two of them and the rest of the world so moved him that he fell back in his chair in wild wonder, as he looked out at the bluebells coming up through the bed of the old pond. He felt like singing. He felt like putting on a Joe Tex album. He felt like drinking.

It came up on him like a snake.

Strikingly fast and deadly.

He counted eight breaths. He looked down for what he could do with his hands. Finding nothing else he could hold on to, he reached for a different anchor. "I love you," he said into the phone, hearing her soft breath in his ear.

"Darren, the things I said about your mom—"

"Yeah," he said gently. "You were definitely wrong about her... because I'm pretty sure she testified in front of the grand jury. I just got out of lockup this morning."

"What?!"

"It happened when I was with her in Nacogdoches, when I was look—"

"Jesus, Darren, are you okay?" He felt her alarm through the phone and was embarrassed by how much it pleased him to know she cared. "You were indicted?"

"I will stand trial, yes," he said. "But listen, you were right about the other thing. The missing girl, there was a story there, a reason to drive up to Nacogdoches County."

Only he wasn't so sure anymore what that story was.

He told her about the past few days chasing down every lead on Sera Fuller, the mixed messages from her family, the oddness of Thornhill and them seemingly blocking his investigation, Lieutenant Wilson telling him in no uncertain terms to back off.

But Randie was stuck on the indictment and what it meant, what his lawyers were saying, and was Frank Vaughn really trying to convict him on an insanely flimsy case. "Obstruction on a murder case that's been solved for years. It's ridiculous."

She was coming home, she said. There was no way he would do this alone.

He heard *home,* and his breath caught, a thousand butterflies waiting to take flight. "The proposal, Randie," he said. "Marriage, I'm serious about—"

She took a breath and let out a low humming sound that did not enough resemble a tune of joy to Darren's ears. "Let's just talk when we see each other again."

He felt his insides seize, felt a hot stab of fear.

"Okay."

"Okay," she said.

As they said their goodbyes, Darren admitted he felt he'd made a wrong turn somehow. "I still don't know where the girl is, if I maybe misread this whole thing, and now the lawyers want me down in Houston to talk about the case and strategy."

The reality of standing trial hit him all over again.

"I'm just glad you tried, Darren," Randie said. "You made enough noise, talked to the girl's mother, that someone is going to send this up the chain, and maybe hearing it from someone else..." *Not a disgraced former Ranger,* he thanked her for not saying. "Maybe they'll listen to her mother if she starts asking questions about finding her kid."

"Yeah, maybe." Though he still felt he was dragging a weight behind him, felt the heft of work undone. A young girl, possibly sick, not anywhere he could name.

"But I'll see you soon, okay?"

"Okay," Darren said on the back of a sigh. Because there were nearly ten hours between Marfa and San Jacinto County, and it seemed at this moment the distance between Mars and Mother Earth. The whole conversation had a dreamlike quality. Would he wake tomorrow alone to find that Randie had never even called him, that he was actually already drunk now, dreaming up how things could have gone if he'd held on tight to any wagon that would keep him dry? He heard her say his name through the cold device in his hand. "It is not my intent to be proposed to over the telephone."

It had a lilt in it, her voice.

It held a teasing joy.

"Yeah?" he asked, a bigger question in that one syllable.

"Yeah."

Before they hung up, she said his name softly, then, "I love you too."

The favor she had bestowed on his soul cut through the gray of the past few days.

He looked out over the back acres of his family's land that God and circumstance had allowed them to lay claim to for a century when really the swath of rolling green and the thick stands of pine, scrub oak, and hickory trees belonged only to itself. By grace, Darren had been born to these Texas woods. By a twist of fate, a few messy knots of history, he and his family had made a life on this land. The yields too many to name. Family and home, soft breezes making a heated day worthwhile. Music and meals out on the back porch. Books and schooling. This land had given him everything. He hoped whenever his time came, he could report he'd been a good steward, that he'd done his piece to make the land of his birth a place of beauty and possibility. He owed the earth beneath his feet that much and more. Lemon-yellow rays of sunlight striped the back of the property, and Darren felt warm. Brand-new. He was safely pinned in place at home. Still, he used an old trick, tossing the keys to his truck in the freezer — this time *not* to make him think twice about driving after a drink but to discourage driving to get one in the first place. Inside, he poured himself another cold glass of water from the sink and then made himself a sandwich with the butt of a loaf of bread folded over salted tomatoes from the garden and one of his sweet peppers.

Plate in front of him on the old Formica kitchen table, he looked up more about the super PAC Keep America Working. They'd registered themselves in 2013, the same year Thornhill had opened, and were dedicated, their website said, to "making labor work for everyone." There were quotes from Henry Ford and Ray Kroc and Sam Walton, all platitudes about the virtue of hard work, the untapped power in America's men. And women, Darren supposed. Keep America Working had a fundraiser coming up soon, the same fundraiser at which Joseph had told Carey-Ann Thorn he still wanted to give a speech. *Still* suggested a change in original plans. *Because of a missing member of Thornhill's model family?* Tickets were available on their website, starting at one thousand dollars, tables for ten grand. Held not at a Hilton in Dallas or the Four Seasons in Austin. Not a Marriott or a Radisson. No, the fundraiser was being held in the gymnasium of Thornhill High School, which further cemented the connection between Thornhill and the Keep America Working political action committee.

He finished eating and took a call from his lawyers' office, setting a time to come in next week. He wondered how soon they could get a trial on the books. Nothing would be gained by giving Vaughn more time to look into Bill King's confession.

He hung up and moved to the couch, his eyes growing heavy after eating.

And a night sleeping on a metal bench, sitting up with his back to the wall.

He slipped into sleep, his skin sun-kissed and his belly full.

He woke in total darkness, no idea what time it was.

It was a noise that had stirred him, a creak in the floorboards.

Night had fallen before he'd turned on the porch light, so it was in blackness that he sat up from the couch where he'd been lying. His eyes began to adjust to the dark at the same time he sensed he wasn't alone. There was a bend in the air, a sense of motion. Just as Darren's eyes took in the wisp of moonlight coming from the windows on the back side of the house, he realized he'd left the back doors open. His heart beat a two-step in his chest, picking up speed. He remembered his attorneys' warnings about some idiot with a gun coming after him just to make a point, snagging a trophy of a buck, black and traitorous. He was a sitting duck out here. His Colt was on the kitchen table where he'd laid it after bringing it in from his truck. To get it would take more time than he had if someone had breached the property, was in his house right now.

He strained to hear more.

There were crickets outside, a pleasant percussive buzz.

And the low hum of the old Frigidaire.

But other than that, there was nothing. It was a quiet so stark it ached, made his head hurt trying to make sense of it, the certainty that there was another soul in this room with him. He started to speak, but then thought better of it. Instead, as quietly as he could, he stood from the couch, praying his middle-aged knees wouldn't make their opposition audibly known. He moved from the living room to the kitchen, had made it all the way to the entryway when he heard a voice in the room. "Was it worth it?"

Ronnie "Redrum" Malvo was sitting at his grandmother's table.

Squat and compact as Darren remembered him in life, with an unkempt mustache and hair lying in greasy swirls across his pointy head, and mean eyes, so blue they were nearly as white as ice floes. Darren could see straight through them.

"I musta put down ten of y'all in my time," Malvo said, licking lips that were crumbly looking, dry and flaky like bark peeling off a river birch. "Niggers on my belt."

He gave Darren a wry smile. His teeth were cloudy.

They looked like they were made of smoke.

"And yet you staked your career, your life, on making my killing look clean. Lying and hiding evidence when you coulda just said the nigger shot me and claimed the victory, admit that I probably had it coming, that some things just need killing."

Darren felt his face flush, burn with the truth beneath the accusation, the part of him that wished he was as ruthless and brazen as men who would take his life without blinking an eye. "I never hid anything," Darren whispered in the dark. "It was Mack that did that. I was just protecting him from going to prison for shooting your ass."

"That Breanna gal, you mean."

Malvo lit a cigarette that Darren didn't know he had.

It materialized as quickly as Malvo himself had.

"So I'm asking, was that worth it to you? If you end up in a prison cell over all this, ABT at your back, when you got time to sit and think on it . . ." Malvo took a long drag and blew smoke in Darren's direction and asked, "Would you do it again?"

That Darren didn't have an answer was the red-hot coal of his discontent.

He wished he had the stones to publicly admit he didn't give a shit that Ronnie Malvo was dead, and he wouldn't let a black man go to prison for killing him. But he didn't and Malvo knew it, and he hated the man for making him feel like a coward, one who was comforted by his own principles. Principles that Darren, despite himself, still believed were the last line against chaos and violence. Cops shouldn't lie.

Nobody in power should.

Keep your cases clean, son, he imagined his uncle William admonishing him now.

What he might have warned if he knew about Darren's misdeeds.

Leave no meat on the bone, nothing they can make a meal of.

William didn't live to see Darren wear the badge, but Darren had started his career following in his uncle's footsteps, policing as his uncle had preached. The power of the badge, its ability to provide protection for all Texans, rested on leaving no daylight between what was righteous and what was *right*. Being above reproach gave moral ground to black men with badges and guns, ensured their future role in the state.

"You a fool, Mathews," Malvo said. "Let a cracker-ass piece of shit like me make you doubt yourself, doubt your instincts . . . even about that gal out to Nacogdoches. When, deep down, you know something is wrong, don't you, boy?"

He cracked a smile, his lips peeling.

"Go on, look outside."

Darren shot up in bed, awakened by his own fevered mind.

He grabbed the Colt .45 by the side of his bed and crouched through the house.

He swore he could smell tobacco and stale sweat in the air, traces of Ronnie Malvo. But the house was empty, the scene conjured by Darren's dream state, the torment coming from inside his own mind. The feral chatter of his own making.

Look outside.

Pistol at his side, he walked out on the front porch of the farmhouse, moving only by the light of a crescent moon as he came down the stairs. Beyond the hulking shape of his Chevy truck, he saw the silhouette of a sedan, low to the ground, a faint stream of smoke curling out of the car. Darren crept along the side of the vehicle, raised his gun, and tapped it against the driver's-side window. Behind the wheel a white man started and had his weapon out and pointed back at Darren in the time it took Darren to realize it was a Thornhill cop, one of the men who had escorted him out of the town.

"Oh, shit," the man said.

He was young, hair the color of wet sand.

And his hand shook as he and Darren faced off.

"The fuck are you doing on my property?"

Darren motioned for him to roll down his window, again knocking the nose of his weapon against the driver's-side window while scanning the car's front seat.

In the dark, he could make out a few items of clothing and bags of chips and Mountain Dew. "How long have you been out here?" He knocked on the window again, as the young man managed to keep his gun aimed in Darren's general direction while throwing the car into gear, nearly taking off Darren's left foot as he sped off toward the red dirt road that led away from the house. Darren raised his gun and debated shooting out his back tires, stopping him long enough to viciously punish the man for making him afraid in his own home. But it was a violent impulse that would gain him nothing.

He had the information he needed.

The town of Thornhill was definitely keeping tabs on him.

And Ronnie Malvo was right: Something was very wrong.

25.

RANDIE HAD a house key.

Bestowing it had been one of the first signals that he was serious about this thing, serious about having her in his life for good, that his home could be hers if she would have it. He'd watched her work it onto a key chain that also had a key to her place in Chicago, a copy of which she'd given him in kind. He wished he could be here to greet her, spend long, winding minutes holding her in a tight reunion. But she said she'd be all right alone. She understood what he had to do. How could she not? It was partly her concern for Sera that had set him on this path in the first place. "Do what you got to." The trust in him, the pride in her words, was something solid he could hold on to as he climbed into his Chevy, heading back to Highway 59. The whole ride to Nacogdoches County, he drove with his windows down. Texas had taken it down a notch, and the air, though still close and kissed by the dampness of the fall season, was mercifully cool. It smelled of hay and the iron, blood-rich scent of red dirt. It cleared his head, let his mind circle back to Rey and his tales about life at Thornhill. Darren wanted to know more.

⋆   ⋆   ⋆

Rey had finally responded to one of Darren's texts.

He'd sent directions to the remains of the old lumber mill.

It was only when Darren made the long trek into the woods, ducking beneath the bough of a cottonwood as he came upon a clearing, that he realized that Rey was living out here. He had finally run away, Darren thought as he came upon a makeshift tent. It was a blue tarp, pierced through on two sides by sizable tree branches that were staked into the soft earth; the other half of the tarp was thrown over one of the remaining walls of the old sawmill. Amid the awesome beauty around it, it was a paltry shelter, a humble cathedral in the middle of the East Texas woods. The air was cooler here, almost cold. And it felt sharp and clean. It brought to mind crisp water that tinkled over river rocks in Garner State Park, where Darren had once camped as a kid. The crystalline, gem-like grandeur of nature unsullied, wild and free. "It was our special place." His and Sera's, Rey said. He'd emerged from his structure and expressed admiration that Darren had found the place on his own. Darren said he knew his way around East Texas woods. They held a natural logic for him, and as long as he could see a snatch of the sun's rays, he knew he could find his way home. His tongue tripped on that word. *Home* and all it conjured. "They find you?" Darren asked Rey, meaning the Thornhill authorities. *Is this why you're now living in the woods?* Rey shook his head and said he'd gotten in front of the problem. He didn't want his folks getting in trouble, didn't want to jeopardize his brother's education, the medical care his mother received.

Then he shrugged. "I could do worse for a few weeks."

Darren took in Rey's campsite, likely the scene of whatever had gone down Labor Day weekend out here. "So, Sera...turns out she's something of a fighter."

"Wouldn't be alive if she wasn't."

Wistful longing sank into Rey's expression. "I mean, if she is still . . ."

Darren was quick to tell Rey the blood on the shirt wasn't Sera's, that she'd likely fought back against the boys, and *girl,* who had bad intentions. "She's tough, huh?"

Rey smiled. "She can be," he said. "But she's goofy sometimes too. Fun. It always feels like she knows she's living on borrowed time." She knew she likely wouldn't live past fifty, he told Darren, that she would never be an old lady. She was really grateful for the medicine, the life it made possible. "She actually got into schools all over the country," Rey said. "But Thornhill offered to pay her way through SFA, and she wanted to be close to her doctors here. This new regimen she's on, it's been a game-changer."

"Her mother suggested she had some health challenges this semester."

"She wasn't feeling as good as she had been." Rey nodded.

"For how long?"

"Since the school year started."

Rey picked up a stick about the length of a baseball bat and used its ragged end to stoke the smoldering embers in a small firepit he'd built out of rocks and old bricks from the mill. It gave off a scent of burning resin that was strikingly pleasant.

"It's beautiful out here," Darren said.

Rey showed Darren what was left of the old sawmill.

"I wanted to study it," he told him. "If I'd been allowed to stay, if I'd gotten the kind of deal that Sera did with SFA, I wanted to look at the environmental impact of that and also mill towns back in the day." He liked to talk about this kind of stuff with Sera.

"That why you wanted her schoolwork?" Darren said, remembering what a big deal Rey had made of asking about Sera's notebooks, wanting to get a look at them.

"It was a thing I helped her with," he said. "Something for one of her classes. She asked me if I could find any of the families that had left Thornhill suddenly, families like mine that had come in when the town and the company were brand-new. I managed to find a couple. Sera kept all the notes, all those phone numbers. I wanted them. If I can't be with my family within those walls, maybe I can reconnect with people I once knew, ones that moved on." He still needed some kind of community.

"I'm sure your folks would leave Thornhill if it came down to it," Darren said. "Don't think they want you living alone out here in the woods, pretty as it is."

"My mom is close to becoming a citizen. That comes through, they're set there. That means a good school for my brother, free health care for the whole family."

"Your mom," Darren said. "You said something about her being sick?"

"It's the plant — the work is hard. And you smelled it. Plus, she was worried about my ass, the family breaking up." Rey ran his fingers through the thick black waves of his hair. "But, yeah, she's diabetic. It runs on *her* mom's side. And has high blood pressure." For which she received treatment at the Thornhill medical center, Darren confirmed.

He felt something roll in on a breeze, a wind of sudden understanding.

"Didn't you tell me that some families were feeling sick before they left?" he said, remembering, as he mulled something over in his mind.

"It's the plant, like I said. There's no telling what shit they're inhaling in there. It's bad enough it's in the air for all the families, the kids that don't even work there."

"And Sera was working on some kind of project about all this?"

"She wrote a paper," Rey said. "For an econ class she was in."

He would do this for Sera.

He would go back to his mother's home.

They'd never actually returned Sera's belongings to the Fuller family. They were still in the house she shared with Pete.

Bell's aging Nissan wasn't parked in the driveway of the house on Lanana Street, Darren thanked God. He was prepared to go through her if he had to, but he was afraid of what he might do to her on the other side of a night in the San Jacinto County jail. The house's front door was open, and through the screen, Darren could hear the whinnying neigh of a horse and the shrill pop of a gun as he came up the porch steps. Pete was watching a Western, the volume sky-high. Inside, Pete was on the couch, long legs stretched out in front of him. A man Darren couldn't have picked out of a lineup a week ago. Pete sat up and said, "Who is it creeping around out there?"

He set a ham sandwich down and reached for the TV remote.

"Your nephew," Darren said.

He hung in the doorway as Pete shut off the TV. The two men stared at each other, neither sure what the protocol was here. Did a fatal break between mother and son mean that Pete and Darren had no relation either? Darren didn't know, but he would step no further over the threshold until he was assured that she wasn't in the house. "Ain't gotta worry," Pete said, reading his mind. "She's gone."

Bell was out on a job interview. "You're good, if this the way you want it," Pete said in a way that quietly invited Darren to consider that he might be making a mistake, that in this lifetime, you only get one mama.

"I'll be in and out," Darren said, heading toward his mother's bedroom, where they'd sorted Sera's things when he'd arrived at this house. He wanted to be done and gone before she returned home, he said as he entered the blue bedroom where Sera's belongings were stacked neatly between sheets of wax paper, the way they'd left them.

Methodically, he laid out the items in a grid across the bed, re-cataloging it all in his mind and working his way to the school notebooks and papers. He started scooping these together in their own separate pile as Pete leaned into the room. "Not gon' stop you," he said. "But don't think I'm not gon' tell it, second she walks in the door. It ain't no lies between me and my baby sister. However it is between y'all."

"Lies, Pete," Darren said. "That's all it's ever been with me and my mom."

"Aw, now, you shoulda seen how she was tore up after they took you to jail."

"She tell you the part she played in getting me arrested?"

Pete wore a wounded expression, hearing this, upset by someone speaking so acridly about his sister, his lifeline. His whole world. "She would never hurt you."

"Too late."

"The woman she is now, not a drink in almost two years, she wouldn't —"

"Let me ask you something," Darren cut in, "when she went to San Jacinto County a week or so ago? How many days was she gone? 'Cause she came to see me around the exact time it appears there was a grand jury hearing testimony about whether or not to string my ass. And she just happened to be in San Jacinto County."

Darren felt a flame of anger licking at his ears, making him hot.

"That's a hell of a coincidence, don't you think?" he said.

"In her own way, she loves you —"

"She's the one who gave them the gun in the first place."

"Gun?" Pete now looked thoroughly confused, wore the expression of a child that had wandered off into the world and gotten lost. "What gun you talking about, son?"

"Uncle Pete," Darren said, using the term as an endearment to soften his tone. He just wanted to get Sera's schoolwork and get out of there before Bell returned. "I'll be in and out of here in just a few minutes. Why don't you go back to your program?"

Pete hung his head and nodded.

Then he shuffled back into the living room.

Darren went through the rest of Sera's things, making sure he'd missed no other school notebooks or papers. His hand brushed against the bottle for Sera Fuller's prescription for Lenarix, the sickle cell medication that her mother said had changed her life, made college possible. He pocketed the bottle and then scooped up all of Sera's schoolwork. A few moments later, he walked down the porch steps with Pete following behind him, looking distressed, as if he'd had a chance to mend Bell and Darren, and he'd blown it. He stood on the porch, his good hand gripping the paint-chipped railing.

And because he was still angry, Darren turned back to his uncle Pete.

"She even made up a story about how my father died, did you know that?" Darren heard the curdling bitterness in his voice and hated himself for taking this out on Pete. "If he didn't go to Vietnam, how did he die, then?"

"Oh, son."

This time, Pete's voice took on a note of pity.

Darren was the confused child now, the one who was lost.

"You trying to catch her in something when dead is dead, son. That pain don't know or care the why or where of it. Life is wild, son, ugly and crazy, then as it is now. People are doing the best they can. And maybe I don't know all that's gone on between you and your mama, but I feel grateful it swung you by here, even if just for a little bit."

Darren didn't respond, just kept walking to his truck parked at the curb.

It's not that he didn't want an uncle Pete. He just needed at least one person wholly on his side, who saw Bell for who and what she truly was, and that wasn't Pete, whose voice carried all the way into the cab of Darren's truck as he climbed inside.

"Looking just like Duke, boy."

Darren closed the truck door on Pete's last words.

He felt a sour thickness in the back of his throat, as he felt tears he didn't understand well in his eyes, a pressure building in his skull. He was newly gripped by a longing to hear the circumstances of his birth from the one man in all this he had so rarely considered: his daddy. Darren "Duke" Mathews. Something he could never have.

26.

IT HAD started simply enough: Rose-Marie Stein, née Hammel, a first-year professor in the economics department at Stephen F. Austin, had expressed interest in the fact that Sera Fuller's family lived and worked at Thornhill, a place she'd had only vague information about, though no one driving past the town on Highway 59 could miss it, this mix of industry and residential living. As Stephen F. Austin University had various disciplines of study — agriculture, logging and its history in the state, and environmental science — that the community of Thornhill seemed to encompass in one way or another, Professor Stein suggested Sera write a paper about the town and her family's experience there to demonstrate how she might approach a major in medical humanities, a catch-all field of study that a student could easily get lost in without the strong guidance of an adviser. Sera was precociously bright and curious, and she had a vested interest in medicine as a business and wanted to study public policy as it related to health care and how it affected millions of Americans, many with chronic illnesses like her. Sera said she'd come up with a take on the return of the mill-town model to twenty-first-century industry and present it at the start of the term. From there, Professor Stein said she'd see if Sera was serious about pursuing a degree in medical humanities and decide whether she would serve as her adviser.

"The Mill-Town Model and the Future of American Industry" by Sera Fuller sat on the passenger seat of Darren's Chevy truck. He'd pulled into a parking spot in Nacogdoches's town square, across from a gazebo. Sera's schoolwork was spread all over the truck's cab. The paper was surrounded by spiral notebooks, all of them bent and a little stained from having been pulled out of a trash dumpster. There was red ink across the front of the paper. Left-leaning cursive writing. Only it wasn't a grade or even an accolade.

No *Well done* or *Nice work*.

Instead, written across the title page: *And you have actual evidence of this?*

By now, he'd read through the notebooks twice, and he'd read Sera's paper four times. Her research had started in her own home; she'd rifled through her parents' "office," a tiny nook in a corner of the kitchen where her dad kept a lockbox of important papers, birth certificates and such, and on top of it sat a weathered manila folder with a copy of her parents' employment contract with Thornhill, as well as years' worth of monthly statements they'd received, an ongoing ledger of sorts. Since she'd lived there, Sera had never understood how, if they finally had housing and her medical bills were taken care of—the single thing that had most destabilized their family's economic situation—they had so little money left over for all the things she'd dreamed of when they were desperately poor and homeless. Trips to the movies, clothes that weren't secondhand, or a computer newer and faster than the clunky desktop that came one to a family at Thornhill and on which she had written this very paper, an exercise that finally explained her family's predicament. Inside that manila folder had been news that her parents were being paid less than minimum wage. Sera wasn't sure how this was legal, though she noted that Thornhill considered rent on their three-bedroom house, a flat fee for health care, and a technology package that included internet, cell service, and a satellite dish as part of their salary, and it appeared they were being taxed on this total rather than the three dollars an hour they took home in pay. Darren also wasn't sure it was legal, if this was allowed under the Fair Labor Standards Act. But it felt all kinds of wrong. To Sera as well. She had found that it was the same for Rey's family next door.

If the professor agreed to be her adviser, Sera said, she'd like to more closely study the economic model, whether and how it was profitable for companies like Thornhill, whose housing costs were stable, yes, but for whom the cost of employee health care was an ongoing variable, especially for families like hers, where a nonworking resident commanded a considerable amount of health-care costs. She was also curious about Thornhill's plans for residents who aged out of traditional hourly skilled labor. Inside the paper, she'd included a photocopy of her parents' monthly statement for this past July. Joseph and Iris Fuller *together* had made only seven hundred dollars, even though their take-home taxable pay was listed at two thousand dollars with Thornhill amenities included. The company also had a program to cover the cost of taxes for any family that came up short, treated as a low-interest loan. Over the four years that the Fullers had lived there, they had a balance of over forty thousand dollars that they *owed* their employer. It was, Darren thought, modern-day sharecropping. Sure, each family had its basic needs met, but they had nothing else to show for their work. No wealth was being created, no legacy or security for a future generation that didn't turn its bodies and labor over to the Thornhill corporation. They lived at its mercy and its perceived benevolence. And if they were fired, they would leave through the gates with nothing.

Which was what happened to the other families Rey had told Darren about, families that had moved to Thornhill when it first opened its plant in Nacogdoches County, families with members who were mostly undocumented like Rey. Except, according to Sera's report, they didn't leave so much as they were drug out of their homes in the middle of the night, put on buses with blacked-out windows, and driven as far away as Mississippi to the east. One family ended up north of Kansas. With Rey's help—after he'd peppered his mother and stepfather with questions about anything they could remember about the families who'd worked and lived at Thornhill with them, where they'd come from, where they had other relatives—Sera was able to get in touch with three families that had left Thornhill suddenly. They each reported a terrifying scenario. Days of feeling unwell, groggy, and lethargic. They'd missed work and believed *this* was the reason for being fired and removed from the premises in the middle of the night. It had all happened fast, and they were weakened by unexplained illnesses and in no position to demand answers to the questions that were hammering in their chests. *What was happening? Where were they being taken?* For years they'd had good jobs, housing, and medical care. That it all came to a brutal, inexplicable end fit the capricious image they held of life in the United States, a country that didn't guarantee half as much for its own citizens. Who were they to demand more? Most had moved on. Found work when and where they could. Only one man, who was by then separated from his wife, living on his own, and doing shift work at a pork-processing plant in Nebraska, held any bad feelings about Thornhill. "They used us," he told Sera. "When they started moving in families with papers, Americans, I knew that they would get rid of us. There is no way to have a business *legalmente aquí con nosotros.* When the shit gets real, they're not gonna have us in it."

Darren sank into the front seat of his truck.

The cab had grown warm, even with the windows cracked.

The sun overhead was baking the roof of the Chevy. He could feel its warmth radiating above his head, which was overheating in its own way. Thornhill not paying its workers a living wage, running what sounded like a tax scheme, busing migrants out in the middle of the night. But there was another more pernicious thought running underneath all of it for Darren. So many reports of people feeling ill. People who got their health care from Thornhill, a company they counted on for their survival. He thought again of the look on Iris's face when they said they'd found Sera's *pills,* the shock and the abject terror . . . because she knew then what Darren didn't yet. That the pills in Darren's pocket, the ones that Bell had found in the dumpster behind the Rho Beta house, were likely the very thing that was making her daughter sick lately.

Which was why, on a day that he was supposed to be in Houston meeting with his lawyers, as a trial date had finally been proposed, he was pulling into the parking lot of Thornhill High School. There were camera trucks and catering vans and dozens of black cars. Escalades and Town Cars and Chryslers. Darren was in the rental car Randie had arrived in at the house in Camilla yesterday, when she'd kissed him and listened as he ran through his plan, agreeing that his Chevy would too easily draw attention to his presence. Her rental was thankfully a modest American-made sedan that fit in with vehicles that had carried politicians and lobbyists to the Keep America Working fundraiser. He'd put on a navy suit and the only pair of dress shoes he owned and driven through the back entrance to the town, the one Rey had told him about.

The arches of his feet ached, and his toes were pinched against the tight leather. He missed his beloved boots, but the shoes and the suit and the flag pin he'd dug up were part of a costume to get him in the room, to get him in the same rarefied air as Carey-Ann Thorn. Because he was now convinced that she knew where Sera Fuller was.

The event was in full swing when he entered the back of the gymnasium. The room had been remade into a simulacrum of a ballroom. A bluish-gray carpet rolled to all four corners, and there were dozens of round tables topped with crisp white linen and centerpieces of bloodred roses and chrysanthemums and aster. Servers were carrying trays of the evening's main course, asparagus-stuffed chickens that might have been processed at the foul-smelling plant on the premises. Darren remembered how Carey-Ann wouldn't touch the stuff at the Fullers' home. She was already on the stage when he arrived. Her whitish-blond hair that he once took for a sober gray shone beneath stage lights that had been brought in special for the event, drawing Darren's attention like a lighthouse, a target in a storm. She stood behind a cherrywood podium, wearing a shift dress the color of dark berries, a rich purple that, as she spoke, Darren realized was a nod to her political message of bipartisan unity. She was addressing a room in which Darren spotted a number of politicians, including Sutton Fielder, the Republican from Maryland, and two Democratic congresswomen from Texas. Darren, who hung by the entrance to a staging room for the caterers, stepped to his right as a waiter walked past him carrying a tray of dinner entrées. The flat, almost plastic scent of food prepared in bulk sickened him a little, the sight of a gummy-looking sauce on the bed of each plate.

On stage, Carey-Ann Thorn continued her speech. "This movement, this mission we're on, it's a big tent," she said. "And you're all here because you are believers in something better for our country. We can bring manufacturing back to the U.S., taking on China and Mexico, bringing all of that business back here. Letting the private sector provide for this nation's citizens. Education, housing, health care. We free families from the burden of having to constantly grind, only to barely get by. That this is happening to good people in one of the richest nations in the world is unacceptable. It's un-American. This country's workers deserve care and protection. We save families from the direst situations; men and women who were in shelters are now in two- and three-bedroom homes, happy to have good jobs, their kids in good schools, having access to world-class health care. When I look into their eyes and hear them say, 'Thank you' . . ."

She paused here, gathering herself against a show of rising emotion.

"Well, as a mom, I just could not be prouder of what E.J. and I have created with the Thornhill model." She took a deep breath and looked out across the room filled with *believers,* as she had called them. Then she raised a hand as if she too had heard the gospel. "When I hear moms thank me for giving their family a chance, it gives me the energy we're all going to need for the fight ahead, the fight for legislation at the federal level to make this model work not just for businesses but for the families that want this. We need your help securing a new class in Congress to make it easier for businesses to have flexible and cre-ative pay structures." To the applause that broke out, Carey-Ann Thorn smiled wide, then placed a hand over her heart in a gesture of love and humility, her appreciation for the potential converts in this room. Then she showed a video of a new model Thornhill family. They were white, but otherwise identical to the Fullers. Mom, dad, two kids. An older girl and a boy. They shared a testimonial about the dad having been laid off during the 2008 recession, just like Joseph Fuller, the fam-ily struggling financially for years, growing more and more desperate, scraping by without steady housing, until they heard about Thornhill. The family applied and were accepted earlier this year. After, Darren thought, all the undocumented families who had helped Carey-Ann Thorn and E. J. Hill shape and stress-test their business model had been conveniently removed. And just in time for the push for political support for legislation to protect Thornhill's right to decide how to pay its labor force. On-screen, the mother of two dabbed at her eyes.

They were so grateful in the video, this family.

The men and women in the room clapped when the testimonial ended, and Carey-Ann Thorn returned to the spotlight at the podium. "Compassionate capitalism is not only possible," she said, "it's in the best interest of every life it touches."

Darren felt the words rumble in his chest before he shouted them out loud.

"Except you switched her meds!" he said, stepping from the shadows toward the circle of light on the stage. "Sera Fuller... make sure you tell the people that part too."

Lenarix, the miracle drug that had made Sera's college life possible, didn't have a generic equivalent. It's why it was so important that Thornhill covered the cost for the family. But the drug didn't come in a pill form, which was why a mother who had let her daughter start managing her own doctors' visits, going to them alone, had panicked when Darren mentioned finding Sera's *pills*. The real drug came only in a powder, to be mixed with food or drink. Whatever pills Sera's Thornhill doctor had given her, it was *not* the medicine that had given her a new, pain-free life.

Darren's words had cut through the audience's applause at the end of the presentation. Heads turned, and he felt eyes on him. Whole tables were either checking the dark edges of the room to see what the disturbance was or staring at the stage, gauging Carey-Ann's reaction. Stage lights may have blinded her vision, but Darren swore she knew who had spoken, if only by the tight smile on her face, the flint of anger in her eyes. Darren stepped further out of the shadows but got no more than two feet before he felt the hollow nose of a pistol at the base of his skull.

★ ★ ★

He was held for nearly an hour in a greenroom backstage, which was just a coach's office into which someone had shoved a vanity and a card table laden with a fruit basket and bottled water. Two beefy men in all black, not Thornhill PD, had thrown him onto the concrete floor, roughing him up as they searched for a weapon. He was unarmed, though. The Colt he'd left with Randie. He had a single gun and a single woman he loved, and he'd felt better leaving her alone with a pistol, a choice that cut both ways, he knew. He prayed his instinct to protect her wouldn't be his undoing now.

The door behind Darren opened and he heard the click of a woman's heels.

Carey-Ann looked tired under the harsh overhead lights.

Darren rose to his feet. "Just tell me where she is."

Carey-Ann sighed as she sat at the vanity table and reached into a camel-colored Chloé bag and pulled out a pill bottle. Her hands shook slightly as she opened it and poured a single white circle into the palm of her left hand. She slid it between her molars and crunched it into a powder she then ran over gums. She was silent a moment, waiting for whatever it was to hit her bloodstream. Then she cocked her head and regarded Darren as she might a windup toy that had gotten itself stuck in a corner, ramming over and over into a wall. "Frank Vaughn has become a friend of mine, a future soldier in our movement. And it's my understanding that he has a pretty strong case against you. I would think a man walking his last days outside of a Texas penitentiary would be more cautious. I don't know what you think you're doing, but I want you gone, for good this time, or I'll testify against you my damn self."

"The phones you give families," Darren said, "the computers—you're watching everything, is that it? You knew that Sera had shared the details of the company with a professor at SFA? Her education coming back to bite you in the ass, is that it?"

A tiny vein on Carey-Ann's forehead rose like a swelling river.

Her eyes narrowed.

"'You're mistaken'...'I don't have the faintest clue what you're talking about'...'You sound paranoid, Mr. Mathews.' Which one of these gets this over with faster?" She gestured like she could do this all day. Placid denials.

"The families you moved," Darren said. "Sera's meds, the fact that Thornhill is practically charging people to work for them, I don't care about that right now. I only care about the welfare of a young woman, a kid, barely nineteen. Someone's child."

"Whose father has known where she is this whole time," Carey-Ann said.

"What?"

But he knew it was the truth before the word even left his mouth. He thought back to his first meeting with the Fullers, how oddly Joseph behaved, aggrieved by Darren's inquiries, the concern over his child's whereabouts, concern that Joseph didn't share. Looking back, Darren realized there was disgrace in Joseph's expression.

"I believe in what we're doing, Mr. Mathews. This is the future. Agriculture, manufacturing, tech. Hell, we might bring customer service phone banks back to the States. There's not a corner of industry that can't make use of this model," Carey-Ann said. "And I'm not going to let a kid, as you said, a young girl who was obviously unable to handle the rigors and stress of higher education, question what I am building."

Darren listened to Carey-Ann, chilled by her callousness.

The way she'd used Sera, the Fuller family.

She looked at Darren as if she was suddenly irritated that they were still talking. She owed him nothing. "You have no idea how close we are to making this happen. Next year's election goes my way, and we'll have the votes to change a few laws, making Thornhill a new model for every major employer in this country."

"You fucked with her medication, you could have killed—"

"People are starving!" she shouted. For a second the cool facade broke, and Darren caught a glimpse of the deep caring she had tried so hard to manufacture on stage. It was in there somewhere, and it was real, an impulse toward good that had rotted along the way. "There are families in this country literally starving right now. People who have worked their entire lives and can't afford to live in this country. Why shouldn't my company do what their government can't or won't, Mr. Mathews?"

"You could have killed her."

"Every crusade has its casualties."

She stood then, smoothing the front of her dress. When she finally spoke, she was calm again, politic. "Sera experienced a setback in her journey with sickle cell disease, yes. We wished the Fullers could represent Thornhill tonight. But such is the nature of her illness. Stress and"— she paused for a second and then continued pointedly—"drinking, these are terrible things for a condition like hers. But be assured that she is resting, well cared for, and Thornhill is, as ever, paying for it all. The Fullers are in our prayers. They are Thornhill family." Then she lifted her bag and started for the door.

"Good luck, Mr. Mathews," she said, in a way that suggested he would need it.

27.

WHEN GREG finally got the information off Sera's cell phone, two things became clear. One, that Sera Fuller was indeed a fighter. She had given as good as she got from Kelsey Piper. To the Rho Beta president, who had indeed been bullying Sera to keep her quiet, she had never backed down, texting Kelsey, I'm gonna tell and your bf is an asshole and they will kick him off campus for this, maybe you too. And when Kelsey hit back, telling her to Keep yr fucking whore mouth shut, Sera told her she'd gone to the Nacogdoches Police Department to file a report, ending her text with Paper trail, bitch. Darren, when he heard this, had smiled. Sera had stood up for herself. As long as she could . . . until a month or so without the real medicine she needed caught up with her. The night campus police had come to confirm her report of harassment by Kelsey, she'd been sick for days. So much so, she'd let her battle with Kelsey go. Campus police had had to conduct their interview while she was in bed. The second thing that became clear looking at Sera's phone records was that she might have known something was wrong with her medicine. "She didn't want to go home," Greg told Darren when he recounted the info he'd gotten from his contact at the FBI. "At least that's what she told her mom."

Sera had been feeling bad for a few weeks, and she texted her mother that she felt like her body was cutting itself from the inside out. She guiltily confessed that she'd tried alcohol, adding, **Please don't tell Dad.** But she wondered if something more serious was going on. She texted her mom a week before she was last seen: **Maybe i need to see a new doctor.** It's possible she'd figured out what was happening to her and had reached out for help from the one person who had always made her feel better when she was most ill, who, despite everything, was still her safe space. *She's a daddy's girl,* Iris had said. According to Greg, Sera's last call on her cell phone was to her father, Joseph.

The case of Seraphine Renee Fuller ended in a hospital room in Conroe, hours south of Nacogdoches, where she'd been for more than two weeks. Darren had missed the hospital by two counties in his first canvass by phone, when he hadn't believed Sera could get farther than that on her own. He was right: She hadn't. Conroe had been her idea, but her dad had driven her. It was as far from Nacogdoches County as she could make it in her condition when she and her father spoke on September 13.

She was in a double room when Darren finally found them.

He had to pass by a woman in her fifties with cellulitis so bad, her lower legs were red in spots, a purplish gray in others, with cracks so deep they looked like swollen fruit about to burst with rot. She did not make eye contact with Darren, who had to walk through her "room" to get to the other side of a curtain, where he'd been told he would find Sera Fuller. His was just another of the many faces who passed through by the hour and he was as good as any nurse or medical assistant to ask after the can of apple juice she'd requested "a good long while ago now." Darren pressed the call button for the woman's nurse, then turned to the curtain that cut the tiny room in two, behind which he could hear the soft murmur of Joseph Fuller's voice. He halted. He wouldn't enter without permission. And maybe if Joseph had known it was him, he wouldn't have grunted out a *yes*. Behind the curtain, Sera Fuller was alive, her skin ashen and dry. Her mouth was slack, chin jutted toward heaven. But she was beautifully alive, no matter how weak she looked. Darren scanned the monitors in the room.

"Is she okay?"

Joseph, who sat beside his daughter's bed holding her hand, didn't turn his head at the sound of Darren's voice. Just answered the question softly. "She's being sedated, to manage the pain." He said something low in his throat to his daughter, words Darren couldn't hear. Joseph kept caressing the skin on his daughter's left arm, kept whispering things to her that Darren couldn't make out. "I'd hoped we could get her better in time for the KAW fundraiser. I wanted to show off my family, what all this has only ever been about for me. To show folks how far we'd come. From homeless to this little gal here in college, first in our family," he said. He lifted her hand and kissed it, rubbed the back of it against his cheek. Darren realized he was using her hand to wipe away his own tears. Joseph Fuller's eyes were red. Beneath them, there were dark, puffy pads of flesh rubbed raw by the crumpled fast-food napkin he pulled from his pocket to wipe his eyes. "This is bad," Joseph said. "But we've been here before. She's come out of a crisis like this before. She refused to go back to her doctors in town, just flat out refused, begged me to get her to a hospital somewhere. She was so bad off, I didn't fight her none. I even took out a credit card so I could pay for it, since the only insurance we got comes through Thornhill. But then they found out she was sick, and they offered to pay. I thought she'd get a few days of treatment here and then we could still be at Carey-Ann and Mr. E.J.'s event, telling folks how they changed our lives."

"And why do you think that is?" Darren said, hearing a nurse enter on the other side of the curtain, reminding the patient she was not allowed apple juice but she would be happy to bring her water. "Why do you think Thornhill is paying for all this?"

He gestured to the hospital room.

"What I just said, they wanted us to speak at the fundraiser thing. They wanted Sera feeling well enough to be there too. They wanted us," he said. "They wanted *us* to be the face of the Thornhill way of life."

" 'Movement,' " Darren mumbled, quoting Carey-Ann.

"Yes."

"They want to push this kind of thing all over the country."

"Good," Joseph said.

"You need to have doctors here run blood tests to see what medications were in her system when she was admitted. I don't think it's Lenarix she's been taking—"

"They think she got behind on it, wasn't taking it on time or something."

"Why don't you have them run a test for exactly *what* she was taking?"

Joseph gingerly set his daughter's hand back on the bed. He took the time to rearrange her blankets, tucking her in as he might have when she was a small child. Then he turned and looked directly at Darren. And because, somewhere deep down, it had already occurred to him—which was why he'd agreed to bring her all the way to a hospital in Conroe and *not* Thornhill—he said, "They would have no reason to harm my child. Carey-Ann has treated my family with nothing but respect since we moved there, has treated *me* with respect, as a man who can provide for his family. No handouts."

Darren felt deep sadness for how little Joseph Fuller thought his life should command simply for existing, when part of organizing ourselves into tribes and nations was to lend a hand, to protect each other's human dignity. It was grace, not charity.

But not for Joseph Fuller.

He insisted, "Everything my family has out there is because of my hands, my body. I spent way too much of my life being treated like I'm begging the world for every little scrap, too much time being looked down on for what I couldn't give my family. All the talk about what black men can't do, won't do, and even Obama talking down to blacks, all while his whole insurance thing put us in the streets. We were homeless, man. I had my family, my *children,* living in a car." His voice caught and his face sank with humiliation that he rearranged into anger. He sat up and said, "I'm not gon' follow any politician who don't see me as a man with value. They welcomed me at my first Trump rally," he said, "the one I took my boy to. That's what I want my son to see. People not looking down on me for what I don't have, assuming I need a handout to make it in this world. I'm a man," he said, still arguing with himself. "And that's what they saw in me, a decent man who just wants to work for what's his."

Darren tried to think of words to explain that he was not required to do anything exceptional to deserve his country's favor. But in the end, he saved his breath.

Joseph Fuller was too far gone.

"They said we might get to speak in front of Congress someday."

"Sure," Darren said, nodding in a way that feigned assent as an exit out of this conversation. Then he glanced down at the bed, where Sera slept a peace that was nearly terrifying. He said a small prayer for her, a plea to God not to withhold blessings because of her father's need to be seen as a man. And he made her a promise. He would turn in her notes, her paper, and the photocopies of the payment structure of Thornhill Industries to ... well, he wasn't sure *who* yet. He was no longer a Ranger, and Greg was no longer FBI. But he promised someone would see it. He wouldn't let her investigative work be in vain. On his way out, he looked at Joseph one last time. "Do me a favor, man. Run the blood tests," he said. "Not for me, not for you. Do it for Sera."

Camilla

Five Months Later

THE NIGHT before his trial, Darren's lawyers hosted a dinner for him at the farmhouse, if you could call it hosting when he'd done most of the cooking. A brisket he'd smoked for six hours the morning before, his breath steaming in the February cold, plus a hash of nightshades from his garden done up with garlic and a criminal amount of butter. Randie had put two hens in the oven and made a pitcher of hibiscus tea and raspberry lemonade. And after grace was said by Justin Adler, who had been in rabbinical school before becoming a lawyer, they all gathered in the dining room off the front parlor. It was a room rarely used, and besides Easter and Christmas, he didn't think the room had ever held this many people. Randie and Darren, Justin and his law partner, Nelson Azarian, two of their aides and a paralegal, plus Greg and a girl he'd started seeing, allowed into this intimate gathering because Darren's lawyers were trying to juice the numbers for the trial. They wanted the gallery filled with people who knew and loved Darren, or who at least gave the appearance of strong support. Lisa had promised she'd be there tomorrow, but Darren told her it was okay if she couldn't make it or just didn't want to. If it felt too weird. Wilson, Darren's old lieutenant, was noncommittal, and Darren understood. He was aware of the bind it put Wilson in — publicly showing support for a former Ranger who might be fully disgraced when the verdict came in. But privately, he'd told Darren he was in his corner. He believed he was a good Ranger, William Mathews's nephew after all. William's twin brother was back in the house tonight, for the first time in years. Darren's uncle Clayton was uncharacteristically taciturn this evening, quiet and with his head nodded in Naomi's direction mostly, speaking in low tones to her alone. It was an acknowledgment of the strain between him and his nephew, but it was also age, Darren thought. He hadn't seen Clayton since he'd had his heart surgery, and his uncle looked diminished, humbled by time. Naomi was by his side, seated to the right of Darren, who sat at the head of the table. He looked at the group of people going into battle with him, not a single one of them knowing that he was living in the gray of guilt over this case: a dull ash when it came to knowing about the weapon Mack had disposed of and a dark charcoal when it came to Bill King's manufactured confession.

He had been prepared to confess to his attorneys if the trial prep included any discovery that suggested that Vaughn was going to bring up evidence specifically about Bill King. Darren worried that to get an obstruction conviction against him, Vaughn was going to reopen the Ronnie Malvo murder case, which would lead to him challenging Bill King's confession. But Justin and Nelson suggested that Vaughn's strategy was to tell a jury he needed to convict Darren *in order to* reopen the Malvo case. Months of prep told them so. As did the fact that Frank Vaughn was spending most of his time making cable news appearances and campaign stops, frequently bringing up his intolerance for Black Lives Matter rhetoric, even and especially when it was coming from inside the heart of law enforcement. Since Darren's arrest, there had been a failed impeachment trial against the president, and it both emboldened and made sloppy men like Vaughn, who Darren's lawyers decided was out over his skis. They had grown increasingly confident that this case was just as they'd originally believed: an elaborate campaign stunt. After grace, they stood and toasted to Frank Vaughn's folly.

The morning of, he woke at dawn.

Randie was awake and holding his hand. She kissed his knuckles and ran her thumb over his skin, which was damp and clammy. In rising sunlight coming through the window on her side of the bed, he saw his grandmother's ring on her left hand, and he broke into a smile he felt deep in his chest. It parted bones. Uncaged him in every way. He thought back to the first time he'd laid eyes on her in Lark, Texas, the way her presence made him feel both undone and yet settled somewhere deep inside himself. She had adopted his lawyers' optimism and rose to make them coffee. She would be with him in court all day, had cleared her schedule for the next month or so, though Darren's lawyers had told them they couldn't imagine the case going more than three days. She was borderline cheerful this morning, kissing his shoulder in the kitchen.

The first half of day one of the trial was a mere reestablishing of the facts of the Ronnie Malvo homicide case, the case file read aloud by the investigating officer, a sheriff's deputy with as much finesse as a fifth-grader called on to recite a passage from *Huck Finn* cold. Behind Darren sat his posse: Greg along with his girlfriend, plus Clayton and Naomi. Lisa was sitting in the back, clearly on the defense side but many rows behind Randie. Rutherford "Mack" McMillan had left about twenty minutes into testimony that brought back some of the worst days of his life, when he'd been suspected of murder. It was too much for him.

Darren was numb through most of the proceedings.

The courtroom was ice cold, air-conditioning running in the dead of winter. Even the ceiling fans turned overhead, blowing cool air over the defense table, stiffening his muscles. He was aware of hope in his peripheral vision, felt its presence in the air, but he was too scared to reach for it, to dare turn his head, even when he felt Randie's reassuring hand on his shoulder as Judge Pickens called the lunch recess. She'd prepared sandwiches with roasted peppers and turkey, and the plan had been for the same configuration of supporters to have lunch together at the farmhouse, as there was hardly a restaurant in the tiny town of Coldspring that could hold them all. Darren spent much of the lunch break in his bedroom alone, his nervous system shot to hell.

He had thought to just close his eyes for a few minutes.

But he woke an hour later with his boots hanging off the edge of the bed, curled over on his side, his left arm asleep. He heard someone calling his name. It was his uncle Clayton, saying, "I'm sorry, son." Darren sat up, his face hot and creased. *What?*

He walked on stiff legs into the living room, where they were all standing around the kitchen table laden with lunch plates greasy with oil and the dust of kettle chips. No one was speaking. They were each of them, the lawyers and their team members, Lisa, Greg, and Naomi, staring at Darren, who stood with his uncle's hand resting on his shoulder, the part he could reach. Darren had been taller than him since the tenth grade. It was seeing the look of dread on Randie's face that made it finally hit him that something had gone terribly wrong. His first thought was someone had died. But wasn't everyone he loved in this room? Clayton sighed. "It's your mother, son."

Darren felt as if the floor were coming up to his face.

He felt his knees buckle, felt a sting in his eyes.

"Dead?" he managed.

"No," Justin said.

Followed by Nelson, who said, "Testifying."

His first thought, he was not even the least bit ashamed to admit, was a drink.

A warm bourbon, neat. If there were ever a time to break a foolish promise he'd made to himself, this was it. He caught Randie's eye, and she sensed his struggle.

"I'll make a pot of tea," she said.

Justin and Nelson told him to have a seat, not to panic.

Bell Callis had not been on the original witness list, which had led the team to believe that, despite Darren's worst suspicions, she had played no part in the grand jury evidence against her son; it was partially the reason for their bright faith that the trial was merely for show. But now word had come down that she had been added to the witness list last minute, and his lawyers would immediately go before Judge Pickens to try to block this or at least buy time to depose her. Darren suddenly found himself in a chair at the kitchen table, having no memory of the steps it took to get there. "It won't matter, it won't matter," he kept saying, over and over.

Clayton was furious. "This woman has in every way put her own anger, her own petty grievances, ahead of your well-being. But even I never thought she would go this far." Then, with a scolding tone he couldn't conceal, he said to Darren, "I have told you, son, again and again. You can't have anything to do with her."

"Got it, Pop," Darren said, his voice barbed with its own fury.

What was he supposed to do about any of that now?

Now that his entire life had arrived back at its nascence.

His life in his mother's hands.

"Let her talk," he said.

He told his lawyers not to fight it. There was no point in deposing her, as you could no more get the truth from her than you could get pee from a tree. Their best bet was to simply discredit her on the other side, on cross. He would get on the stand himself, if need be, to speak to all the times and variety of ways she had lied to her son. He could show the battle wounds of having been born to Bell Callis, would drag his uncle Pete into this if he had to. The whole of the Callis line was full of fabulists and criminals. "Under no circumstances are you getting on that stand," Nelson said.

This whisper-thin case was the State's to prove. Darren didn't have to legitimize it by defending himself against a weak stream of smoke in the air, against mere insinuation.

"We won't let you," Justin said.

"It's my case, my trial, and I'm saying let's get this over with. Give her another day or two, and she'll have placed me on the grassy knoll in Dallas." He stood from the table, one hand on the Formica top to mask how much his legs were shaking, how weak he felt. He'd never felt so scared. But what choice did he have? "Let's just get this over with."

She took the stand on the second, and what would ultimately turn out to be the last, day of the trial. Vaughn was wearing his finest suit to date, a slim cut he didn't yet have the figure for. But they were nine months out from election, and his transformation was nearly complete. A modish haircut that better suited his face and the new clothes, plus he'd laid off bread or beer, Darren guessed, as he recognized the recent lack of bloat in his own face. He had seen the same in his bathroom mirror these past months. Vaughn's mood was soaring. He'd worn a smirk since the bailiff had called court to order, a look that so spoke to a perceived shift in his fortunes when it came to the case that Darren's lawyers began to whisper speculations that Bell Callis was maybe a surprise to the DA as well. They still believed she hadn't been a grand jury witness, but who was to say she hadn't reached out to Vaughn during the trial, offering herself up at the last minute to, under oath, link the gun more directly to Darren? He had spent a sleepless night preparing himself for this very outcome, going so far as to show Randie where he kept his important papers. The house was paid for, but there would be property taxes to pay. He added her to two of his bank accounts and gave her the name of a man down the street who had a riding mower and might take care of the grass for a couple of twenties.

The tomatoes in the garden were heirloom and the last living thing his grandmother had touched, besides him and Clayton. "Watch the leaves when you water them. They'll burn." He asked her to please keep them going.

Bell was wearing an outfit similar to the one she'd had on when she'd walked back into his life months ago. Khaki-colored polyester pants and a cardigan. She wore no jewelry, not even a watch, and her hair was pressed and oiled. It had grown since he'd last seen her, the day of his arrest. She set her hand on the Bible and swore to tell the truth, her eyes lifting and meeting Darren's as she did. He felt his stomach drop.

Then she sat in the wooden chair and placed her hand on the railing in front of her, as if bracing herself.

She answered one question correctly, the one that gave her credibility, that explained her whole reason for being in the courtroom today — yes, she had been the one to drop off the snub-nosed .38 at the district attorney's office, the one that ballistics had proven was used in the Malvo murder — and then she proceeded to lie in response to every question Frank Vaughn asked. No, she did not leave an anonymous tip about finding the gun on the property of the defendant. She couldn't imagine where anyone would have gotten that idea. "I found that little piece out back of the motel I used to clean. Knew enough not to hold on to it. Seemed right to turn it in."

Vaughn was patient at first, believing that she was nervous in court, what with her son looking right at her, but as his direct examination continued, he grew red about the neck, and his tone became sharp. "Ma'am, did you not tell me that you had information that was pertinent to the case against this defendant? Do I need to remind you that perjury — that's not telling the truth in here — that that's a state crime in itself?"

"Sir, I wouldn't never tell a lie on God."

She invoked the Bible three more times as Vaughn tried to get her to return to whatever she must have told him she knew about Darren Mathews hiding a gun to get him to put her on the stand. The red-hot flush of his neck rose to his cheeks and at one point a sheen of perspiration shone on his upper lip. He broke several state rules of evidence, but each time Darren's attorneys made like they might object, Darren shook his head. He mouthed the words he had said the day before: *Let her talk.* It took him a while to believe it, but once he realized what she was doing, a warm rush of relief enveloped him completely. She never made eye contact with him again, selling the part of her testimony that she and her son were estranged and therefore she had no reason to protect him. "And I don't know that I appreciate you questioning my character, sir."

She held firm that she couldn't understand where Vaughn got the idea that Darren had anything to do with that pistol. Vaughn approached the bench seeking permission to treat her as a hostile witness, but by then Judge Pickens had lost his patience. He asked if Vaughn had another way to ask the same question he'd been asking for the past ten minutes, and when Vaughn conceded he didn't, Darren's lawyers passed on a cross-examination and by the next afternoon the case went to the jury.

The verdict was in before the sun went down.

A lie had haunted Darren for years, and a lie had freed him.

The celebratory dinner at the farmhouse was smaller than the one pretrial. His attorneys had to get back to Houston, and Lisa declined to join them. Greg gave him a hug at the courthouse and an update from his buddy at the Bureau office in Lufkin who'd opened a file on Thornhill. None of the families in Sera's notebooks wanted to talk, and the Fullers hadn't come forward with information about their daughter's health status. The feds were wary about digging into a private citizen's health-care records without true probable cause. And anyway, Carey-Ann Thorn and E. J. Hill were donating to enough 2020 candidates that Greg's buddy at the Bureau was afraid that digging into their business dealings would give the appearance of a witch hunt, a new favorite phrase coming out of DC. "But I'll keep trying," Greg told him.

Lieutenant Wilson called Darren before he was even out of the courthouse parking lot. He offered his congratulations and told Darren not to be a stranger, come by the Ranger office in Houston sometime. Darren hung up, his body still shaky from the adrenaline.

In the end, the dinner was just Clayton and Naomi.

And Darren and Randie.

No one had had any time to cook, so barbecue and catfish plates from G.W.'s on the way out of town would have to do. Darren couldn't imagine a better way to taste freedom. They sat around the kitchen table eating straight from the Styrofoam containers, their biting hunger covering the initial awkwardness among the four of them, the cloud of hurt feelings that hung between Darren and Clayton. His uncle had been around Randie for days now, but Darren still caught him watching her, making quiet notes, he thought. Of what, he didn't know. But Clayton was studying her.

Darren braced himself for a barbed shot of criticism before the night was done.

But when the two men were alone in the kitchen, sharing a pot of ginger tea instead of a bottle of Jim Beam, Clayton surprised Darren by saying, "There's a peace about you with her around. Even with all this mess with the case. You look good, son. You look happy," he said, making his approval known. "And if she had anything to do with you quitting the department—"

"Wilson asked me to come back," Darren said.

He hadn't told anyone yet. Not even Randie.

"Son, if you haven't learned from what just happened—"

"Let's don't, Pop."

Clayton sighed and sipped on his tea. "Well, I like her," he said. "And kicking the drinking, if that's to do with her too, then I'm happy for you, son."

"It was Mama."

And then, because he wasn't sure that was entirely true, he said, "It was time."

Clayton looked at him over the rim of his cup, sensing his nephew working his way up to something. Bell's time on the witness stand had reordered their universe, had both reinforced and completely undone the story that Clayton had been telling him for years. His mother was a liar, yes. But she had done something to save her only son. And because

Darren now felt a tiny pulse of trust in her, after all that had come about during the Sera Fuller case, he said, "My dad...Duke...he didn't die in Vietnam, did he?"

Clayton sat his cup on the Formica table, the same one he'd eaten off of when he was in high school. He ran his finger around the rim, his brows knitting together.

"She told you."

"Why didn't *you*?"

His uncle's shoulders hunched, his body rounding in on itself like he'd taken a sock to the gut. His face was low, the color sallow, the expression one of distress. Pain.

"You lied to me my entire life," Darren said.

He was tender all over.

And his hands were shaking.

"It was William," Clayton said, invoking the uncle they both knew was Darren's favorite, the one after whom he'd patterned his entire life. The former Texas Ranger, first black one in the state. The man Darren had long considered his North Star, the phantom voice that had been in his head for the past three years, admonishing him for the liberties he'd taken, the extralegal power he'd wrested from his badge.

This didn't make sense. "What?"

"Duke was in love, despite it all," Clayton said. "What me and William thought about the Callis people, the fact that our mama and daddy didn't like it either. But it was you, son, the fact of you. A baby was coming, and he would not leave his son for a war he didn't believe in, and he wouldn't leave Bell. You were his family now, he said."

His mother had been telling the truth.

Not even her turn at his trial could have prepared him for this. Not just the fact that Bell Callis was capable of the truth when it really mattered, but also that had things gone differently, he might have been raised by Bell and Duke, a small boy cocooned in the threesome of their family. It allowed for the possibility that Darren had love at his core, that love was, in fact, in his blood. That love had made him. He'd so often felt like an orphan who was *lucky* his uncles William and Clayton *had decided* to love him. This belief had come out in couples therapy too, how much of Darren's life he'd spent feeling only marginally wanted. "You were so loved, son," Clayton said.

He couldn't hold it, not then. Not yet.

But he was distantly aware that nothing in his life would be the same.

"What about William?" Darren said.

"Duke's deferment got lost in his transfer from Waller County, where he was in school at Prairie View. He reapplied in Nacogdoches County, but people were taking all kinds of liberties, and I believe the local draft board *conveniently* lost a lot of paperwork that would have kept young men out of the war. But either way, he was drafted, meant to report for basic training, and he refused. He just never showed up."

"He was AWOL?"

"Don't know if you can call it that if you'd never officially become a member of the armed services. But what he was doing was dangerous. He could have been arrested at any moment. And, for William, who'd served early in the war and who had an eye on moving up in law enforcement, who'd been talking about becoming the first black Ranger since he got out of the army, for William, it was also an embarrassment."

"And a professional liability," Darren said. His throat closed as soon as he said it. He felt strangled from the inside out. He understood at once that having a brother who deserted his military duties would have been a problem for an ambitious William.

Across Clayton's face, Darren saw behind the rage over William becoming a Texas Ranger. Rage Darren had always attributed to Clayton's belief that his brother had died in vain, because Clayton didn't respect the Rangers, didn't believe they were worthy of his brother. Darren felt childish for not realizing that the grief wasn't just for William; it was also for his baby brother, Duke. For all Clayton had lost.

In the other room, he heard Naomi showing Randie old quilts in a chest his grandmother had kept in the front bedroom. Their voices were dulcet and lighthearted.

Darren felt like he was drowning.

"He never got caught, Duke," Clayton said. "He hid out for a while with Bell and her brother in Nacogdoches, even stopped going to classes at SFA to not draw any attention to himself." His grief sat on his chest, and he sighed deeply. Hurt and confounded. "When William applied to be a Ranger, years later, I guess he thought it made more sense to just let folks *believe* Duke had been in the service. All of this was before computers. Why draw attention to—"

"So he lied to the state." Darren looked around the farmhouse, the rooms he'd followed his uncle through, sometimes riding his back as William played horse to his cowboy, rooms where he'd taught Darren the way to comport himself as a man.

"And to me," Darren added.

"Yes."

Clayton pushed aside his teacup and reached for his nephew's hand.

He held it softly. "I know you've heard me say all kinds of things about my brother, things I maybe shouldn't have said in front of you," he said. "Grief is a beast of a thing. And I have been angry with him for years. Angry with all of them, my whole family, since I'm the last one left."

"You got me."

"I hope so," Clayton said. "I was worried there for a while."

Darren laid his other hand on top of Clayton's, so they were gripping each other.

"But you have to understand, your uncle William believed deeply in that badge, in what a man like him, a black man, could do as a Texas Ranger. The whole of what he felt called to do, to take care of black folks' lives, to protect and keep them, meant he needed a seat inside the most powerful law enforcement agency in the state. The older I get, I see him so clearly. I see his heart, Darren. Not doing things the way I might have done, but everything he did, he did for love of peace and justice. He dedicated his life to protecting black and brown folks in Texas. And if he had to lie to do it . . ."

Darren pulled his hand back.

He needed a bit of distance to process all he'd just heard.

His uncle William as a deeply flawed and deeply principled man.

Randie's throaty laughter floated in on the air from the other room. It was an anchor to hold on to, knowing that her arms awaited him tonight. It gave him the courage to reach for the final piece in this. "How did he die, then?" Darren said. "My father."

It was a car accident on Highway 59, the same road that Darren had loved his whole life. Duke had run down to San Jacinto County to help with the cotton harvest on their father's land. Granddaddy had been short of hands that fall of 1973. Clayton had come in from his teaching duties at UT Austin in the legal department; even William had taken a few days off work as a young state trooper at the time. All three brothers worked side by side as they had all through their childhood, calling out to each other across rows, teasing Clayton about his noto- riously slow speed. Boy could count more scratches on his hands than bolls in his bag. Despite the drama among the siblings, the strife about the war, the brothers knew by then that Duke had a child coming, and there was a moment of real peace among the brothers. It was all love. It was on the drive back up to Nacogdoches after, back to his girl, that he'd been hit by a truck and spun off the road. He died there at the scene. Bell, Clayton said, had been the one to identify his body. And again, age and a heart condition had made Clayton wiser to what that might have done to a young pregnant girl newly alone.

"Yeah, I wasn't but sixteen," his mother said two days later, as she sat on the porch of the house on Lanana Street, where Darren had come to say . . . well, *thank you* hadn't sounded right, since her actions on the witness stand were to undo what she had set in motion in the first place. But to say something more complicated. That she was his mother, and he didn't always understand her, but today he understood her better than he ever had. The drinking came on after Duke's death, she said, after she felt everything she ever wanted ripped away from her. And it made her mean and spiteful. To him, she told the full truth: She had given the gun over to DA Vaughn with the intent to get back at Darren, for what exactly, she didn't even know. "I was bitter and drunk."

"I know."

"Ain't an excuse."

"I know."

"But I'm sorry, son," Bell said. "For all of it. I should have been there for you."

"I had a good life," he told her.

This time, she said, "I know."

It was a final acknowledgment that she was in no position to raise him, drunk and angry and scratched all to hell inside by grief that clawed at her day and night.

"You want a coffee, a Coke, Dr Pepper or something before we go?"

They had been having this conversation looking out on Lanana from the porch, feet up on cardboard boxes. Bell and Pete had, painstakingly, only three good arms between them, packed up the house. They were moving to, of all places, Thornhill.

"My number come in," Bell had said to him.

He'd warned her off their scheme, and more specifically about all the reasons the powers that be over there had to retaliate against anyone related to Darren Mathews. He told her that she wouldn't make any real money, might even come out upside down.

"Money ain't something folks like me and Pete see coming our way in this lifetime. We just trying to get by. Both of us getting on in years, and here's a place providing health care that we can't afford no other way. We'll be in debt, maybe, but we'll be alive. Ain't a whole lot this country got going for people like us, son."

No matter what he said, she couldn't be moved off it.

She wanted what she couldn't get anywhere else. *Security.*

"It's not the paradise you think it is."

Bell nodded and said she didn't care about carrying debt into the afterlife, didn't imagine God would greet her with a ledger on the other side. She would check all her and Pete's meds, she swore. Darren wondered if they could all pay into a family plan together, words tumbling out of his mouth before he'd thought any of this through.

"Let me help you," he said. "I don't have much, but —"

He stopped short of inviting her to live at the farmhouse, her and Pete. He would have to discuss it with Randie first. But Bell waved off the thought of any help from her only child. She didn't want charity, she said, and Darren felt a thick sorrow for all the ways she too was gripped by the idea that there was something noble in not needing help in this world, that self-reliance was an American virtue to be treasured. When we all needed each other more than ever, Darren thought, would only make it through whatever was coming next if we knew enough to lean on each other, lend loving hands.

But Bell insisted she was good. "I can take care of myself."

They hugged when they parted ways and made jokes that there would be no Thanksgivings at Thornhill. The thought of a holiday season with his mother made him nervous, a little. A lot did about the year ahead: 2020. His free-floating anxiety had returned of late, waking him up in the middle of the night, each breath a sharp stab of desperation. He couldn't get enough air in his lungs to calm his nervous system.

But he had Randie. He had a hand to hold.

He gave his uncle Pete a hug on his good side, and then he got in his Chevy and headed south, home to his soon-to-be wife. They had set a date for next month, something quiet, just the two of them on the back porch of the farmhouse in Camilla. It was her favorite place on the property, and they'd spent many mornings and nights out there, depending on the weather, the mercy of the Texas sun. They had an early dinner on the back porch tonight. Randie had grilled some fish. She thought the cuisine of East Texas would kill them both if they didn't mix it up with some lighter fare. Darren prepared the salad. And they carried their plates outside, plus two mason jars filled with a tea she'd made with cloved oranges. The sun was starting to set, and the light was a holy gold, the breeze tinkling the wind chimes in a way that brought to mind church bells and angels. It was cool, mid-February now, and they'd brought out his grandmother's quilts to lay over their laps. After a few bites, Randie said, "So, you going to go back to work?" There was no judgment in her voice, no nudging in one direction or another based on her opinion, which she had yet to voice to him.

Darren shrugged. "Maybe I'll go back to law school."

He'd been thinking about this a lot since learning about Thornhill. The kind of crimes for which a badge and a gun weren't the answer. Crimes that happened in state legislatures, crimes of Congress, the laws that needed to be probed and put to the test in courtrooms daily. Would that reignite his hope that the country could reach for its best impulses again? If his gun wasn't the answer, maybe the law was, the Constitution, old as dirt, but, like the blood and sweat–soaked land of his ancestors, the red dirt of East Texas, still capable of bearing fruit. "Either way, I have to tell you something," he said.

He finally confessed it to Randie, to the wind, to the soul of his imperfect uncle.

He'd framed Bill King for the murder of Ronnie Malvo.

"I know," Randie said.

"You *know*?"

"Yes."

The nights he'd been blackout drunk and said things to her on the phone—he'd told her then. It had been his shame and self-hatred about it that scared her, not the fact of what he'd done. She still saw Darren as a hero, *her* hero, a man who could right big wrongs. And she didn't care how he did it. The crimes against black folks, against her late husband, justified the means. She supported his decision to turn in his badge, if that's what he wanted. But she had never once thought it necessary. "This life is yours, to decide how you want to add your piece to our time here." And either way it wasn't anything that he had to decide tonight. No, he didn't suppose he did. Right now, there was a setting sun. There was the wintergreen grass, the air wet as always, but soft this evening like a kiss. There was his garden to get into tomorrow, a call to check in on Rey, who was working at a tire-manufacturing plant in Dallas and going to community college. And he would reach out to Greg about Thornhill again and what could be done to hold them accountable. Because there was no doubt that there would be service in his life; it was in his blood. Be it boots on the ground as a Ranger or boots in a courtroom, his uncle William's words still held true.

The nobility is in the fight.

Acknowledgments

I want to first and foremost acknowledge the grace I have been given in this lifetime by being born into a family of dynamic, creative, hard-working, wily, confident, visionary, sweet, and sensitive black Texans going back over five generations. It has been the blessing of my life to know the pure heart of Texas at its best. Its spirit of open arms, of fellowship and protection — *love* — values that even its worst charlatans in power cannot undo. I'd like to take this moment to honor two of my relatives in particular.

In 2023, we lost my "aunt" Lennette Benjamin, who was my mother's "sister cousin" and one of the funniest women I ever met. She was an absolute hoot, who also happened to be one of the foremost sickle cell physicians in the world. She dedicated her career to pain management for patients struck by the disease, and she improved the lives of thousands of people with her medical acumen, with her humor, her straight talk, and her deep love and caring for her patients. As a kid, I thought Lennette was the coolest. As a woman, I am in awe of what she gave the world.

In 2022, we lost my darling Precious, née Willie Jean Perry, aka Willie Jean Birmingham. She was my grandmother and one of the great loves of my life. She carried herself with warmth and wisdom, was full of front-porch philosophizing that kept her heart and soul safe in ninety-three years of living in rural East Texas. "Things ain't so bad they couldn't be worse" was a favorite saying of hers and a reminder that even in the worst of times, goodness can be found. Precious was the East Texas sun, the sweetness of a Southern peach, the beauty in the flight of the eagle that nests in Coldspring in San Jacinto County. I was blessed that she was my grandmother.

I would like to thank Josh Kendall at Mulholland Books and Rebecca Gray and Miranda Jewess at Viper Books in the UK for their counsel and their confidence in me. Thanks as ever to Richard Abate, who helped bring Darren Mathews into this world, along with Reagan Arthur. Thanks also to Dr. Cheryl Arutt for helping me psychologically weather some of the most difficult times in history and for always helping me be brave.

My forever thanks to Karl Fenske for always holding my hand. And my eternal love, awe, and respect for my Clara. Mothering you is the best thing I've ever done.

About the Author

ATTICA LOCKE is a *New York Times* bestselling author of five novels, including *Bluebird, Bluebird,* which won the Edgar Award for Best Novel. She is also a winner of the Harper Lee Prize for Legal Fiction and the Ernest Gaines Award for Literary Excellence, and she has been short-listed for the Women's Prize for Fiction and nominated for a Los Angeles Times Book Prize and an NAACP Image award for her work as a novelist. Locke is also a screenwriter and TV producer, with credits that include *Empire, When They See Us,* and the Emmy-nominated *Little Fires Everywhere,* for which she won an NAACP Image award for television writing. She co-created and executive-produced an adaptation of her sister Tembi Locke's memoir, *From Scratch: A Memoir of Love, Sicily, and Finding Home,* for Netflix. A native of Houston, Texas, Locke lives in Los Angeles, California.